Released

The Romani Realms Series

Series

Book One

by Mia Fox

Released, Book I, Romani Realms Series by Mia Fox

Published by Evatopia Press

http://www.evatopia.com

8447 Wilshire Blvd., Ste. 401, Beverly Hills, CA 90211

a division of Evatopia, Inc.

ISBN: 978-1-62378-087-6

Cover design by Eden Crane Design

http://www.edencranedesign.com/

Interior book design by Bob Houston eBook Formatting

Bob_Houston@hotmail.com

See other titles by Mia Fox at www.miafox.net.

Stay in touch with Mia Fox

Twitter @MiaFoxBooks

Facebook www.facebook.com/MiaFoxAuthor

Dedication

For my parents - Johanna and Bernie

Acknowledgements

I am so thankful for the kindness, support, and encouragement that I have received from the following amazing friends and family:

Eden Crane -- for shaping my idea into a cover more beautiful than I ever imagined.

Ginelle Blanch and Gabriela Warner -- for being the two best betas a girl could ask for. Without a doubt, your eagle eyes, attention to detail, and uncanny ability to keep track of changing time eras made this book better.

Lizzy Ford -- you just might be the bravest person I know. Thank you for giving me the courage to play in the indie pool and ensuring that the waters were welcoming.

"James Bond" -- for your secret service.

And, to our three cherished children...thank you little ones -- for always believing in me.

Chapter One

Sometimes one must take drastic measures when their own survival is at stake.

People are always going on about wanting to travel and see the world, but let me share something I once heard from my mother – be careful of what you wish for because it might come true...

When I was just knee high to a grasshopper it seemed that grass was always greener in someone else's pasture. I wanted to go to faraway places and live a life of luxury. But that was before I met Sultan Shahryar and agreed to be his queen back in 1706. Talk about the honeymoon phase ending quickly. It ends up my life in that Persian palace lasted only 1,001 nights, before my stories ran out and the Sultan lost interest in me. The only way I could save myself from beheading was to end up here – shrunk to the size of Thumbelina and hidden away in a dusty bottle, floating through oceans and seas to land in 2013 on the shores of Malibu.

So, I survived, but was it worth trading my life for this kind of...existence? Every time I enter a new realm, I find myself wondering: what was I thinking?

As usual, my thoughts were reeling with images of people and places, while songs I had yet to learn pounded my psyche like a surreal music video. It happened every time I entered a new Realm -- my mind played catch up, preparing me with visions of major events. Atrocities mixed with celebrations, joy along with sorrow. The visions came in flashes and snippets--two planes hitting New York's twin towers, the U.S's first black president taking the oath of office, and to my surprise, Queen Elizabeth II celebrating 60 years as Britain's monarch.

I rested within the confines of my home, a cobalt blue bottle encrusted with a diamond butterfly. I intuitively knew that my release was imminent, but something was different about this time. The voices I heard today were those of two eighteen-year-old girls from unremarkable backgrounds.

I closed my eyes and concentrated on their voices, willing my mind to see them.

A delicate hand turned over my bottle and traced a finger against the faint lines that bore my name...Suzette. But it was impossible to tell which girl had held my bottle in her hand. Just as quickly as it arrived, the vision altered and my mind's eye drifted more clearly to the girl called Samantha. She was thoroughly absorbed in her shopping, browsing through racks of other people's discards with purposeful intent, plowing ahead with determination.

Every once in a while, her green eyes would twinkle with life as she would flip a wave of gorgeous red hair over her shoulder, letting her friend know that she was on a mission.

The other girl, Charlotte, observed her with serene patience and simply shook her head in the negative each time her friend held up a dress. Undeterred, Samantha moved quickly, bouncing from one rounder to the next, believing the perfect dress was waiting for her. Charlotte seemed the more grounded of the two and willed the ordeal to be over. This mundane shopping expedition hardly seemed like a vision worthy of my talents. I struggled to focus my mind on who would become my next Releasor, but it was useless. Their conversation and gossip flooded my mind as if the volume had been turned up. It was all I could focus on and the image of the two of them was the clearest vision I'd had in months. Although I had yet to be released, I could observe them from within my bottle, much in the same way they watch television.

"I'm going to find it. Somewhere among these racks is my perfect dress -- probably something utterly amazing that one of the uber-rich women of Malibu wore once and then decided to send it here because they couldn't possibly be seen twice in it." Samantha continued to thrust hangers across the metal racks, as she sighed to herself, "Their castoff could be my prize."

Charlotte stood nearby, her arms pulled in tight to her sides as if fearing she might accidentally brush against something that was contagious. "I thought you said that retro was out?"

In contrast to Charlotte's cautionary stance, Samantha whipped around. "Just because these clothes have been worn, doesn't make them retro. For all we know, they could have been brand new just a week ago. Anyway, I told you...I saw this perfect dress in my dream."

Taking a deep breath, Charlotte paused before carefully finding the right words. It was obvious that she had years of experience dealing with Samantha and knew that when her best friend had her heart set on something, it was near impossible to sway her. "Maybe you should be a bit more open-minded? How can you hope to find a dress that you saw in a dream? Let's go to the mall, and I'll help you find something just as wonderful, and not nearly as...dusty."

"Did I mention that the dress of my dreams looked suspiciously like the one that Giselle Bundchen wore in the last Victoria Secret fashion show? Maybe it's here."

Not used to causing waves, Charlotte nervously twirled a lock of her hair around her finger. "Yeah...wasn't that dress just a bit revealing?"

"Your point?"

"Well, maybe you should look for something more...you. You know, Giselle probably has personal shoppers, trainers, make-up artists and umpteen people who help her look the way she does. We're just sifting through a dirty thrift store looking for the last dress she wore publicly."

"That's where you're wrong, Charlotte. We're on the cusp of an amazing experience."

"Sam, I say this with love in my heart, we are not on the cusp, we're in the abyss of averagedom."

For the first time since walking into the store, Samantha interrupted her search and placed her hands on Charlotte's shoulders. "Just look at us," she said turning Charlotte toward a horribly distorted mirror that had seen better days and made both of them appear misshapen. "There is nothing average about us."

Charlotte stared at her reflection and considered her straight blonde hair that was more white than golden and extended below her shoulders. In contrast to Samantha's fiery looks and personality, Charlotte maintained a quiet reserve. Her Nordic looks and icy, pale blue eyes magnified her cool demeanor. But in spite of looks that could be considered eye-catching, Charlotte fixated on her flat chest, long legs and lean arms, appendages that many girls would like, but she saw as being boyish especially in the understated outfits that graced her closet. Today's ensemble was no exception -- a pair of faded jeans and a plain, white tee.

Samantha stood next to her, hair flowing as wild as ever, a smile that dared anyone not to return it, and the green eyes, sparkling as if to say they didn't give a damn what anyone thought of the houndstooth skirt she paired with red cowboy boots because she liked it and that's what mattered most to her.

You're both beautiful. You may not see it, but I do. From within my bottle, I was smiling at them.

Charlotte answered, always the diplomat, "You're right. We don't look average, but I'm starting to think that maybe we should strive to be more like the majority. Isn't that what average really is? Just think how nice it would be to fit in for a change, have a boy look over his shoulder at us, and I don't mean in a worried, are-those-girls-stalking-me way."

Samantha held tight. "This one might work," she said holding up a pale pink strapless dress. "Oh wait a minute, there's some sort of dark smudge over here," she said examining the offending spot.

Charlotte tried a different tact. With deliberate slowness and a pleading quality to her voice she spoke. "Sam, that looks like mold and I left my hand sanitizer in the car. If that doesn't convince you, then consider the fact that prom queens don't shop in thrift stores."

For the first time since stepping into the Melrose Avenue shop, Samantha stopped her search. "See, that is where you're wrong."

Shaking her head, Charlotte answered back, "No, I'm sure I'm right about that fact. I don't see Ashley or Jessica or any of the other fembots here. Sure, I try to avoid them at all costs and I'm not one to emulate their less than friendly social skills, but I do think they're onto something by insisting to only buy clothes before other people have worn them."

Samantha took a delicate sniff of the dress in question. "The musty smell is very slight. I'll just dust on more talc." Samantha said, pretending to shake an invisible bottle over her head.

"Talc? That's so granny."

Samantha inhaled deeply, either an attempt to embellish a feature that was less than prominent or out of defeat. "Listen, you've made your point. I've only got one more rack to go. If it's not here, we'll go."

"Thank you. I'll wait for you in the car." But Charlotte only made it as far as the next aisle before she looked straight at me, that is, at my exquisite bottle which sat atop a shelf. "Hey, you've got to see this."

Well butter my bread and call me a biscuit...I had envisioned Samantha becoming my next Releasor, I thought to myself, as Charlotte reached to lift my bottle. I waited and watched them admire the beauty of my home. It was bright blue, like the Caribbean Sea and beautifully shaped with a long, graceful neck leading into gentle curves like those of the most beautiful woman.

Charlotte held my bottle. Turning it over, she could see where someone many centuries earlier had carved my name into the bottom. She traced her finger over the name and then let it drift to the clear, delicate stones that formed a magnificent butterfly, wings spreading as if indicating my desire to be released from its confines. She couldn't know just how much I wished I was like the butterfly.

Samantha peered out from between the racks of

clothes. "That is so cool and it would look perfect..."

"In my room," Charlotte finished her thought.

"Yeah, but it's like me, so vivid," said Samantha, moving her own hand over the handle that stretched along one side of the bottle. "It really matches my stuff better."

The girls each held a hand to the bottle, seemingly at a standstill. I waited with baited breath to see for sure which one would become my Releasor.

Until Ryan and Josh, two of the hottest boys from school, happened to enter the shop causing Samantha and Charlotte to both instinctively drop to the floor, hidden from their sight.

Myself and my beautiful bottle were all but forgotten. I slid out of their hands and rolled across the floor. I was feeling like a burr in a saddle at being flung across my bottle in that manner. They were lucky magic bottles didn't break, or I would be homeless. I prayed their carelessness hadn't chipped one of my precious butterfly's wings.

"We can't be seen in here," Samantha whispered. "Not by them."

"That's what I've been telling you," Charlotte barely managed while pushing clothes aside and crawling along the dirty floor to the middle of the rounder. "Since when do you care, anyway?"

"You may have a point about the granny smell in here," Samantha agreed, while flicking a dust bunny away with her fingers. "It's one thing to look apart from the crowd, but another to shout out where I found my sense of style," Samantha pointed out.

"Clearly you've come to your senses. Now let's crawl our way out of here."

"Not without our bottle," Samantha indicated the delicate pottery that had rolled across the floor, just out of arm's reach. "Go get it."

Charlotte whispered back, "Now it's ours? You get it."

"You saw it first," Samantha whispered back.

"And, I kindly agreed to share it."

"So, you agree to share it?" Samantha said, earning one point in her favor.

"Yes, I'll share if we ever get out of here with our dignity."

Dignity! I've served heads of state and noblemen, and these girls all but throw me across the store. As I've heard them say in this realm...*I am not a happy camper*.

Samantha paused to sneak a peek at the boys. "I wonder what they're even doing in a place like this?"

"They're over by the jewelry counter. Probably buying something for you know who."

The exit was in sight, but Samantha wouldn't drag herself toward it. "I have to know why they're here."

"Sam no. It's social suicide if they see us here."

"Yeah, but jewelry is a bad sign. It means they really like the fembots. Come on," Samantha started shuffling across the floor to gain a closer vantage point. "Grab the bottle and follow me. We'll buy it when they leave."

"Sam, Sam!" Charlotte hissed in a tone only a dog

could hear. "Damn it," she said defeated, cradling the bottle while inching closer to the two boys they considered god-like creatures.

The thrift shop's jewelry case ran along the store's side wall, just in front of a meager changing room. Samantha indicated the small closet with a nod. The girls abandoned crawling for the more distinguished tip-toeing method of getting across the shop.

I couldn't help thinking that after dropping my beautiful bottle, a wee bit of embarrassment might do them good. I concentrated on the shop owner, a woman whose looks could be described as an artifact in itself, and smiled to myself when I heard her call out in their direction: "I'll be right with you, dears."

"We're just looking," Samantha mumbled, grabbing Charlotte so they were both standing with their backs to the boys, but it was too late.

The boys turned to see Charlotte, who was trying desperately to brush lint and dust from her clothes while Samantha tried in vain to smooth her mane of hair, which after crawling across the floor looked even more like a burst of flames than usual. As the four of them took a moment to size each other up, it was unclear which party seemed more ill at ease.

It was just like me to leap before looking. I thought seeing the girls feeling a bit ill-at-ease would please me, but now my heart went out to them. I didn't want my next potential Releasor to feel badly. In spite of what I've been through at the hands of humanity over the years, I still hold a soft spot for people.

Samantha decided to break the silence. "Hi, what are you guys doing here?"

"Ryan's getting pressured to buy jewelry for Jessica," Josh blurted out. "He's totally whipped."

"Dude, it was your idea," Ryan retorted and then added, "Because Ashley got him to do it last month."

"Wow, they're really lucky girls," Charlotte said.

"Yeah, they must really appreciate you both," Samantha said with an edge in her voice, only to receive an elbow in the ribs from Charlotte.

"Actually, we're returning stuff," Ryan said. "The girls aren't into vintage. They think it's just old."

"I love vintage," Samantha gushed. "I love the history behind these pieces. I just imagine who might have worn it first."

"That's really cool of you to say," Ryan said, smiling at Samantha.

"Yeah, but that's what creeps out our girls," Josh interrupted. "So, you two, like shop here or what?"

Samantha opened her mouth to speak, but Charlotte quickly put an end to the possibility. "No, we wouldn't wear old stuff either. We just saw this in the window and thought it was cool," she said holding out the bottle. "We've never been in here before, isn't that right, Sam?"

Samantha rolled her eyes at Charlotte. "We should probably let you guys get back to your returns. "See you in lab, Ryan."

"Sure see you later, Sam," he said and gave her a gentle punch in the shoulder.

Charlotte turned to Josh, "Good luck finding something for Ashley. If you ever want another opinion, I can help. I mean, I know what kind of stuff girls like her would want."

"That's really cool of you, Charlotte. Thanks, I'll let you know."

Samantha and Charlotte watched with longing as two other girls' boyfriends left the shop. "Real smooth, Sam," Charlotte noted. "They obviously will never think of us as normal girls."

"Not true. Ryan is so much better suited for me than stuck up Jessica. He's into culture."

"But he doesn't see you in that way. He punched you in the arm," Charlotte argued.

Samantha continued to make her point. "It was a cry for physical contact in the only way he felt comfortable. I'm much more approachable than Jessica. Besides, you're one to talk. 'Oh Josh, let me help you buy something wonderful for your girlfriend and then just throw me in the garbage when you're done with me.' Could that be more degrading?"

If I had a side to pick, it would probably have been Samantha's. Josh wasn't the type of man I wanted for my Releasor. Of course, nobody was asking me. I had lived over three hundred years and regardless of the time period, the life of a Genie was always the same. People want wishes, not advice.

"Stop it. It isn't like that. I'm happy to just be a friend to Josh and help him out."

"Sure you are. Anyway, I've only got five dollars on me and this is ten," Samantha indicated the bottle that was still being passed between the two of them. "So we really are sharing it. We can keep it at both of our houses, every other week or until one of us decides to redecorate."

"Fine. At least the trip wasn't a total waste. Here," Charlotte said, placing her five next to Samantha's on the counter in front of the store owner.

"There's an interesting story behind this one," the old woman noted. "See this filigree work along the handle? The Faberge eggs from the courts of the Russian Tsar used to feature this type of work, but I suspect that this remarkable piece is even older. And the butterfly design?" she said indicating the front of the bottle. "Nearly every culture has associated the butterfly with the soul."

"How's that?" Samantha asked.

"Aristotle gave the butterfly the name psyche, the Greek word for soul. Egyptians said the winged ones were symbols for the human soul. It was also the name of Eros' human lover," she said with a wink. "You may find yourselves with those cute boys after buying this find."

"That's doubtful," Charlotte said dully. "But tell us more."

"Well, the Aztecs associated the butterfly with the soul of the dead."

Yes! I did a little dance within my bottle. I loved the butterfly and all it stood for, which was why I worried about the girls chipping it.

"Charming," Samantha scoffed. "We kind of hoped to find love in this life."

"Shh, let her finish," Charlotte scolded. "Go on, please."

"As I was saying, dears, the Aztecs along with Native South Americans and even Russians, believed that butterflies were all associated with the happy dead."

"Happy dead?" Samantha asked.

Charlotte added, "Isn't that an oxymoron?"

"It depends on how you view your current life," the woman replied patiently. "These cultures passed down the belief that butterflies appeared to calm people or to assure them that all was well with their dearly departed. Butterflies flock to flowers for this same reason."

"And what is that?" Charlotte asked, shivering involuntarily.

The woman gave a hearty chuckle as if the girls' ignorance of this subject somehow amused her. "Only men of high social ranking bought flowers..."

Samantha interrupted with her usual glibness. "That must be why I'm not on the florist's delivery route."

"Sam, let her continue," Charlotte said. "You'll have to excuse her."

"Well, it was considered bad manners to smell a bouquet from the top. Only respectable women knew this and therefore, if they were going to take a whiff, they would always approach a flower from the side in order to leave the top for more supernatural souls to enjoy the fragrance. The butterflies know this as well and that's why they always flutter lightly, but never hover too long. Yes, this bottle is certainly a find. Enjoy it," she said, placing the now carefully wrapped bottle on the counter between them.

"Oh, and one last thing," she called out as the girls were nearly outside the door, "As good as butterflies are, white moths are their opposite, vengeful and typically representing an unsettled or trapped spirit. Be safe, girls."

"Uhh, sure. We'll remember that," Samantha called over her shoulder before whispering to Charlotte, "talk about weird."

It's not weird, Samantha, I answered in words I knew she couldn't hear. There are bad humans and even worse spirits. The difference: humans eventually die, but a vengeful or angry spirit is able to follow you throughout time and Realms. Crossing one meant having to look over your shoulder for eternity.

They left quickly, holding their sweaters around themselves for there was a sudden chill in the air. The leaves were turning colors, signaling the beginning of Fall and for the first time this year, the sidewalk carried a spilled palette of oranges and reds.

"Can we walk a little faster?" Samantha asked, now buttoning her sweater as she walked.

Charlotte picked up her pace. "Definitely. I've got chills from that old woman."

"By the way," Samantha added, "I don't think I ever want to go in there again."

"Well, that's something," Charlotte said, a smile appearing for the first time in the last half-hour.

Chapter Two

My visions were coming in on two simultaneous channels. I had spent the last hour listening to the fashion and social problems of two teenage girls, but the innocence of their shopping expedition seemed short-lived. A woman's voice had also mentioned white moths. That creature, along with that of the black bird, was the preferred form taken by demon gypsies, those who had used black magic to grant themselves extended life and supernatural powers.

As I was still yet to be released, it was unclear what these thoughts had to do with me. I could sense the girls had taken possession of my bottle and their proximity made my heart pound with unexpected force. I longed to be released, but not under these circumstances. I had always been owned by men and not just ordinary ones, but men of impending greatness. Never before had a woman, let alone a girl, had the fortitude to spend time in my presence. I wondered which one of these girls was about to release me. I pondered who would be a better match for me: Charlotte, who was sensible although perhaps too methodical, or Samantha, the one with a wild streak that either couldn't sense condemnation or refused to acknowledge it. Neither seemed the type to cavort with demon gypsies so I couldn't figure out why the two visions were intersecting.

From the darkness of my bottle I could hear the foreshadowing sounds of screeching tires, a girl's screams, and the caw of blackbirds. Something harrowing was about to happen to these girls and I prayed that my release wouldn't be too late. That's when it began -- the unmistakable rumbling that I have heard throughout time brought on by the demon gypsies controlling the elements.

The girls sat on the floor of Charlotte's bedroom, choosing to peruse a gossip magazine rather than focus on homework. It was their evening ritual brought on by a lack of desire to be alone since neither lived with a traditional family. Ever since her parents died in a car accident, Charlotte had been a ward of the state. But now that she was eighteen, she decided to live alone rather than stay in the foster system. A similar situation befell Samantha once her mother discovered her father having an affair. Both parents decided to find "me" time, which meant her father had accepted a job that kept him on the road for 340 days a year, and her mother chose to live off the alimony and travel, insisting that Samantha was better off on her own, away from the "toxicity," as she put it, of a bad relationship.

The girls were enjoying a bowl of popcorn while sharing their answers to the magazine's monthly romance quiz, when their procrastination from homework was brought to a halt by the sudden rumbling of an earthquake.

"Oh my god, Sam, did you hear that?" Charlotte's voice was panicked and Samantha, usually full of bravado, barely squeaked out a response.

"Where are you?"

In an instant after that first horrible crackling sound, the lights went out and all was black, but certainly not quiet. The sound of dishes falling to the ground, glasses breaking, and a relentless rumbling occurred.

"Sam, I'm here. Give me your hand."

The girls extended their hands, desperate to find each other in the darkened chaos. When they finally found each other, they held hands tightly, willing the shaking to stop. But it didn't.

They sat holding each other, huddled in the doorway leading to Charlotte's room, hoping the structure would provide added support. The house creaked and heaved as if deciding whether to continue its fight against the forces of nature. At the far end of the bedroom stood a six-foot tall armoire with glass doors that banged open and closed. The bottom half of the armoire was made up of drawers that tipped forward and emptied unceremoniously onto the floor while the top portion was for display and housed an assortment of delicate china dolls, framed pictures that flew directly towards the girls, and decorative vases and bottles, including mine, the one they had just acquired. Suddenly, the entire armoire itself started to topple and without thinking Charlotte rushed toward it, desperate to keep it from falling.

"Charlotte, no!" As Charlotte headed toward the armoire, Samantha instinctively ran as well, pushing her out of the way. In spite of her efforts, the armoire fell forward pinning Charlotte's leg underneath with a sickening thud. And then all was quiet.

"It's over," Samantha finally breathed. "Are you okay? Charlotte say something."

"Oh my God, Sam, what can I say? If you hadn't shoved me, it could've been my head stuck under here."

"You're welcome. Let's get you out."

As Samantha moved across the room, Charlotte could hear the sound of crunching glass. "Wear shoes!"

"Yes mom," Samantha replied with sarcasm. "Geesh, even when pinned to the ground you have to be the sensible one," she said struggling to gain leverage on the offending armoire. "But, trying to steady this monster piece of furniture in the midst of an earthquake probably wasn't your most rational moment."

Charlotte grimaced in pain while trying to slide her leg out from under the splintering wood. "I thought the bottle would break...the new one. I just felt like I had to hold onto it."

Well tickle me pink. With that one statement, I

knew that these girls were my destiny. One had saved my bottle; the other had saved her friend. Both were acts of complete unselfishness, the opposite mission of the demon gypsies, who no doubt had arranged this earthquake in an attempt to destroy me once and for all.

Inch by inch, Samantha leveraged the armoire to slide Charlotte's leg out from underneath it. A nasty bruise had already come up and the splintered wood had made a pretty decent gash along Charlotte's thigh, but otherwise she was okay.

"You did this for that bottle?" Samantha reached a hand to her temple, shaking off the disbelief. "I feel a headache coming on."

"I knew how much you liked it. It's brand new -- actually, really old, but new to us," Charlotte noted. "But Sam, you're bleeding—badly. Come on, let's get cleaned up."

The two held each other as they made their way to the bathroom and the first aid kit. When they returned to Charlotte's room, they surveyed the disorder around them. It was as if someone had ransacked the place. Every drawer was turned out. Every picture frame was broken into pieces. Miraculously, the only delicate object that remained intact was the bottle with the butterfly design.

"You keep it," Samantha said. "You nearly lost your leg for this bottle."

"You took a hit on the head for it," Charlotte pointed out.

"No, I took a hit on the head for you."

I felt my bottle being replaced on the shelf, steady and safe. And yet, I was still no closer to being released.

"It is pretty," Samantha said rotating my bottle. "You should definitely keep it here. I can admire it when I come over. We're lucky that wasn't the 'big one'."

"It was big enough for my liking," Charlotte said while gathering up the broken glass. "What do you think? I'd say it was at least 7.0. I guess there's no point in turning on the T.V. I'm sure the power isn't back this quickly."

"Probably not," Samantha concurred, and then went to the window to check out if the neighbors' houses had light.

"Sam, you should stay away from the window in case there's an after shock. The glass could shatter."

"I don't think so. Look," Samantha said indicating outside.

Charlotte's house was the only one in darkness.

"It's impossible," Charlotte said not believing what they were seeing.

"There's an explanation. It's the seismic waves. They hit like every other house or something. The force is stronger for some than others," Samantha said more convincingly than she felt. "Still, I better go and check on my house, just in case."

"Yeah, but your head...maybe you shouldn't be alone right now. Do you need a doctor?"

"I'm fine. Unless...are you afraid to be alone?"

"Don't be ridiculous. I'll see you tomorrow."

As she left Charlotte's home, Samantha noticed two moths, tempting the porch light with their proximity. The thrift store owner's words rang in her mind and she hesitated for a moment, nearly deciding to ring the bell and come back inside, but decided it was silly to fear the idle ramblings of an old woman. Nevertheless, she walked quicker, pulling her sweater around her against the sudden chill in the air and feeling very aware of the night and its solitude.

Samantha rounded the block, and then as if her nerves weren't already on edge, two enormous blackbirds swooped low, practically cutting off her path before gaining height once again to perch in a tree above her. They cawed from the tree top, and with the exception of their cries, the street was oddly quiet. She had expected to hear sirens in response to the earthquake or at least increased traffic from those hurrying to check on loved ones, but there was only the sound of the wind.

And, then the same creaking rumbling that was the prelude to the earthquake started up again. The leaves of the trees rustled angrily; branches collapsed and flew in every direction from a forceful wind; and suddenly, the trunk of an old oak split causing the tree to fall and block half the road. It wasn't the falling tree that nearly ended Samantha's life; it was the car that swerved out of its way. The driver had instinctively moved to avoid it, but instead, careened onto the sidewalk and in spite of Samantha's fire red hair that shined brightly even in night, the driver either didn't see her or simply didn't have enough time to avoid the inevitable. The car slammed into her with a force that threw her into the air and caused her body to fall like a limp doll.

Had the two of them released me from my bottle I might have stopped her from being hit, but as it was, all I could do was close my eyes and watch the scene on the street unfold in my mind, wondering why I was connected to this girl.

Samantha lay unconscious on the pavement. Her legs were both bent behind her body at distorted, unimaginable angles. Blood oozed from a nasty gash at her temple. The blackbirds immediately descended on her, tag teaming their efforts of lapping up the crimson river and maliciously playing with her hair, pulling and pecking a few strands loose as if wanting to return home with a souvenir of the atrocity.

"Stop it! Get away from her!" the driver of the car stumbled toward Samantha's body, shooing away those nasty blackbirds into the night sky. "Oh my god, what have I done? Somebody call an ambulance!"

He shouted this last plea at the group of neighbors who had assembled to find out what the commotion was about. The crowd grew as police, a fire truck and an ambulance arrived on the scene. Within minutes everyone had a job to do. The police were taking statements, the fire crew worked to remove the fallen tree and the two paramedics tried desperately to save Samantha's young life.

The two blackbirds flew low, attracted by the carnage. One even dared to swoop in on Samantha's body yet again. A fireman swatted at the overly zealous bird, which only led it to dive bomb again, extending its talons against his cheek.

"Damn it," he exclaimed.

"What's wrong?" one of the paramedics asked, looking up.

"Just some stupid bird actually scratched me."

"Want me to look at it?" the paramedic asked.

"Nah, I'll be fine. Just take care of her," he said motioning to Samantha.

The blackbirds cawed loudly and flew away from the gathering crowd. At the end of the darkened street, they shape shifted back into their bodies, the devastatingly beautiful Raven and Phineas, two demon gypsies who had plagued me for centuries.

Black magic had not only given them extended life beyond many centuries, it enhanced their very appearance, making them irresistible to humans. Raven, with her shining black hair and eyes that appeared just as dark due to her pale complexion, smiled at Phineas. I found it fitting that an obnoxious cartoon character from this time shared his name. Yet in truth, Phineas was far too handsome for any other similarities to be compared.

His mesmerizing green eyes, which were as deep in color as emeralds, bore into hers. Pleased with the destruction they had just caused, Raven tilted her head upwards and smiled suggestively at the golden-skinned, sandy brown haired teen who was her lover and partner through the ages. Phineas wrapped his strong arms around her and cradled the small of her back before lowering his lips onto hers. They remained hidden in the shadows, careful not to let their display be publicly seen. Although their was no blood or relations shared between them, only a mutual desire for power and control, they preferred to keep up the ruse of being step-brother and step-sister. The lie allowed them to live together without raising suspicion, especially since they looked no older than eighteen.

"This is so much better than one of those stupid Malibu High School parties," Raven said.

"You almost got hit," Phineas said. "You should be more careful."

"Ahh, I love it when you worry about me. Here, taste..." she said pressing a finger to his lips. "There's still a drop of that hot fireman's blood on my fingertips."

"Raven, that was reckless."

"And you're a spoil sport."

Their conversation floated on the air. I may have still been imprisoned, but I would be able to hear the demon gypsies even if I were at the bottom of the ocean. I was connected to them whether I liked it or not and for centuries I had witnessed their destruction. I knew that my time to reappear would come soon and there was no doubt that either Samantha or Charlotte would instigate it, although given the circumstances I couldn't hold out much hope for poor Sam.

The best I could do was to keep listening and hoping to learn what they were planning.

Phineas motioned to the activity at the other end

of the street. "What a mess." Raven nodded in agreement, "That tree must've been a hundred years old. I so hate that so much of it had to come down. It was a lovely view from those branches. I'll miss perching there."

"I meant her."

"Oh that," Raven said with a shrug of her shoulders. "What choice did we have?"

"Well what are we supposed to do now? That car totally took her out. Were you able to read her when we were, you know...," his voice trailed off as if disgusted by the thought of his own carrion activities.

"Don't be so squeamish, Phin. Redheads are deliciously spicy. Why do you think I had to have some of that fireman? She was like an appetizer," Raven whispered in his ear, and then playfully teased his lobe with her tongue.

"And...?" he prompted.

"And, I don't know if she's the one. She certainly doesn't look very impressive right now."

Samantha was sprawled on the ground, her breathing becoming shallow. Raven extended her arms high above her head, and with eyes closed in prayer she suddenly altered back into bird form with those arms becoming wings that swirled the wind and used the cold night to pull the air from that poor girl.

Raven controlled the element of air to suck the life from Samantha. There wasn't much I could do as technically she wasn't my Releasor yet and the air in my bottle was terribly thin from my efforts to gain sight of her life. Yet still, I focused my energies to save her.

Phineas hissed from the shadows at Raven. "Stop it. You've done enough damage."

Raven transformed back and met him at his side. "Ahh, you're such a softy. It's really endearing."

She was right. Phineas was a young demon gypsy, alive for only a century and a half. He was aligned with Raven, created by her and dedicated to serving with her. He was strong and smart, an expert at mind-control and illusion, but it was obvious that the newer tricks such as shapeshifting still left him tired.

But Raven's powers were another story. It was mind-blowing to see how easily she shifted. She could inhabit and then come back again without any sign of stress or exhaustion. If she hadn't developed the habit of using her powers for evil, I could almost admire her for the way she had developed them. They had certainly increased from the last time we met. I paced my bottle thinking about how unreal it all was. Sure, it had been 300 years and naturally people change, but one would think that someone's true essence wouldn't. How we were once such good friends and to see Raven the way she is now, was beyond belief. I longed for the way we were, thinking back to those earlier days.

Raven was among those to experience the atrocities of the Salem Witch Trials. She was the first person to be tried alongside an animal. It was her dog,

Pixie, and the grief of it nearly killed her, particularly since she knew that no magic had been performed. Back then, people didn't know how smart dogs were or that they could learn so many tricks. But John Proctor, Raven's lover of the time, knew this and taught her many things about life.

He was a tavern keeper and he and Raven fell deeply in love, in spite of the fact that he was already married. I warned Raven what the townsfolk would say if they found out, but she insisted that they weren't doing anything wrong. I still remember the first lie she ever told me. "John isn't interested in me. He's just being kind in giving me a job," she said.

Maybe. I came into the tavern looking for Raven one day and caught her and John in a kiss. And not just any kiss. This was a full blown, lip lock and later that night, when she and I sat on my bed gossiping for hours, she admitted that she loved him. The kind of love that ripped open your soul and would make you do anything for it. The kind that I had never myself known.

Obviously, John could never offer to marry her because he already was with his wife, Elizabeth, and back then one didn't separate. But he promised to take care of Raven by giving her a job and paying her a wage three times what the other barmaids received. He also gave her his time. I worried about her future, but she seemed so happy. Pixie was a Maltese and a gift from John. She became their child of sorts. Not only did John teach Raven the ways of the world, he taught Pixie tricks so that for the first time, Raven had a way of supporting herself. She would take Pixie into the town square and that sweet dog would dance for everyone who gathered. Then, she would command her to jump into her arms, just as John had shown her, and Raven would bid her audience goodbye and go home to spend an afternoon lying in bed with John. For a short period, it seemed they would get away with it all. Until the afternoon when she was followed by one of Elizabeth's friends, who suspected that her relationship with John was more than platonic.

Soon after, this woman invited the Salem Magistrates to the town square to watch Pixie perform. She was declared a familiar on the spot. At the time, I wasn't even familiar with the term "familiar." They put Raven on trial along with Pixie, and insisted on knowing who had taught the dog such tricks. They said she was a witch's partner and as such she was capable of doing a witch's dirty deeds and would grow to not be satisfied until she had commanded a person and bewitched them. Raven said it was ridiculous, but still she wouldn't give up John's name. And this is where our friendship died. Because when the Magistrates ordered Raven and Pixie to death by hanging, I couldn't stand by and let it happen. I just wouldn't.

Raven expected me to remain quiet, but I begged her to be reasonable. I can still recall our conversation.

"I couldn't bear if something happened to him. Let them take me alone. What good is it if we're both dead?"

"Because if you give him up, you will save yourself!" I implored her. "Or, try out your new powers."

"I don't have enough control over them yet. And besides, why would I want to go on living if he weren't here by my side?"

I looked at my dear friend tenderly, and spoke the truth. "Raven honey, he doesn't love you in the same way that you love him. You just said you were willing to die for him. Then shouldn't he do the same for you?"

"Perhaps he will," she insisted. "But then what would be the point? We wouldn't be together. Don't you see, Suki?"

"But he's not worth dying for. For God's sake, he's married. You're lucky they haven't called you his whore."

She slapped me hard after that comment. Her hand stung my skin, but I'm afraid what I did hurt her heart.

"You can hate me as much as the day is long, but I can't let you throw your life away. We found each other, which given our unusual makeup accounts for a lot. Our lives move through the ages by magic." I reached out to hold her hands, "You and I are like grits and butter. We belong together and I couldn't bear to lose you."

"Well, except I'm a Gypsy, not a Genie. Don't forget the difference."

I had been through this with her before. "It

doesn't matter that my powers are a gift from the gods. Those gifts and my immortality came with a price of two lives. I have to live with the grief that I cost my parents everything."

"Poor little Genie," Raven said shaking her head.

"Stop it, Raven. If anything, your powers will one day become more impressive than mine because they are self-taught. You studied and sacrificed yourself to the gods and in return, well, you know what you can do."

"Yes, and then I crossed over."

I nodded, knowing what she was implying. It was the undying truth that part of her was demon, which meant a darkness resided within her. It was something that she would always have to fight or it would take over.

"Please Raven, don't let your gift go to waste. I beg of you. You are the closest thing I have to family, the only person who can live on with me."

"Then you of all people should love me enough to let me go," she replied simply. "And, considering what I may one day become, to do otherwise is pure selfishness."

It was a comment that cut me to the core for every Genie knows that the only wish that cannot be granted to a Releasor is that made out of selfishness. A wish must be the opposite -- of pure intention.

I shook off the hurtful comment and persevered. "I'm looking out for you, not myself. If I thought there was any way this would end well, then I wouldn't say anything, but they will hang you or burn you at the stake and if the latter happens, you know as well as I that you may not survive for another life. I have lived through centuries, losing one person after the next. I can't form attachments or fall in love. I only have you, Raven, and I don't want to lose you."

"Don't you see? If you do this to me, then you've already lost me. He's going to leave Elizabeth, and then he'll come forward for me."

"I'm sorry, sugar, but he won't."

And those were the last words we spoke. Our friendship ended over a love, but I couldn't let her risk her life for a man who wasn't worthy of that love. I told the Magistrates that she was influenced, but clearly not possessed by the Tavern Keeper John Proctor. But poor Pixie...I never expected them to take her sweet dog so that she had nothing left. They asked who was responsible for teaching Pixie and I had to finish what I started.

John was found guilty of infidelity, witchcraft and high treason for it was said that Pixie could command an audience even of council officials. The Magistrates agreed that Raven was only a pawn in his plan to expose Pixie to innocents. As such, they spared her, but ordered both John and Pixie to death. Raven never forgave me, and in some way, I have never forgiven myself. It was the last time I saw her, but her effect on me has lasted throughout the ages. Because of our fight and my guilt over what caused it, I've never allowed myself to fall in love as retribution for taking that joy away from Raven.

Raven took in the activity of the busy street. The paramedics were lifting Samantha's body onto a gurney and calling in their arrival time.

"Looks like the show's nearly over," Phineas said. "Ready to go home?"

The macabre scene turned Raven on and she smiled lustfully at Phineas. "I'm going to do such things to you tonight." She wrapped her arms around his neck and trailed her tongue from his collarbone up his neck.

"Stop it. There are still people here. *Sis*," he said pointedly. But he couldn't hide the involuntary shudder that hit his body with each of her kisses.

"So you want to play make-believe games? I can role-play," she said kissing the length of his neck. "Besides, they're kind of busy talking about the nearly dead chick."

Phineas pushed her away. "Not here."

"You can be such a bore. Doesn't this make you feel anything? They say a mind is a terrible thing to waste and after witnessing what ours just did here, well, I'd say that's a very true sentiment. You have to admit, it's pretty cool," she said motioning toward the fallen tree and everything left in its wake.

"Alright, you are amazingly powerful."

"We are, darling Phin. I couldn't have arranged the car to come around the corner at precisely the right time without you. You should have rewarded yourself, as I did. So tasty."

"Don't go all vamp on me. I don't know why you find road kill so appealing."

"I'm just fascinated with humanity."

Phineas looked amused. "I can tell."

"They're so fragile and yet, they go on and on talking about empowerment and being strong."

"We were human once," he reminded her.

Raven nodded her head, but continued to argue her point. "For a brief time, I lived as humans do, but it ended when that miserable Genie took away everything that was my life. Power is so much better than humanity and I'm not talking the kind that is born unto Witches or Genies. What we have is something to be proud of. Gypsy powers. We've died for it. We study it. We've learned to cross over and control the elements with our mind. Yes, our minds...we can even use them to control others. Isn't that an intoxicating thought?"

"I suppose it is satisfying to know that we've worked hard for what we are, rather than it just being handed to us," Phineas admitted.

"It's well deserved ego, my brother. Our powers have been nurtured and they have the potential to feed and grow from others. I want that Genie's powers once and for all."

"But she hasn't been released. It's obvious or this," he said motioning to the street, still littered with broken glass, "wouldn't have been so easy."

Raven took a red lip gloss from her purse and seductively applied a healthy sheen to her pout.

"She'll show up soon. We'll just hang around the hospital and wait for her."

Phineas couldn't take his eyes from her lips. It was the reaction she was hoping for. He shook himself out of his reverie before speaking. "Maybe you should have been a bit more patient. We can't really visit Samantha in the hospital when we've only been here a week and haven't even become friends yet."

"Then you better figure something out. Maybe you can focus on her friend, Charlotte. Seems to me she's ripe for the picking."

"She's got her eye on Josh."

"She can eye him up all she likes. Nobody can resist your charms, especially when you take control of their little brains," she said angling her body closer to Phineas.

His arms automatically drew around her and pulled her closer to his chest. He pressed against her, feeling at home in her embrace. They kissed passionately, unaffected by the tragedy in the air.

"Are you sure this isn't one-sided?"

"What do you mean," she said nuzzling his neck. "Can't you tell how I feel about you?"

Phineas looked away from her eyes, not wanting to be influenced again. Careful with his words, he answered, "I know that I'm devoted to you. So much so that when I'm with you, I do things that I'm not proud of."

Raven cocked her head back and laughed slightly. "You're still in touch with your humanity, even after all these years," she said with slight amazement in her voice. "That is so cute."

Phineas pushed away from Raven. "Enough."

"I didn't mean anything bad. I admire that about you. It shows how strong you are."

The ambulance was leaving the street, its lights and blaring horn fading in the distance. The driver of the car that hit Samantha had been taken down to the police station. And even the last of the gossiping neighbors had gone indoors leaving Raven and Phineas alone in the darkness. "You didn't answer my question," Phineas pressed.

"It's ridiculous. We only have each other. It's a long, painful life if you're alone. So Phin, don't question me. You have no idea what I'm capable of. Just get busy because Little Miss Bottle Stopper is about to be popped into our world. This is the first time we've had a head start on her."

"Do you always have to be so in control?" Phineas asked as he grabbed Raven by the wrist. His anger was palpable, but Raven could even use that to her advantage.

She surveyed him hungrily. "Not in all situations."

He reached for her, pulling her body closer to his. She responded by pressing her lips against his and wrapping one leg around him, pulling him in closer *there* too. Phineas had no chance of staying angry.

"I guess we understand each other," he spoke softly. "But you better hope Samantha pulls through because we need her thoughts if we're going to be successful." He moved his hand onto her back, reaching underneath her thin top. "You're beautiful, but cold."

It wasn't clear whether he was referring to her temperament or temperature, but it didn't matter to Raven as long as she got what she wanted.

"Phineas, I do love you," Raven replied. "It's just hard to let go of the past, which is why I need to make Suki feel what she did to me. I need your help, sweet Phin. Do it for us and everything we've been through together. You know that I love you. I chose to save you. That says something, doesn't it?"

Phineas slowly ran his hands up her bare arms, letting his finger trace the length of her neck and then along her jawline. His eyes rested on those red-glossed lips and he kissed her once before taking her hand and leading her down the quiet street to their ocean-front home. They stood on the driveway of the Mediterranean-styled mansion that was decorated in a sleek, minimalist style that matched Raven's lack of warmth.

Raven paused to lean against the front door, a massive glass fixture decorated in swirls of wrought iron. "So you're not mad at me?"

Phineas stopped a moment to face Raven. "It's hard to stay mad at you. You're all I've ever known."

He said the last sentiment almost wistfully as if he longed for some other type of love in his life. Regardless of what may or may not have been in his heart, his mind and body told him to take Raven inside.

Chapter Three

Some people foolishly think that stumbling upon a Genie's bottle and unleashing her power is a random act of coincidence when in reality it is fate. The girls I was about to meet appeared to be your typical, average teenagers, but I knew that if the demon gypsies were circling, flying in their animal form – whether that of blackbird when they wanted to swoop in, or quiet as a white moth when they surreptitiously gained access to a home -- then these seemingly ordinary girls were actually quite exceptional. How their destiny would affect our world was yet to be seen, but I was sure to be a part of it. That is, if Samantha pulled through.

I needed Charlotte to get me to that hospital, but the girl had been a basket case ever since hearing about the accident. If I could only occupy her thoughts, I might be able to get to Samantha before the gypsies returned for her. Of course, I couldn't know for sure that either of the girls would be my next Releasor, and if I were wrong and I entered Charlotte's psyche, then I may not return for many lifetimes. It was a risk I was willing to take.

I concentrated on my bottle's history, the magic of the butterflies that could carry a thought on the wind, and imagined Charlotte at peace. In her dreams, she wouldn't remember Samantha's accident. She would only see herself running through a beautiful grassy field with the butterflies trailing behind her. Whereas the gypsy moths brought darkness, butterflies were used by Genies at the opposite end of the spectrum.

Charlotte smiled in her sleep. Butterflies of lavender and blue tickled her arms and she felt weightless as if she could fly next to them. Samantha was in the field too and everything was beautiful. Flowers were the colors of the rainbow. The sky was a clear, light blue and they were running freely with the wind in their hair. It was a feeling of total elation in a world of peace. There were no memories of Samantha's accident, until Charlotte's neighbor, who was looking for her cat, rang the bell and woke her.

"Charlotte dear, have you seen my Caesar? I think all of those sirens must have scared him," her neighbor spoke while peering behind bushes. "How is dear Samantha doing? Such a tragedy."

Charlotte struggled with the thoughts from her dream and stared at the woman in confusion. "What do you mean?"

"The accident. She's at the hospital. You remember that, don't you?"

But Charlotte didn't know anything about the tree, the car or Samantha caught up between the two. Her kindly neighbor explained it all patiently and suggested that Charlotte see her own doctor after school. It made no sense and the only person who understood what Charlotte was thinking was lying in a coma. With the memory of the dream I planted in her mind, Charlotte rushed to get dressed hoping that it was a positive sign. I willed her to take my bottle with her. She was just about to leave, but stopped suddenly and eyed the bottle, just as I had hoped, and thinking that it would be a nice gesture to bring it to Samantha, she placed it inside her backpack before heading out the door. She moved with renewed purpose and I had hope that she would release me in time.

When Charlotte arrived at school, throngs of students stopped her in the halls to inquire about Samantha's state of being. She was considerably more popular than just a week prior.

"They're all fakes," Charlotte mumbled to herself while attending to her jammed locker. She shoved against it harder that usual, relishing the pain inflicted upon her shoulder. If she could take away any of the pain that Samantha was feeling she would.

"Hey, easy Tiger. Can I help you with that?"

She looked up to see Josh smiling down at her. "Thanks. It just gets stuck sometimes."

With barely any effort, Josh had the door flying open. It was the kind of typically cool behavior she would expect from him. And then, as if to prove how undeserving she felt of his attentions, Charlotte removed one book only to send the others careening onto the floor.

"Let me," he said bending down.

"You don't have to, really. The bell rang and I'm sure you have better things to do."

But Josh stayed and picked up her books. "So I'm sure you keep getting asked this, but how's Samantha? You must be pretty shook up."

"I'm going to visit her after school."

"So she's seeing visitors?

"I called the hospital this morning. They said she was in and out of consciousness, but showing signs of improvement. Her nurse says that she can probably sense people, so I want to go there just to you know, talk to her."

"Would you mind if I came along to keep you company?"

Without thinking, Charlotte blurted out, "Why?"

Josh laughed. "Because you nearly lost your best friend and I figure you might need one right about now."

"I could certainly use a friend. Thank you." Charlotte smiled for the first time since learning about Samantha, until Ashley, Josh's girlfriend, rounded the corner and headed their way. Her deliberate gait didn't go unnoticed by Josh either.

"I gotta run, Charlotte, but I'll meet you in the far corner of the parking lot after school."

Charlotte knew that Josh could wait undetected by Ashley if he met her there. Although she didn't like the fact that he felt he had to sneak around to spend time with her, she was thrilled nonetheless that he even wanted to. She decided to help matters. "I've got independent study for last period so I'm heading over there early. Do you mind meeting me there?" And then seeing Ashley glare in their direction, she asked again, "Are you sure you want to come?"

"Stop asking. I'll even buy you a delicious cup of hospital coffee," he said before hurrying to Ashley.

So here's the deal. I've got one potential Releasor in and out of consciousness. Another one who has no idea that demon gypsies are after her. And both are totally infatuated with unavailable guys. If this is indeed my next assignment, it couldn't be more challenging. And tell me, why is it taking so long to be released? I am in severe need of a skinny latte, or sushi, perhaps a cupcake, or any of the other amazing foodie delicacies that have crept into popular culture since I was last sprung from my bottle.

Honestly, it's been nearly twelve hours since I willed Charlotte to dream of Samantha and see the two of them happy again. I had no real connection to these two, and yet I found myself praying for Samantha's speedy recovery. Even though we hadn't been properly introduced, I already cared about these two. There was something about them -- some undiscovered talents within them, something I have a lot of experience in nurturing.

It reminded me of the time back in the '50s when Frankie Avalon and I were hanging out at the beach. It took Frankie awhile to get used to my magic and before he did, he thought that I must have come from another planet. Yes, it was me who inspired that cute little "Venus" song. Anyway, one day I left the beach early, which seemed like a horrible mistake at the time because that Annette caught his eye. But later I came to realize that when one door closes another opens because I was headed home on my Harley in just a pair of cut-off jeans and a bikini top when I stumbled upon a very sweet and stranded young actor, Jack Nicholson, by the side of the road. His car broke down so I told him to hop on and hold tight.

Jack was not the mysterious dark horse that people now know. He was quite shy about holding a scantily clad Genie. But during that ride home he got inspired by my curves as well as those of the road. With the speed of my Harley hugging each bend of Malibu Canyon we rode until nightfall and he said that he had never felt such a thrill. It's no surprise that he signed up the very next day to a little film called "Easy Rider." He was nominated for his first Academy Award as a result of that film and my dear Jack told everyone that it would never have happened without the inspiration of a certain Genie. I changed Jack's image from squeaky clean to down-right dirty and it hasn't failed him yet. Now I'm not saying that Samantha and Charlotte should float down that river, but maybe they could use with dipping their toe into the water. I paced my bottle and used all of my intuitive powers to will the event of my release into action when suddenly the air shifted and it became noticeably hotter. I felt the constriction around my neck that occurs when meeting my Releasor is imminent. Like a baby coming into the world, being unleashed is tiring and risky. There's a moment in time when the air leaves my bottle and forces me outside, and yet I'm not real to the human world. It is the period in which I am vulnerable. During that continuum, I am neither here nor there. Like that baby, I wait to take my first breaths of the human world.

For some reason, this time my struggle was greater. I tried desperately to grasp a vision of Samantha or Charlotte, but the image kept fading back and forth between them as the interior temperature of my bottle threatened my existence. Perhaps it was because there were two potential Releasors and the spirits had not decided who would do the deed.

"I hope you can hear me, Sam," Charlotte whispered. Various hospital monitors were hooked up to Samantha's pale frame, beeping regularly within the otherwise quiet room. "I brought some things to brighten up this place. I've got Cuddles, your first stuffed animal that has definitely seen better days, and I brought our bottle over too. I thought we could decide whose house should get it first. So, here it goes."

Charlotte held one hand around my bottle's body and then used her other to carefully hold Samantha's hand over its neck. She watched her friend lying still and thought of happier times.

"Please don't leave me, Sam," she said aloud. "We have been best friends our entire life. You are a part of me and I am a part of you. Wake up. Please God, she has so much life to live. I would give any part of my life for her. Please, let her wake up."

It was just the type of unselfish plea that makes this Genie's day. With that request, the air in my bottle stirred, finally giving me the extra push I needed to be released. I inhaled deeply, pulling the oxygen from the room just enough to put Charlotte into a deep sleep. Before she knew what had happened, she was hunched over Samantha's bed without ever releasing hers or Samantha's grasp on the bottle. Out I popped, just in time to change into the cutest nurse's uniform you ever did see. With ease I entered the thoughts of the rotation nurse and willed her to place me on Samantha's case.

I looked from Samantha to Charlotte and found it hard to believe that these were the same girls I had been listening to over the past week. Samantha, who was so full of bravado, remained so still with one foot in this life and one daring to tiptoe into another. Charlotte enjoyed the sleep I had instilled in her for she had fought it so much during the last few days. Normally quiet and reserved, she had fought her fears with such bravery in order to remain strong for Samantha. The two of them deserved a reunion and I was looking forward to our introduction.

I placed my hands on Samantha's temples willing the energy I've garnered from centuries of living to enter her body. I could feel her growing warmer underneath my touch. I slowly exhaled over her head causing the air to stir like a halo above her. With that, she inhaled my breath and her heart began to beat on its own.

I gently woke Charlotte, who opened her eyes just as I was disconnecting Samantha's leads.

"What are you doing?" Charlotte asked in a panic. "She's not...I can't lose her."

"Of course not," I smiled. "She just plum doesn't need these ugly things anymore."

Taking that cue, Samantha slowly fluttered open her eyelids, and Charlotte released tears of joy.

"Oh Sam, you're back. God I missed you," and Charlotte reached over to hug her.

"Can you believe all of this?" she said looking around the room. "I'm so tired and yet, I feel like I haven't eaten in forever."

"Now I know you're going to be okay," Charlotte smiled with relief.

I have to say, it was one of my happiest releases. Those two girls were as sweet as a summer watermelon. "I'll get you some applesauce and saltines. Sound yummy?" I said in Samantha's direction. "Oh, and Charlotte, there's a boy due to arrive any minute. Remember? Maybe you want to freshen up."

"Was he here earlier?" Charlotte asked in a panic. "I hope he didn't see me sleeping and drooling."

"No, he hasn't been here yet. In fact, I've never met him, but I do think he might be sweet on you and he's on his way."

"How do you know this?" Charlotte asked.

"Not now, sugar. You've got to get yourself together and I need to take Samantha's vitals."

They both gave me a funny look and since I'm horrible at keeping secrets, I conceded. "Alright, if you insist. It's a pleasure to meet both of you. I'm Suzette, but my friends call me Suki. Oh, and I'm a Genie. Actually, your Genie," I motioned toward the bottle, it's beautiful butterfly design glowing softly in the light from the hospital monitors. "I'll just take that back, part of the deal and all."

For the first time they noticed what so many before them had seen -- my aura, a pull that brings people in and invites them to be inspired. They took in my long brown hair that falls in shiny waves down my back and my wide-set, brown eyes framed in long, black lashes that begged an explanation. "My eyes can see things more clearly than most people. You'll learn that about me, as well as my other talents because it seems that I have been released by not one, but both of you. It's a regular party here. Have we got lots to talk about or what?"

Chapter Four

Samantha spoke first. "I got hit in the head, well actually, hit in the head, run over and thrown a few hundred yards. Is that right?"

"And you're not really a nurse?" Charlotte asked.

"Yes," I said patiently.

"You're a Genie?" Samantha said with doubt.

I nodded again. "It's a lot to take in," I admitted. "Some humans don't believe in Genies, but I am living proof that we exist. In fact, I've lived for over 350 years serving many a fine gentleman. I was originally born in ancient Mesopotamia, now Egypt, but my formative years were spent in the South. I'm a Macon, Georgia girl at heart. But I've told you all this."

"Yes, and we don't believe you," Samantha said sitting up quickly, only to get a head rush and slump back down.

Charlotte was still feeling protective and as such, she made her first request, which I was obligated to obey. It's a pity that the first wish is always wasted in this way. "Prove it," she said.

"Is that a wish?"

"Yes," she repeated and then rolled her eyes

sarcastically, "I wish you would prove yourself."

"As you wish."

Charlotte and Samantha glanced at each other, neither knowing what to think and weighing the possibility of truth or hoax, back and forth.

"I will prove myself, as you wish," I continued. "Close your eyes and give me your hand," I said to Charlotte. She did as I said, allowing me to read her memories.

"You were born Charlotte Renee Osbrin. Your parents perished in a car accident. You've been in and out of foster homes ever since, until last year. You're doing fine on your own, except the obvious fact that you won't allow yourself to rely or get close to anyone.

"That can be construed as opinion, not fact. And you could have found out about my parents from reading an old paper," Charlotte interrupted.

"I'm not finished. You will be convinced. You regret not telling your father something before his death. You never kept secrets from him, but you did in the case of a boy who you fell in love with. At least you thought you were in love, until you were faced with having an abortion."

"Oh my god, Charlotte. You never told me about that," Samantha exclaimed.

"It was before I moved here," Charlotte explained. "It's in the past and it doesn't prove anything. She could have gotten a hold of my medical records."

"Actually, you didn't use your real name. Did you?"

That's when the look of realization hit Charlotte's eyes. "I'll continue. The boy betrayed your trust. He didn't stand by you, and so you were relieved when three months later your father was transferred to California. You entered Malibu High where you met Samantha, found a true soul mate and friend for life, and that important shoulder to lean on when your parents passed..."

The girls were silent, ruminating over the truths that I had dispelled.

"But you're strong," I continued. "You'll get past your pain. You'll learn to trust -- maybe starting with me. You have a future of importance before you. I don't know what is involved, but I do know that it's why I was sent to you. Now do you believe me?"

"There's no way you could know the things you know," Charlotte replied carefully.

"That was pretty amazing," Samantha joined in. "Do me," she said sitting up quickly before slumping back down.

"Well as for you, Samantha, you shouldn't sit up so fast or get overly excited. You're healed, but still weak. Don't be concerned, it's a human thing," I said fluffing her pillow.

"That's not what I meant," Samantha huffed. "Do the freaky psychic thing."

"Psychic? I'm a *Genie*. I have guided people for centuries. I'm not carnival sideshow."

Charlotte sat on the bed next to Samantha. "So, are we like the first to release you?"

"Goodness, no. I've been a muse to sultans,

generals, famous artists and actors..."

"And now us?" Samantha asked, implying the obvious.

I nodded. "We'll figure out the reason," I said taking their hands in my own. "Say, when was the last time either of you had a manicure?" I turned my attention then to Charlotte's exquisite complexion. "You have remarkable pores."

"Uhh thanks, I think."

"But, you could still use some make-up. You know, just to enhance your natural beauty. And you," I said turning to Samantha, "have you ever thought about a Brazilian blow-out?"

"I like my curls," Samantha said.

"You're right. They're unique. You just need a good wardrobe to help you pull off the whole wild child look. The minute you two get out of here, what do you say we do a make-over?"

"We're good," Charlotte answered swiftly.

"I do declare, I have no idea why any girl would refuse."

"Yeah about that...that accent," noted Samantha. "You've been all over the world. You could have stayed anywhere, and you chose the South?"

"I wasn't always in the South, but it's where I prefer to be. Well, there and a wonderful little English village where I was released about one hundred years ago...Uckfield."

"Uckfield?" the girls asked in unison.

"It's a quaint little village in East Sussex, England. Beautiful place. And, it's where I met and became engaged to Charles Dawson. He was the only man who I have been released to that I also fell in love with.

"You haven't been in love for one hundred years?" Samantha asked incredulously.

"Love is the bee's knees. It doesn't just land in your lap everyday. Anyway, I think I'm better off without it. My judgment became clouded when I fell in love. Charles was a romantic. He saw what I was capable of doing and decided that he wanted to make me proud. After all, he was only a gravel pit foreman in Piltdown, which was near Uckfield. His job didn't matter to me, but he knew that I had been with head's of state and he was desperate to make something of himself. He said that he was old-fashioned and wanted to provide for us without the use of my powers. He was the first man to accept me for who I was without ever trying that old trick of using the last wish to ask for more wishes. That doesn't fly, by the way. Wishes have to be used for goodness.

"What? You can't make up new rules about wishes. Everyone knows that people wish for..."

But I had to interrupt Charlotte quickly. "No they don't. I am not inclined to stay with someone I can't help or who doesn't help the world around them. And people of that caliber do not wish for money or harm to come to others or...for more wishes. That's a rule. My rule. If you've heard differently, then it's just a fairy tale."

Samantha and Charlotte sighed. "Okay, so you're our Genie, but pretty much anything we would want to wish for we can't have. Is that right," Samantha asked.

"No it's not that bad. When you learn a little more about why I'm here, you'll want to do the right thing, which is take your time with the wishes. You only have three, well now two, so you don't want to mess up because what you wish for will affect those around you. This is why I'm usually with people until their deaths. It can take a lifetime to figure out the most pure and wonderful of wishes."

"Terrific," Charlotte said with a roll of her eyes. "So go on about Charles."

"Well, he came home one night from the gravel pit and told me that he had made a scientific discovery that would ensure his place in history. While digging one day, his workers discovered human bones."

"Gross," Samantha said.

"Bloody bones?" Charlotte asked.

"Don't swear. I don't condone that type of language."

"I didn't mean it that way," Charlotte explained. "Was it a murder?"

"Oh, I see," I said realizing my mistake, but then again, I was on edge recalling the story of my one love. "No, this was what the newspapers and scientists of our day called 'the missing link.' Charles was obsessed with the find. He dug by himself for days after that first bone fragment was discovered until he found more and pieced together an entire skull."

"How could it not be murder?" Samantha

repeated.

"Although the head looked human, the jaw stuck out meaning that the find supported a theory among England's scientific circles that evolution began with the brain. Overnight, Charles was the toast of the town. And, he did this all on his own. I was so proud."

"So what happened?" the girls asked.

"One night, he said that there were men who doubted his discovery and we needed to leave England right away...tout suite. I didn't understand why we had to leave, but Charles said that he didn't want to be a part of a community of naysayers, and besides he had a brother in Louisiana. I had never been to the United States and he said that it was time he introduced me to his family, not as his Genie of course, but as his wife. How could I argue? He proposed and that night we were on a plane.

"It was the first time in my entire life that I found myself speechless. I may have been 250 years old, but I was acting like a school girl. Charles was wildly successful as a result of his own doing. I was planning a big Southern style wedding with a Scarlett O'Hara dress and his family didn't even care that I was immortal. I let my guard down and for the first time, I thought that I could have real love in my life. Everything was perfect. But, I was wrong and it didn't last."

"Your relationship?" Samantha asked.

"His career?" Charlotte piped in.

"None of it," I answered. "There was a man who hunted us like a rabid dog --Franz Weidenreich. He had been examining what had become known as "the Piltdown Man" and he reported that it wasn't a missing link, but a manufactured hoax developed by Charles. He said the skull consisted of a modern human cranium and an orangutan jaw with filed-down teeth. He said that Charles not only fiddled with the bones, but planted them in the gravel pit himself to be found later so that he could take the credit."

"Was it true?" Samantha asked.

I couldn't answer at first. Even after all these years, the memory of the betrayal was too much. "I didn't want to believe it, but eventually I couldn't deny it. Weidenreich was an anatomist and he didn't give up easily. For thirty years, he pursued his theory that Charles had fooled everyone. I finally asked Charles if this was the reason we left England and came to the South. It seemed like the people Franz was working with were closing in on us as if we were a couple of bank robbers."

"But I thought you said you were happy," Charlotte questioned.

"For awhile everything was as it should be. His family showed me true Southern hospitality, not to mention amazing Southern cooking. I could eat sweet potato pie from dusk until dawn and be content as a pig in a mud bath. But I couldn't ignore the signs around me. After all, even though Charles never wanted me to use my powers, I still was a Genie and I couldn't just turn off my intuitive powers like a water spigot.

"For awhile the accusations stopped, but then

someone else would bring them up again. Talks about Piltdown Man being a hoax usually corresponded to talks about Charles receiving a knighthood or being elected to the Royal Society, both lifelong dreams of his. Eventually, it was proved that Charles brought Arthur Smith Woodward, who was keeper of the geological department at the British Museum, to the site after he had planted the skull fragments. Not only had Franz questioned him, but French paleontologist Marcellin Boule and American zoologist Gerrit Smith Miller did as well. Charles felt like the entire world was against him and that he had let me down horribly."

"Well, he kinda did, didn't he?" Samantha noted.

"How could you love a fraud?" Charlotte asked.

"I guess love really is blind, especially if it's given without taking anything in return. As I said, Charles was the only person in 250 years that never asked anything of me other than my love. That is a pretty powerful aphrodisiac."

"So, when everyone said he was a fake you broke up?"

"No, it wasn't that simple. Charles even planned the end of us. He even fooled me."

Samantha looked at me questioningly. "How can he fool a Genie? I thought you had all sorts of powers."

"Yeah, what are your powers, anyway?" Charlotte asked. "I mean, if we're to trust you, shouldn't we know?"

"I suppose you're entitled. I am first and

foremost an Intuitive, a muse if you will. I innately know a person's true nature and I influence them to achieve what is best for them."

Samantha broached the subject of Charles' death. "But you weren't able to help Charles."

I nodded. "He didn't need much from me. His true nature was a loving man with pure intentions. He gave me unconditional love, something that nobody before him has been capable of. It's just that he fooled the world in his quest to prove love to me. I said I can influence thoughts, actions are part of free will. In other words, you can lead a horse to water, but you can't make him drink."

"So what else can you do?" Charlotte forged on.

"I obviously am immortal. In order to survive so many years, I have been gifted with an ability to trigger forces of nature – water, air, earth, and fire. I use my gifts foremost to protect my Releasers, and if they deem necessary, then to grant three wishes."

"Necessary?" Samantha asked.

"Sometimes protection and guidance proves to be more beneficial than a fleeting wish. I stay as long as you are alive and have wishes still to use. I am now connected to you."

"How Zen," Samantha said.

"Quite," I agreed. "There is one more ability I haven't mentioned. Love and the desire humans have to find it. For obvious reasons, men are a bit more easily influenced in this area. In time, you will learn to be aware of the power of influence within yourselves."

The girls seemed to mull over what I was saying

as if they were already weighing the benefits of a quick fix wish or being associated to someone who has lived for more than three centuries and has a range of supernatural powers to assist them through the rough waters of their teenage years.

"You can teach us? And help us figure out why we Released you?" Samantha asked.

"To a degree," I replied carefully. "I have centuries on you and I'm immortal. But even though you are human, you still have some intuition. You just need to tap into a part of your brain that is dormant, unused."

"Suki, how did Charles fool you?" Charlotte asked cautiously.

"He pretended everything would be alright, all the while planning his own suicide. He even faked that by making it a long, drawn out event."

"How? How can suicide be drawn out?" Samantha asked in disbelief.

"He pricked himself with a rose bush and then allowed the thorn to remain. Ironic really. He used to say late at night that those men who hunted him were thorns in his side. He was the one who first said that phrase. And it gave him the idea to end his life. The rose bush thorn remained for days until he was sure that it had infected his bloodstream, but even then he pretended that nothing was wrong. He must have been developing the fever, but he carried on working in the garden, helping with chores around his brother's house, until he finally succumbed to the sickness of septicemia. It's a brutal condition. The body develops an inflammatory response by the immune system that affects the blood, urine, lungs, and even skin. Blood poisoning takes over and by the time it was discovered in Charles, it was too late to stop it. But he knew that would be the case and it was as he wanted."

"What happened after he died? How did you end up in your bottle and belonging to someone else?" Charlotte inquired.

"I didn't retreat to my bottle right away. I had come to love the South and I wanted to remain close to Charles' family. I needed them and I remained with them until his brother became an old man. I didn't want to see him die and so before he became too elderly, I asked him to confine me to my bottle and throw me out to sea. I was discovered about five years after that time, but I haven't found a man like Charles in the last century."

The mood was somber after my story. It wasn't like me to open up so much, but I had never been released by not one, but two people. And, it was a new experience to be around teenagers who walk around with bravado, but are actually innocent. They deserved a healthy dose of truth considering what they were about to become involved with. For it was just after I concluded my story that Phineas, dressed as a hospital orderly, spotted the three of us chatting like long-lost girlfriends and ducked into a nearby room before I could set eyes on him.

Chapter Five

$\mathcal{H}$ere's the thing...when you're as gorgeous as Phineas with his high cheekbones, eyes the color of emeralds, and hair color that perfectly matches his golden skin, it's easy to sweet talk your way into human resources and land a job as a hospital orderly. He probably flashed his dimples and they no sooner threw the uniform at him. Forget about background checks, job experience, references or the niggling little detail that he and his revenge-seeking lover were responsible for nearly killing one of the patients, he was in. Rules were meant to be broken for people who looked like Phineas.

But I, on the other hand, was immune to his charms. Raven was vindictive and dangerous, but in a sense, Phineas' actions were even more reprehensible. He was willing to let Raven teach him black magic and use it to support her goals. I suppose he felt he owed her his second life and so he would spend his immortality serving her needs. In my mind, it just made him seem weak in spite of his growing powers.

I quickly excused myself from the girls' when I suddenly sensed the presence of danger. It had been centuries since I had been in contact with the twins, but images of them passed in front of my eyes. I tried to keep my mind on Samantha and focus on her getting better, but a warning kept haunting me. If it were true and Raven and Phineas were nearby, I couldn't allow either of them to get close to Samantha considering her weakened condition.

I hadn't let my mind think about them in so long that I had nearly tuned the memories out. I rationalized that it had been too painful to keep remembering the past, but this time was different. I focused on hearing Raven's thoughts out of necessity for the girls' safety, not for any cause relating to my own past with them.

Like tuning into a radio channel, I could hear Raven and Phineas as their conversations pertained to the girls. Their voices filled my mind louder now as I had been released by the girls and therefore, had a direct line to any ill wishes relating to them. Charlotte and Samantha were now my responsibility and as such, I intended to find out why Raven and Phineas were taking such an interest in them.

Phineas was rounding the corner, headed directly to Samantha's room while wheeling a crash cart that yielded enough electricity to stop her heart rather than its intended purpose of a jumpstart.

"Phineas, you look good for someone pushing 130 years. What brings you to these parts?"

He bore his eyes into mine, deciding the best course of action. And rather disappointedly, he chose none. "Hello Suzette. Does Raven know you're back?"

"I assume she'll hear about it. You two are still sharing a few brainwaves? Tell her I say 'hi'."

"This doesn't concern you, Suzette. I don't personally have issues with you, but my loyalties lie with Raven so maybe you should just take a vacation," he said making little fluttering motions with his arms.

"So, who are you visiting?" I tried to sound nonchalant just in case I had been wrong and he wasn't yet aware of Charlotte and Samantha.

"Just hanging," as they say these days. "I also wanted to check on a poor girl named Samantha." He pointed to his i.d. badge. "It's my job to make sure all patients have everything they need."

My eyes flashed anger and the pleasantries were finished. "Stay away from them, Phineas."

"Suzette, you should really take your own advice."

"That's going to be pretty much impossible. Those girls are my Releasers."

If I wasn't mistaken, Phineas experienced surprise at the news. So he was once again acting on Raven's instructions.

"Were you involved in nearly turning Samantha into road kill?"

"I was just leaving," he said retreating into an open elevator.

"Good and take that cart with you. If you think it's getting anywhere near her, you're sadly mistak...," but the doors closed before I could dish out the last warning. Phineas had only just disappeared when my heart started beating fast.

It wasn't like me to lose control of my emotions

and he had hardly posed a threat, but here I was feeling like a metronome turned on high. And then all hell broke loose and I realized it wasn't my heart I was feeling – it was Samantha's. I could feel what she felt, see what she saw, and it was all too much for her human heart. Beepers went off, nurses were scuttling about, and down the hall someone distinctly yelled, "She's crashing!"

Genies are gifted with grace of movement and stealth-like quiet. There was too much commotion for anyone to notice my sudden appearance by Samantha's bedside. A nurse ushered Charlotte out of the room, while another shouted again for the crash cart. I shook my head at my own stupidity. Phineas wasn't going to use the cart to pump Samantha's heart into overdrive; he was removing it so that it couldn't save her.

I concentrated on the poor girl lying just before me. That's when I noticed that Samantha's eyeballs were jumping against her closed lids. The frequency of the R.E.M. – rapid eye movement – indicated she was in the midst of a nightmare and it appeared to be a terrifying one that had triggered a heart attack. I closed my eyes as well and entered her dreams.

"No! Oh my God," Samantha tried to scream, but the result was only a whimper. She was too scared to produce any force behind her words. A dark shadow loomed over her. The entire sky filled with blackness as thousands of white moths swarmed and blocked any bit of sunlight. Their wings brushed against her skin. Some became tangled in her mane of curls. They flew into her eyes, making her fall to the ground. And then, the air became stiflingly hot. She tried to stand, but her legs kept giving out as the white moths dove upon her. They seemed to multiply and as if Samantha were a piece of fabric, they landed on every inch of her body and chewed through the silkiness of her skin.

Another silent scream filled my mind as I tried to lead her away from the insects and the hard concrete where she imagined falling. Nothing was working. It wasn't a normal nightmare that people float in and out of. This was a prison encasing Samantha's mind and willing her to die within it. In spite of my own anxiousness to jump into action, I allowed my mind to quiet and take in the silent sounds. I listened carefully to the realm of her nightmare and there, beyond the sounds of thousands of moth wings rubbing together I heard Raven and Phineas' whispered voices instructing each other to torment Samantha's mind.

So this was no ordinary nightmare. It was planted. I wouldn't be able to lead Samantha to a place of peace unless I played them at their own game. I felt the cold of the concrete where Samantha's nightmare had caused her to lie, and then like an artist, I painted a new scene.

I whispered soothingly to Samantha. "Everywhere there is beauty." Soon, the cold feel of concrete was replaced by gentle tickle of a grassy field. I imagined the constant hum of the moths transporting into a gentle whoosh of a breeze carrying with it one perfectly symmetrical butterfly. The colors of its wings magically changing with every glimmer of the sunlight. It started off as lavender and then deepened into an azure blue, before fading lighter to the color of the sky, and fading even further until becoming pink, when suddenly, it would grow more vidid and return to its original state. Its beauty was incomparable to anything else.

"Follow it," I commanded. "It will take you home."

Samantha could see the floating butterfly that led her to my bottle with its own sparkling clear butterfly design. She could feel its coolness in her hands and innately she knew that I was with her. The fluttering of her eyelids slowed, replaced by the floating of the butterfly that led her back to life. As suddenly as the attack started, her heart rate stabilized. Naturally, the doctors and nurses believed it to be medical science. I knew that Raven was behind this and the extent of her powers had grown tremendously since I last encountered her. Back then she thought physical power outweighed mental strength, and she was determined to develop her ability to shape shift.

Given this latest display, I guess she had a change of heart and decided it best to learn a few mind games. Well, two could play those games. I stayed by Samantha's side, contemplating what could possibly have triggered Raven's rage. Could it be another attempt to get back at me, even after all of these years? Taking the life of someone so young and innocent before I had a chance to be of influence would be a distress that I certainly wouldn't recover from easily. Still, it didn't make sense that this was all directed toward me. Raven had other opportunities to come after me in the past. Why choose this moment?

I stayed with Samantha and concentrated on her heart growing stronger while considering whether Raven even had a heart. But keeping me occupied with Samantha allowed Phineas to seek out Charlotte and launch the first step of Raven's plan.

Phineas saw the flash of her blonde hair, so light it glowed like a beacon and would have drawn him near her even if Raven hadn't insisted on it. Charlotte paced the hallways, the worry over Samantha obvious on her face. For a moment he just watched her, surprised by her beauty. She was wearing her usual jeans and t-shirt with little to no makeup. But regardless of her casual appearance, Charlotte possessed a natural beauty that was undeniable. Furthermore, Phineas could sense an inner beauty that he hadn't witnessed ever before. She even moved with grace.

"For God's sake, get a grip," he muttered to himself and then set his mind at the task at hand. There was no point in admiring this girl. She was a job.

"Excuse me," Phineas said catching up to Charlotte. "I have information about the patient in room 1019."

"How is she? Please tell me she's okay," Charlotte said, her voice choked and shaking.

Phineas placed his hands on her shoulders, allowing his touch to influence her. He looked into her eyes and focused on calming her. Her mind was so open and innocent that within seconds, Phineas' powers took hold. He saw Charlotte audibly exhale and smile, and ironically he felt pleased that he had given this girl reason to smile. "She's going to be fine. We're not sure what triggered it, perhaps just the stress of being here. But she's out of danger."

"Thank you. I should go to her," Charlotte said already backing down the hall. But Phineas caught her hand easily in his own. He didn't know why he was looking forward to spending time with Charlotte, but without a doubt he wanted to do just that. Raven had told him to get in with her, which he found pleasurable. He was inexplicably drawn to Charlotte and his hope that she would stay with him had nothing to do with Raven's request.

"She's sleeping. I'm sure if you give her half an hour, the rest would do her good. I'll tell you what, how 'bout I keep you company? Buy you a coffee?" he said, the charm oozing out of him.

"That's very nice of you, but you probably have stuff to do."

Phineas smiled, knowing that Charlotte was interested and no doubt hoping that he would insist, which he did. "Come on. I'm supposed to look after visitors and I'd much rather be with you than the old guy visiting the room down the hall."

The body language said it all. Charlotte twirled a lock of her hair around her finger. Phineas stared directly at her, and then she nodded. To Charlotte's surprise, Phineas held out his hand, and after just a moment's hesitation followed by the sudden blush that appeared on Charlotte's naturally pale skin, she placed her hand in his.

Charlotte's hand was cold when Phineas took it in his own, but immediately warmed at his touch, their connection instantaneous. A feeling of electricity pulsed through her, down her entire spine, and she stopped walking momentarily out of surprise.

"You ready?" Phineas asked, not quite expecting the reaction himself. He chocked it up to Raven's lessons on influence and assumed that she was hovering in bird form nearby, helping him sway Charlotte's mind. Whatever the reason, Phineas was at least relieved that Raven would see he had done as she requested.

After half an hour of alone time with Phineas, Charlotte was giddy. She was just putting her number in his cell phone when Josh turned up, giving Charlotte her first taste of what it's like to be a sought-after woman.

Charlotte half expected Phineas to immediately return to work, but he had his agenda. In spite of Josh's arrival, Phineas decided to lay claim to her attention. He stood by and waited while she awkwardly introduced him.

"It was nice of you to come. Umm, Josh, this is Phineas. He just transferred to our school and he works here. He's been keeping me company."

Josh eyed Phineas and immediately had him pegged as competition. "That's nice of you, but hey, I'm happy to take over."

Phineas took a step closer to Charlotte. "Don't you have a girlfriend?"

The first verbal punch had been thrown. "Don't you have a job to get to?" Josh replied.

"Yeah, I'm doing it. If you had been here earlier, you would know that Samantha's heart just about jumped out of her chest and Charlotte was pretty shook up. Making sure she's okay is my job," he said moving next to Charlotte.

Charlotte attempted to diffuse the situation. "Guys – Samantha is stable and I'm fine." She looked at the time display on her cell. "In fact, it's probably been enough time and I can go back to her room, right?" she asked Phineas.

"Absolutely," he said giving her hug. "Hey, I'm sorry that it took this to bring us together, but I am glad we met. See you tomorrow?"

"Sure. Thanks again."

"That guy is so full of himself," Josh said once Phineas was out of earshot. "I've seen him sulking around corners at school. Something seems off about him."

"He's just being friendly, like he said, he kept me informed. I was totally freaked out. I mean, one minute everything is fine and then Sam's heart goes berserk and it looks like she's about to die."

"She's okay now?" Josh asked, concern showing

in his eyes.

"Yeah, it's weird. Like nothing happened. It was great that Phineas was here to calm my nerves, though." Charlotte eyed Josh to see if her words had any effect on him. She knew he had a girlfriend, but that didn't stop her from still having a baby crush on him, and wanting to test the waters by seeing if just maybe she could make him jealous.

"I'm glad she's okay. Shall we get back to her?"

Josh put his arm around Charlotte's shoulders to lead her toward the elevators. Maybe, just maybe seeing her with Phineas was the inspiration he needed, she thought to herself. And then just as suddenly as the thought hit her, the moment was broken when Josh received a text from Ashley.

"Uh oh," he said aloud.

"Bad news?"

"Well, it's just that Ashley thought I was giving her a ride home today. I didn't mention that I was coming here, and well, she's asking where I am."

"Why didn't you tell her? Charlotte asked, the feeling of dread coming over her.

"I just...I guess I didn't think it was necessary. You helped me in chem lab all last year and now it seemed like you needed a friend."

I felt Charlotte's heart now plummet into her shoes. "Just repaying the favor?"

"No, it's not like that. I mean, you're a really good person. I want us to be friends."

"But, you don't want Ashley to know?"

"It's just that sometimes she gets jealous when

she obviously shouldn't."

"Totally, I get it." Charlotte repeated. "I guess you better go. You wouldn't want to keep her waiting."

"You'll be okay?"

"Yeah, I'll be fine. I'm going to check on Samantha and then I'm going home anyway. There's really no reason for you to be away from your girlfriend."

Charlotte noticed that this time, Josh didn't try to argue with the truth, the way he had when Phineas was around. It wasn't her that he wanted, it was more the desire to win against another guy. Charlotte's mind immediately went to those dating reality shows where 50 some guys or girls compete with each other to be the "lucky" one chosen by the perpetually single, but oh-so-terribly-good-looking person who was hand-selected by producers because of their ability to string along dozens of dates while still appealing to a mass audience.

"Right, see you at school, Charlotte."

As Charlotte watched Josh leave, she wondered how she could be so stupid in thinking that there was something between them. And of course, she felt a bit guilty for even contemplating her own situation right now. Samantha was the one who deserved the pity, after all, she almost died. But, the truth was that Charlotte would much rather hang out here with her because she had nobody to go home to. Charlotte spent far too much time alone, and she longed for what Josh and Ashley had, someone who was waiting on her - someone to love.

The elevator bell dinged, signaling its arrival and as the doors opened, once again Phineas and Charlotte came face-to-face.

"Ha, fate is on my side," Phineas said.

Charlotte smiled a wide grin; thoughts of Josh immediately taking a back seat. Phineas extended his arm, making sure the doors wouldn't close and Charlotte admired the muscles of his bicep.

Phineas deliberately stood in the center of the elevator so that when Charlotte got on she was standing closer to him than would normally be customary.

"I thought your friend came to keep you company?" he asked, not making any move to place more space between them.

"I decided that I wanted to be alone."

Phineas leaned in even closer to Charlotte, his mouth seductively close to her ear. He whispered, "I'll let you in on a secret. Hospitals aren't the most fun place to be alone...unless you find yourself alone with one other person in an elevator."

Charlotte blushed crimson at his words. Her heart soared and without even laying a finger on her, Phineas had caused a delicious tingling sensation to form in her stomach and travel downward. She inhaled out of surprise, giving Phineas the confidence to kiss her cheek, letting his lips caress her pale skin and remain there until the elevator dropped into its place on the floor below.

Charlotte barely breathed. She just stared at this gorgeous boy, hardly believing that he had actually kissed her.

They stepped off the elevator and with utter coolness, Phineas carried on a conversation as if what happened was the most natural thing in the world. "So when is Samantha being released? Is she going to stay with you? Her chart didn't list a guardian nearby, which was weird." It was the information that Raven had insisted he learn and repeat in detail upon his return home.

"She became an emancipated minor last month," Charlotte explained, now having regained her composure. "Like me, her dad isn't alive; her mom's cooped up in rehab, which is a good thing. We've sort of adopted each other, so she'll be staying at my place."

"That's good. Except for one thing."

Charlotte looked concerned. "What's that?"

"I won't see as much of you when she's released."

Charlotte beamed, not used to the attention. Phineas was laying it on thick, but it was working like a charm. "I think I can arrange to fit you into my busy schedule. But, I don't know anything about you."

Phineas looked down, a sudden and unexpected wash of guilt coming over him. He found himself enjoying the conversation with Charlotte. She was witty and genuine. He wanted and hoped to spend more time with her, but in spite of what he was feeling, he launched into the lie that he and Raven had developed for humans.

"I'm not that interesting a subject. My sister and I transferred to Malibu High this year. Our parents are in the military and we used to travel and go to school on bases all around the world, but now U.S. bases are considered targets for terrorism so they wanted us to be somewhere safe and we wanted to enjoy the last couple of years of high school near the beach."

"So if your parents aren't here, then who looks after you?"

"We're kind of like you guys. Our parents signed the papers allowing us to be on our own because it made the most sense."

"Doesn't it get lonely?" Charlotte asked. "I miss my parents."

For a moment Phineas faltered. "I'm different from you...What I mean is, I've got my sister."

"True, but I know what it's like to have an empty house to come home to. We've got a bit in common," Charlotte smiled.

"I guess we do." Phineas said and took her hand.

Charlotte opened the door to Samantha's room to find her still asleep. "Really? It's been like an hour. Please wake up," she whispered. "I have amazing news." She looked hopeful as Samantha stirred, but then sighed in audible disappointment when

Samantha merely turned over to face the opposite wall.

Charlotte paced back and forth, and then unable to contain herself, she "accidentally," but quite on purpose, bumped the bed.

"Oh, you're awake," Charlotte said cheerily.

"How long have you been here?" Samantha asked.

"Not long."

"Like long enough to pace around the room and then decide you needed to wake up a sick girl?"

Charlotte gave her a look to which Samantha burst into a large smile.

"I was awake the whole time. What is with you? You're like a caged tiger."

"Well, I am ready to burst with news, if that's what you mean," Charlotte replied and pulled a chair closer to Samantha's bedside. "Guess who I've been hanging with?"

"Josh?"

"Yes and someone else...someone who makes me want to say 'Josh Who?' and stuck up Ashley can have him."

"There's someone who can do that? Well, spill."

Charlotte launched into details of her time with Phineas, careful to point out every one of his physical attributes, which she had already made a mental checklist of.

"He sounds way hotter than Josh," Samantha agreed. "I say you go for it."

"I would strongly advise against that." Their

backs were to me, so they both gave a slight jump when I spoke. "Sorry, didn't mean to surprise you like that."

"Suzette, how long have you been standing there?" Charlotte asked me.

"Please, call me Suki. How long were you in the cafeteria with that boy?"

I knew darn well that she had been with Phineas this whole time and I felt like a parent waiting up for a teenager to return from a date.

"Why do you want to know?" Charlotte asked totally bewildered.

"I was worried. I didn't know where you were or who you were with."

Charlotte looked at me and then to Samantha, who appeared equally surprised at my declaration. "You're not my mother."

"Don't be insulting," I answered back. "I may be 352 years old, but I do not look old enough to have an eighteen-year-old. I was just worried because you were with Phineas and he is very bad news."

"How do you know who I was with and that he's bad news?" Charlotte retorted. She rolled her eyes at Samantha and exhaled her breath with the annoyance of a teenager. "This is becoming a drag," she said pointing toward me.

"I'm not a 'this'. I'm a person." Charlotte and Samantha both raised their eyebrows at that comment. "Okay," I corrected, "I'm not completely human, but I was once and I've lived with enough of them to know what people feel. Let's just say that I would prefer that you think of me as a person and not a thing, or perhaps a person with extraordinary insight who knows that you...," I said pointing a finger that was in desperate need of a manicure toward Charlotte, "should not be spending time with Phineas."

"Is that his name?" Samantha asked.

Charlotte took over. "Yes, even his name is different and hot. I could fall for him big time."

"You are not falling for that boy, er, gypsy," I said strongly.

"Gypsy?" the girls both asked in unison.

"Isn't that a bit racist?" Samantha asked. "I read in history class that Romanian refugees were often called gypsies by their government."

"He's not that kind of gypsy. He and his sister, Raven, are demon gypsies. They practice black magic. She is incredibly powerful, has lived nearly as long as I have, and gave Phineas second life in exchange for his loyalty."

"What's second life?"

"Immortality. And the longer they live, the stronger they become. They have followed me through the ages, hell bent on revenge."

"He's just a normal guy," Charlotte insisted. "If he were a demon gypsy, like you say, why would he want anything to do with me?"

"I don't know, but it has something to do with the fact that you two were able to release me. It's funny, you seem perfectly average."

"Thanks a lot," Samantha said.

"You don't pull any punches," Charlotte added.

"I don't mean it the way it sounds. What I should have said is that up until now, you've lived a typical teenager's life. I mean, come on, you are in high school. Most of the people, no actually all of the people, who have released me have been on the cusp of something big. That's why you have to be careful and listen to me. You're now my responsibility and I have to keep you safe. You're destined to affect a major change in the world, somehow."

Charlotte and Samantha still looked at me with doubt in their eyes.

"Samantha, I'm pretty sure that Raven and Phineas put you in that hospital bed. And Charlotte, they want something from you too. You can't trust Phineas. He owes Raven his life and will do whatever she commands.

"How do you know all this?" Charlotte asked simply.

"It's a long story and it goes back to why Raven is so angry and against me."

"What did you do to her?" Samantha asked.

"I took away her true love and had her dog killed."

"Why would anybody do that?" Charlotte asked repulsed.

"It wasn't like it was my fault," I explained. "Raven's true love, John, and her dog, Pixie, were believed to be witches. The Salem Witch Trials were a crazy time filled with ignorant people. Anyway, they sentenced both to death and I had information that could possibly have saved them, but I felt with all my heart that speaking out would only get Raven into trouble, and possibly result in her hanging. I kept my silence in order to save her. But Raven said she couldn't live without Pixie and John, nor could she not avenge their deaths so she left for Romania to pursue gypsy rebirth. The next time I saw her was seventy-five years in the future, but like me, she didn't look a day older. She had obviously found what she sought.

"She vowed that one day she would bring the same pain to my heart and until that day, took pleasure only in growing her powers, ending her connection to the human world and playing puppeteer. With each installment, so to speak, of her powers, she grew closer to the black magic and its intoxicating pull until she became filled with more hatred than goodness. The only thing she desired more than growing her own powers was to control other people and the events that filled their lives. But like they say, it's a lonely trip to the top so she decided a companion was needed."

"Phineas?" Charlotte asked.

I nodded and continued the story.

"When Phineas' mother died in childbirth, Raven happened to be the woman's midwife. She had long since left Salem, leaving the puritanical attitudes of the United States behind in favor of a more liberal lifestyle found in Europe. Raven chose Spain because she said the sunny weather might help to improve her disposition, but sadly it didn't. She settled in the city of Seville and her reputation as a midwife flourished.

"It was as sad as a homely girl on a Saturday night that I couldn't visit her because I loved that city. I remember being released in 1492 by the cutest sailor boy named Christopher."

"You mean Christopher Columbus?" Charlotte asked surprised.

"In 1492, Columbus sailed the ocean blue," Samantha recited.

"Cute. Can I continue? We used to sail from the port of Seville to wherever the wind would take us. Of course there were a few times when Christopher would get a bit panicky when we lost our bearings. Men are so funny when it comes to being lost at sea. They just refuse to take directions from a woman, but thankfully Christopher wasn't afraid to show his emotions and when he went below deck for a good cry, I took the wheel and ended up in the West Indies.

"It was just about the best thing we could've hoped for because that place was heaving with all sorts of things that the people of Spain would enjoy and I suggested bringing a little something home to Queen Isabella. Christopher had gravitated to a carved wooden sculpture of a hunter spearing a warthog. You couldn't imagine anything more hideous.

"Christopher, the Queen will think you are comparing her to the likes of a fat pig," I remember saying. "I suggested a pair of beautiful turquoise earrings, which he finally agreed to and she absolutely loved. So much so that she decided that all trade should pass from the West Indies into Spain. Profits started to pour into Seville, and Christopher was made Spain's Chief Expeditioner. You should have seen that boy in his fancy new sailor suit. Gosh, talk about a man looking mighty fine in a uniform. "Sometimes I think Christopher would have been better off looking pretty at state dinners because it wasn't long before he took another wrong turn. The Queen was going to fire him this time, but I suggested we start an import company and soon this place we stumbled upon was called the new world and all of its lovely little goods were distributed throughout Spain. Naturally, there were others who wanted in on the action, but it was only fair that Seville be awarded the royal monopoly for trade. All the merchants from Europe and other trade centers had to go through our port to acquire new world goods. The city's population grew to nearly a million people in the first hundred years after sweet Christopher died. He left quite a legacy, thanks to my navigation skills."

"Suki, what does this all have to do with Raven?" Samantha asked.

"Well, with all those people living in Seville, making babies left and right, it was certainly a good time to be a midwife. Raven became known as the best midwife of all, until Mrs. Giralda died during childbirth. I wish I could say that it was just God's will, but part of me wonders if Raven hadn't planned it."

I noticed the girls' mouths dropped open for a moment, but I continued my story.

"Mrs. Giralda's husband was a wealthy businessman and not the type to stay at home with a child. Raven suggested a solution to ease his burden. A bell tower was just being erected in the Cathedral of Seville, but rumor had it there wasn't enough money to finish the elaborate Gothic and Baroque styled project after the architect had insisted on making it one of the largest churches in the world.

"She suggested that Mr. Giralda put up the remaining funds in exchange for the tower being named in his family's honor. They would pretend that he was grief stricken and wanted a permanent memorial to his loved ones. They agreed to say that not only did Mrs. Giralda die during childbirth, but the baby perished a mere two hours later. Raven would take the baby and leave town and Mr. Giralda would continue to be one of the town's most respected men, easily earning him a new wife. He had no reason to argue since the child was horribly weak. And so, it was agreed."

"People were so whacked back then," Samantha commented. "Let me weigh out the decision," she said holding her hands like scales. "Get rid of my only child after my dear wife dies in childbirth or swap it out for fame?"

"No need to be sarcastic," I reminded. "It happens today too. Anyway, Raven quickly took the child and left, raising it as her own. As she never ages, she waited to instill gypsy magic into Phineas when he was nineteen so that they could live the same age together, as brother and sister, until the end of time."

"Phineas is nineteen?" asked Charlotte. "Sweet! An older man."

"No, not sweet. Sick. He's pretending to be in high school. He is dangerous. He's not even human. There are millions of reasons why you should not have that smile on your face, young lady. Now, let me finish."

"Yes, Suki," Charlotte said dutifully, if not a bit sarcastically.

I had hope that Raven taking Phineas under her wing would place her hatred at bay, but she only worked harder to convert him and erase any traces of innocence from him. I was naïve to think otherwise. After all, what boy of nineteen could resist a beauty like Raven? And since the brother/sister relation was not by blood, Phineas reasoned that his desire for her was natural. He accepted the term "family" loosely. Coupled with promises of mastering dark magic and eternal youth, you can imagine what a powerful aphrodisiac it was to be with Raven. He never stood a chance against her. With each kiss and every dalliance, his ability to stand up against her would incrementally decrease. Unless he ever earned the love of an innocent, which was something that Raven would never willingly allow, he was bound to her."

"So you met Phineas while you were in Seville?" Charlotte asked. "Has he changed much since the 1400s? Was he always so cute?"

"Have you not heard a word I've said? He is dangerous."

Samantha sided with Charlotte. "Dangerous can

be kinda hot."

Charlotte and Samantha giggled like school girls while I laid on my best disapproving look. "Teenagers have such one track minds," I complained. "Anyway, Raven didn't grant him immortality for many years later. She was taking her time and plotting against me. She was angry that my life had carried on. I was sailing around the world with Christopher so she thought I was having the time of my life, at least my current life. In fact, the truth was far different. Christopher developed gout, a type of arthritis that occurs when acid builds up in the joints. Eventually he died of it."

"You know, Suki, have you ever analyzed the fact that every man that has been with you ends up dying a horrible death?" Samantha asked.

"Yeah, with Christopher that brings the number of dead men pretty high, even for someone who has been around as long as you have," Charlotte added.

It had been ages since I found myself rendered speechless. These girls were definitely not ordinary. They may have been teenagers with one-track minds, but in just a span of one day they had hit on the one thought that had plagued my mind for centuries and made me make a promise to never get involved again.

"Humans must perish at some point. To live is to die, but while they are with me I bring about their greatness. As for their deaths, certainly there are extenuating circumstances," I said feeling suddenly defensive. "I mean, Christopher did suffer a bit, but Queen Isabella really should be blamed. She suggested that we go to Valladolid in Northern Spain where she and Ferdinand were married. The city was known for its wild mushrooms and legumes, and Isabella insisted that the healthier diet would improve Christopher's gout.

"Christopher wasn't happy about resigning his post, but I assured him that things would be better for us in Valladolid. "I hear they are fine producers of wine," I said trying to convince him. "Without a responsibility in the world, we can sip from our glasses all day! Besides, it might numb your pain." And so we moved.

"Poor Christopher's gout became so painful that even a sheet on top rendered his joints painful. Finally, my poor dear died at age 54 before I learned that legumes and alcohol were among the foods to avoid when suffering from gout. The queen told me not to feel too terribly. After all, she was the one who insisted he eat beans and peas every night. I merely washed them down with three glasses of wine. Still, I felt a bit guilty for a spell and retreated into my bottle awaiting my next release.

By the time I was set free again, it was two hundred years later, Chris was long dead and the damn witch trials ended my friendship with Raven. I was always sad that we didn't stay friends. Immortality has its advantages, but it's a lonely existence. In time, everyone you love or care about eventually dies. It would have been nice to have a girlfriend. I hoped that in time, Raven would have forgiven me for the whole witch trial debacle, but the grudge continued, and then her darkness manifested itself.

But I later learned that John's sentence to death wasn't the sole cause of our friendship's demise. Raven's anger toward me was as much bred from a broken heart as it was a jealous mind. She coveted the relationships I had with men of means and wanted access to their intelligence and inevitable power. This quest became all consuming and continued to drive Raven even today.

Raven was waiting for Phineas when he returned from the hospital, but he didn't need to tell her how things went for she already knew.

"Never send a boy out to do a man's job," she chided Phineas as soon as he came through the door of the Malibu mansion. She was waiting for him in the stark white living room. She sat perched upon the back of the couch and indeed looked about ready to shift when she could enjoy carrion for a meal. Phineas took note of her position and then as if to make a point, he did a jump onto the couch landing in a reclined position.

"Don't start the minute I walk in. You weren't there."

"Like hell I wasn't. This body may not have been there," she said gesturing from her head to toe, "but in bird form I sat perched seven stories up and heard everything."

"So then you should be happy. I'm in."

"You're supposed to get information from her, but you got nothing."

"Raven, you may be older than the hills, but you still haven't learned patience. I now know that Charlotte is alone. Without anyone in her house, except for Samantha when she's released, the two of them are easy prey."

"Then you should strike at any time."

"But where would that lead us? You want the source of their powers and they don't even know that they have any. We need to take this slowly. Let her invite me over. I'll help her with homework, get to know her, be irresistible. It's called dating, oh but I forget...you're more into taking the guys that you want."

Raven rolled her eyes. "Fine, but don't be too irresistible. And, don't forget that you're not human, you're not a teenager, and you're not going to enjoy dating her."

"I don't know, it could be fun."

Suddenly Phineas grabbed his neck as if a muscle spasm had occurred. "Ouch, I just got the sharpest pain in my neck."

"Oh, poor thing. I know just how you feel. Now tell me that Charlotte isn't going to be a pain in my neck."

"You're doing this to me? How? You never told me you could do this."

"Phin darling, there's a lot you don't know about me. Getting inside people's minds and shapeshifting is just the beginning of my powers."

Phineas bent over in pain. "Damn it!"

"We are connected and if you hurt me, I hurt you."

"Stop it, Raven!"

"Fine," she said closing her eyes and breathing deeply, concentrating. "Better?"

Phineas tentatively rotated his neck from side to side. "It's fine. Geez, you're a jealous one."

"I can't help it. I don't like sharing you, even when I must. Anyway, do you think Suki knows what these girls bring?"

"She didn't let on. But that thing you just did to me...about being connected. Suki does it too. She's connected to the girls. She feels and sees what they see. She knows what they're experiencing."

"Interesting."

"Yeah, she's also really protective and told me to fly the coop, so to speak. She thinks I invaded Samantha's dreams. Did I?"

"Nearly," Raven answered. "Like I said, I was perched outside so I gave you some help, but you were nearly there. You're a good student."

"What's that? A compliment?" Phineas teased, pulling Raven onto him.

"Stop," she said.

"Stop what? Having a go at you or this?" he said moving his mouth to her neck where he fluttered kisses along her collarbone. "You have nothing to be jealous about."

"Mmm, don't stop that." Raven drew her head

back, giving Phineas better access to her throat. Wanna taste?"

"No, I don't. Let's keep things nice between us."

"Don't be so squeamish. You might like it."

In an instant Raven shifted into her bird form. She was already on top of Phineas so it didn't take but a second for her to bite his neck.

"Damn it," he said swatting her away. The blackbird cawed loudly and Phineas knew it was the sound of her laughter. "It's not funny," he yelled to the massive bird that had now flown to the windowsill. His hand went to his neck where a deep puncture was oozing blood. When he pulled his hand away, now covered with his own blood, the bird flew back to him and landed on his shoulder. It moved down his arm to his hand where it more gently attempted to lick the blood clean.

"I'm not into this, Raven. Either shift back or I'll fly myself out of here."

And just as quickly as the transformation first occurred, Raven was back in all of her earthly glory, lounging on the floor, her long legs extended seductively, her arms extended overhead and her eyes pleading with Phineas for forgiveness.

"You taste so good. It's just the first bite that stings a bit. Afterwards, it's all gentleness."

"How am I supposed to go to school with this?" he said indicating his neck.

"They'll think it's a love bite."

"And Charlotte is going to want to go out with me when I've got this souvenir from someone else?"

Raven looked pensive. "Maybe I let my instincts take over for a moment. Sorry. Anyway, young girls are stupid. The jealousy will take over and she'll try even harder to get you."

Phineas walked over to where Raven was lying and stared down at her. "That's it?" he said standing just above her. "That's your way of an apology – to tell me sorry in just a word and insist you did nothing wrong?"

Slowly she got to her knees and tilted her head to look at him. "I have another instinct."

"Will I like this one?"

She reached for his belt buckle. "Most definitely."

It was Phineas' turn to throw his head back in ecstasy. "God, maybe I'm the young, stupid one. I forgive you," he said reaching down to smooth the back of her hair.

"I knew you would," she said pausing to look up at him. "And Phin, when we're done, let's fly over the city. Suki may have saved Samantha today, but she can't be there all the time. I want to know where she is when she's not with them."

Chapter Six

Immortality can be lonely, but it can also give you the ability to meet the descendants of the people one has lost. It gives one hope for the future and in my case, the chance to meet new and interesting people and one in particular, who would prove to be more than a bit challenging to me.

During my first visit to the Los Angeles area in the late 1960s, I fell in love with the beaches, the sunny days and of course, the shopping in Beverly Hills. So later, when the chance to purchase a suite within Maison 360, a very chic boutique hotel with the top floor available for long term tenants, I jumped at the chance. I've always had a head for investments. When I'm indisposed, in other words locked in my bottle, the suite is rented out by the management who then deposits my share into an investment account. It gives me a nice income, nice enough in fact to keep me clothed in the latest fashions. There's nothing worse than an out of touch Genie.

But the best part of the investment is that I've got a place I can call home whenever I'm in L.A. As much as I value my relationship with my Releasers, I need my own space, and nothing beats my penthouse with a view of all the twinkling lights of the city. So romantic. I had just finished sorting out all of my clothes that I had carefully put into storage and realized that being away from my little home away from bottle for the better part of a few decades meant that my clothes were seriously out of fashion. I threw on the one wardrobe essential that never goes out of style, my LBD, and headed downstairs to the restaurant bar on the ground floor of the hotel.

I was wishing there was someone special to share my first night with, when a hand placed a cocktail napkin in front of me and I looked up to see two smiling blue eyes boring into mine.

Let me tell you, it's not every guy that can take a Genie's breath away. In fact, I'm not sure it's ever been done, but this was an immediate connection as if an electric coil attached his heart to mine and suddenly as our eyes met, someone flipped the switch.

"Hi, I'm James. Can I get you a drink? On the house?"

"What have I done to deserve a drink on the house?"

"You made my heart pound."

"That sounds like a line."

"That it does, but I'm not the type to deliver lines. So, can I get you something?"

"Can you take a break and have one with me?"

"If you tell me your name."

"Suzette -- Suki, if you like."

"I most certainly do."

And then as he took my hand to shake it, without any rationality, I blushed. I actually felt my face flush and a tingle go up my spine. I am the lamest Genie of the century. He's only a 25-year-old human. Snap out of it.

I shook my head back to reality. "So, I'll have a …"

"Let me make you the house specialty. It's an absinthe cocktail concoction."

"But absinthe is forbidden," I said without thinking.

"It was…during Prohibition," he said and smiled, exposing the most adorable dimples in all of the world, and trust me, I've traveled nearly all of it. So, I'm crushing over this guy with the strong jaw line, brown, wavy hair, blue eyes, and an oh so terrible strongest chest that I wish I were lying my head against. And, I can't think of anything intelligent to say.

"That's what I meant." I forced myself to concentrate.

"This drink takes a special skill to make. The process," he said looking directly at me, "might as well be called a seduction because it requires careful maneuvering that if done correctly, leads to a beautiful result."

Oh my, did he just say seduction? I'm already there.

"You've done this before?" I asked warily.

"Never with intention," he said and winked at me. Oh my gosh! He is a total hottie. Not only his looks, but he had confidence without arrogance, a combination that was indeed seductive. This was a guy who was intent on doing something for me. It's always been the other way around, and I think I could get used to this.

I watched as James started off by selecting a reservoir glass featuring cut crystal designs. He reached for an absinthe spoon and when I saw its intricate design, I caught my breath.

"It's beautiful."

"A butterfly. It's apropos, because they are beautiful, beguiling creatures that move with grace. It's like you. Now watch."

I was a bit taken aback when James compared the butterfly to me. It wasn't a known fact, but Genies always used the butterfly as our shapeshifting form. They are gentle creatures that flit in and out of people's lives, just like a Genie does and for a moment, I felt melancholy for my bottle with its intricate butterfly designs and the safety and warmth I feel when inside it. But, I was sitting with a gorgeous man who I definitely had the hots for and I wasn't even commanded to be with him. I quickly turned my attention back to James.

He placed a sugar cube into the slotted spoon, put his hand over the butterfly design and then slowly poured the liquid over the sugar cube. He transferred back and forth between the distilled spirit and iced water that was apparently chilled in a specially designed absinthe fountain. The result was a licorice flavored liquid that was nearly the color of emeralds.

"It's amazing. Like nothing I've ever had."

"It's made from a mixture of herbs and flowers. The primary taste comes from green anise, that's what gives it the licorice flavor, and sweet fennel."

Thinking about all the years I've lived and the things I've experienced I could only smile and say, "It takes a lot to surprise me. Thank you."

"Well, it takes a lot to impress me. So thank you, too. I've finished for the evening. Maybe we could grab dinner together?"

I would have normally jumped at the opportunity to spend an evening with a gorgeous guy, taking in one of my favorite towns, but I had work to do. Raven and Phineas were hungry for power; they had already shown their capabilities against Samantha, and for all I knew, Charlotte could be next.

"I'd love to, but I have to take a raincheck. I live here so I'm sure I'll be seeing you."

James seemed disappointed, but if there's one thing I've learned about men it's that you have to troll them like big sea fish. You know, show them a little bait, dangle that line and slowly reel them in or they'll just have their fill and go after the next treat to come their way.

"I understand. Come by and visit when you get the chance."

"Most definitely," I said.

James took my hand to say goodbye and before I knew what had happened, I felt the most electrifying shock. He felt it too for he jerked away at my touch.

"Sorry. I must have rubbed my shoes on the

carpet," he said apologetically.

"Sure. It's probably the wind as well." But there wasn't a branch stirring. Something was different about my life this time. First, being released by two young girls. Then, Phineas and Raven showing up and now, a human releasing such energy onto me. I excused myself and went upstairs, more than a little freaked out.

It had taken hundreds of years for the stars and planets to align and intersect the Tropic of Cancer and the Tropic of Capricorn, the only area in the world without a change in seasons and similarly, the only place where my powers are dormant. It was there that a metaphysical shift occurred catapulting me to the present.

The experience was akin to a really bad case of jet lag and placed me at a distinct disadvantage in fighting Raven and Phineas. I could already pick up on signs that they were listening in on my conversations with the girls. It was apparent that Raven had studied my ability to control the elements and had tried it once or twice on her own. Fortunately, my powers with regards to that still overtook hers. And while I influenced people in an effort to bring out the best within them, she copied that skill as well and used it for her own purposes. This was the only explanation for how Phineas must have landed a job at the hospital and how Raven seemed to already be in with the popular girls at school. They were setting themselves up to infiltrate the girls' lives. It would make protecting them all the more difficult and equally imperative that I discovered why the girls were being tracked by two demon gypsies who have been around since 18th century England.

The only thing I could do was install a sort of firewall around my own home so that at least I could have peace there. It certainly wasn't foolproof, and like firewalls on computers, Raven and Phineas were a bit like a savvy hacker. Eventually, they would figure out a way to spread their virus, but at least it would buy me a bit of time to figure things out. Not to mention, giving me a small slice of heaven unto myself.

I let myself relax atop my bed, looking up at the canopy made of scrolling iron covered with a sheer pink fabric. My mind was spinning and coming up empty in trying to figure out why Raven was here. The confusion kept leading my mind toward thoughts of James. In fact, it was most peculiar that I seemed incapable of getting him off my mind, as if he were willing me to focus on him. Sure, there were worse things to consider. I imagine that staring at him on a hot day is like a tall glass of lemonade, pure refreshment if there ever was one. But it was frustrating that I couldn't get an accurate read on him. I was starting to wonder if this intersection of the stars was diminishing my powers. I was even feeling more...heck, there was no way to sugar coat it...I was feeling more human.

For instance, right now I would have liked to simply act like an ordinary girl and sit downstairs with him at the bar, but what's the point in having supernatural powers if you're not going to use them? I concentrated harder than was usually necessary for me until finally I got a reading.

I felt a chill with a realization that his life was due to intersect with mine at this precise moment. It was impossible. Never had I been involved with one human while being released by another. What's more, my vision showed that his soul was nearly as old as mine. It was an impossibility for a human, which meant only one thing...and so try as I might to find a reason to stay away, I decided that returning to the bar may be the wisest thing to do. If there was a gorgeous bartender whose destiny was meant to be with mine, it was up to me to determine if he was human, demon, or something altogether different.

I was bound to protect Samantha and Charlotte, so taking a bit more time to check out what exactly James meant in this picture seemed par for the course. I grabbed a lipstick off the counter, and decided that pretending to have lost it in the bar would be cause for my return. Yes, as excuses go, it was a bit weak, but at the moment, so was I. I checked my hair in my compact, popped a mint, and headed for the elevator.

The entrance to the restaurant bar was the only business on the ground floor of the boutique hotel and yet it remained discreetly hidden, causing an air of mystery behind "Maison 360." The hotel's lobby was decorated in crisp whites with a wallpaper that featured a thin, black pinstriped pattern that made the only entrance into the bar nearly disappear among the walls. Not even a door knob or sign was posted. The only telltale sign of something more being behind this hidden door was a small peephole at eye level that stared out into the lobby from the inside, and the even smaller buzzer located near it. The fact that the buzzer was also painted white caused it to be practically invisible unless one knew exactly where to find it.

I pressed the buzzer and no sooner, the heavy door swung open from the inside revealing the hidden bar and restaurant that, in stark contrast to the white walls of the lobby, featured dark paneling throughout.

I casually let my lipstick drop from my fingertips and then kicked it underneath a nearby chair before striding further into the bar. I inhaled the woody scent of the furnishings and took note of the ambiance--dark and romantic, somewhat styled like a speakeasy of the 1920s and yet, far more plush. There were couches tucked away in corners where couples cozied up. Another couple drank at the bar and half a dozen more were enjoying meals at private tables.

I took a seat at the bar at the opposite end of the couple and saw with relief that James' painted on smile seemed to take on a significantly more genuine appearance when he looked up and saw me.

"What made you change your mind?"

"I seem to have lost my favorite lipstick. I thought maybe I dropped it here," I said looking down at the ground before stooping to pick it up exactly where I kicked it. "Oh look, here it is."

"Well, just because you found it doesn't mean you have to leave. Stay and have another nightcap with me."

"Alright," I said simply.

"It was getting lonely here," James said, keeping his eyes planted on mine. It was as if we were both trying to size up the other. "Glass of wine or something stronger?"

"A cabernet, would be nice. Thank you."

"You've got it. I have one that I want you to try."

James reached for a bottle with a beautiful label of scrolling vines adorned by delicate daisies whose petals were starting to fall. My eye traveled to the bottom of the label and I caught my breath in spite of myself. There, the petals had pooled into a lush heap and lying atop them was a woman with alabaster skin, brown hair that fell in waves past her shoulders and almond-shaped eyes of the darkest brown accented with long, black lashes.

"It looks just like you," James said appreciatively.

Indeed it did, and I wondered immediately about its origins.

"It's from a little winery in Southern Italy called 'Muse Winery'," James explained. "Seems apropos," he said looking straight at me.

"What do you mean?" I said feeling somewhat put off by his comment. There was no way he could know about me and yet, he seemed to know me through and through. I tapped my finger nervously on the cold, black marble of the bar and he placed his hand over mine. Within an instant of feeling the warmth of his hand over mine, a vision entered my mind of the two of us running through total and complete destruction.

My heart quickened and my instinct was to pull my hand away, but I was drawn to the images playing throughout my mind. I closed my eyes to focus on what danger was associated with James and how it involved me. The moving pictures came fast and I felt the emotions that would someday soon affect James...fear, trust, and an overpowering desire to protect. But why? I was so tuned to his energy that it was impossible to tell if these emotions were his or my own.

Finally, I managed to pull my hand away and gathered by James' expression it was as if no time at all had passed. He was still looking at me happily, pouring the wine with one hand and now reaching for a napkin with the one that had been covering mine.

"And, this wine just beckons to be paired with chocolate. It has a fruity undertone and I happen to have some dark chocolate passionfruit truffles that I picked up on a whim today."

I swallowed hard. "Passionfruit?"

"Uh huh. Want to try?"

"It's my favorite," I answered remembering the

last time I had eaten passionfruit was in Paraguay where the plant that bears this remarkable, purple colored fruit is considered the national flower.

James placed two of the most enticing looking truffles in the center of a white bone china plate, but not before first looking through an assortment of cocktail napkins and deciding on one in a pale shade of lavender and first placing that in the center of the plate. "Now, it's fit to be eaten."

"You go to a lot of trouble for something that is going to be consumed in a mere matter of minutes," I noted.

"Presentation is important. It's all about the illusion of what is to come. Now, you're going to enjoy your wine and chocolate all the more because it appears to be something even more remarkable because I've built it up to be that way."

"Hmm, and what if you've built it up so much that I end up being disappointed?" I asked coyly.

He smiled at me, and then slowly leaned across the bar all the while holding my gaze until his mouth was just inches from my own. I swallowed hard, thinking he was about to kiss me, knowing that I shouldn't even entertain such an act with a mere human that wasn't even my Releasor. And yet, I didn't dare breathe or move a muscle for fear of ruining the moment.

But instead of kissing me, his lips came within inches of my own and continued past my cheek, just grazing my flesh and coming to lightly rest on my earlobe sending waves of chills down my spine. He whispered lightly in my ear, "You wouldn't be disappointed."

He straightened up into his usual stance behind the bar and smiled wickedly, knowing the impression he had made and the effect it had on me. I must have looked ridiculous, probably sitting there with my mouth agape because I couldn't even speak.

"You're pretty sure of yourself."

"That I am."

"Some people might even say that it borders on arrogance."

James shrugged his shoulders. "Those people don't know me. Now go on," he encouraged and gently moved the plate of truffles closer to me.

I picked one up and as I brought it to my mouth, the intense aroma from the dark chocolate hit me. I took a bite, cutting the truffle in half with my teeth and immediately received a flood of sweet fruity juice from the passion flower. It was sheer heaven.

"Now have a sip of that wine," he instructed.

I did as I was told. In a word, it was remarkable. "Oh my gosh, if I told anyone about this they would never believe it's as amazing as it is. I mean wine and chocolate isn't new, but it's never been like this."

"Consider this the first of 'never been like this' experiences."

I nearly choked on the sip of wine that I had just taken. I was considerably more relaxed now and my mind had immediately gone to more intimate thoughts with his words.

In an attempt to restore my lost dignity, I tried a

change of subject. "So passion fruit. Who knew it could be this good?"

"Do you know where the name passion fruit comes from?" he asked.

It was another small victory for James. For the first time, I could truthfully say I had no idea of the history.

I shook my head. "Enlighten me."

"Interesting choice of words. The flower's anatomy was seen as being reminiscent of the torture, otherwise known as the *Passion*," he said huskily, "of Christ prior to his crucifixion."

Leave it to James to turn even this into a decidedly more suggestive conversation.

"The name was given by the missionaries," he continued. "The three stigmas reflect the three nails in Jesus' hands and feet. The threads of the passion flower resemble the Crown of Thorns. The vine's tendrils are likened to the whips. The five anthers represented the five wounds. The ten petals resemble the Apostles..."

"And let me guess, the purple petals represent the purple robe used to mock Jesus' claim to kingship."

"Precisely," he said.

"Interesting bit of trivia. Where did you learn it?"

He shook his head like it was nothing. "I was getting away from it all in Brazil and read about it when visiting a village of the Tapuyos Indians. I called it my Age of Discovery."

I looked at him closely, trying to figure out what was real. It could be that he had just taken an extended trip as young people do, reading about history and visiting sites of interest, but my instinct, which was acutely aware that James was mysteriously unreadable to me, told me that something about him was not as it seemed. I watched his quiet confidence, the way he would get lost in thought as if there were just too many to keep track of and wondered if he was even older than I. Could he have visited the Tapuyos himself and not just "heard" about them?

And then I realized that he had indeed made one slip up when telling his story about a youthful zen of wanderlust. The Age of Discovery wasn't something that James had made up about himself. Also known as the Age of Exploration, much of it was from Europe to Brazil...in the 1500s! Due to travel being so limited at the time, this was a little known fact. I thought about testing him on the subject, but he shot me a sudden look as if to say, "enough."

"Now eat up. Your chocolate is getting cold," he teased while refilling my wine glass.

"Please, I'm fine," I said placing my hand over my glass. "I didn't eat much earlier and I think the wine is going to my head. We wouldn't want that."

He gave me a sideways glance as if weighing how terrible that would actually be and then decided to behave like a gentleman -- at least for now. "No, we wouldn't want that. You should have some food in you. I hope you're not opposed to eating dinner in reverse tonight. Shrimp cocktail and lobster salad sound good?"

I nodded, pleased with his choice and giddy

either from the wine or the fact that I so enjoyed his company. He was learned, good-looking, well traveled. I knew that I shouldn't feel compelled to be with one human when another, make that two others, have released me. But I did.

Now admittedly, I'm a little out of touch on how girls handle dates in modern Los Angeles. I assume they don't go to dinner and then bring the guy back to their place on the first date. Or do they? James didn't seem at all surprised when I asked him upstairs.

"This is quite a suite," he said admiring my view. "It's odd that we haven't met before, considering you have permanent residence here."

Think. Think fast. "Well, I do quite a bit of traveling and I sublet the place when I'm gone for long stretches."

"So you travel for business or pleasure?"

There was something about the way he was looking at me, as if sizing me up before I struggled through each lie.

"A little bit of both. You know, when you love your work it's hard to just turn that part off."

He nodded and I thought the interrogation was over and maybe we could get on with something decidedly more fun, after all, I have been cooped up in my bottle for nearly half a century. But no, that would be too much to hope for as James launched into yet another question, and frankly, seemed quite amused at putting me on the spot.

"I bet you meet some interesting people on your travels." He smiled at me when I merely nodded, and meandered through my living room, stopping in front of a massive oak book case. I was careful to replenish the items on that book shelf with each visit. I'd buy books and knick-knacks from local stores every time I'm back so as to appear with the times. I'd even get a few stock photos and place them in frames so it appears I have friends and family that aren't from the dark ages. I held my breath as James' eyes scanned the shelves. He wouldn't...but he did, the one item he commented on was my bottle, hidden away on the very top shelf.

"That's an interesting piece," he said pointing. "I've never seen anything quite like it. Tell me its story."

Please, this was getting to be a bit too much. I was getting the distinct idea that he knew my story. Alright, two could play at this game. He may have some sort of barrier in place that doesn't let me read him, but that could be broken. All I needed was to bridge the gap, so I moved closer to him. In fact, I turned him around to face me, and stood just inches from him.

Here goes nothing. Drastic times led to drastic measures. "James," I purred, "I'd rather you tell me a story--a naughty one."

That did the trick. For a moment, he was speechless. But I will say, he recovered quickly.

"Have you heard the one about the bartender

who met a most beguiling woman?"

"Sounds promising. What happened between them?"

"I'll keep you updated," he said and then took me in his arms.

He locked eyes with mine and ran his finger down the length of my jawbone and across my lips. And when I responded by letting my lips kiss his finger, he retreated it only long enough to replace it with his own mouth.

He utterly absorbed me with that kiss, making me lose all sense of time and place. My only awareness was that I wanted him. Reading my thoughts, he carried me to the couch and positioned himself atop me. I felt his hardness against me, and although we barely knew each other, the connection was undeniable and I couldn't resist wrapping my legs around his waist, pulling him toward me.

James responded by reaching a hand underneath my hips, and guiding me toward him, bringing our bodies even closer together. But with every electric tingle that went through my body, my brain also kicked into high gear.

Nagging thoughts. I tell myself to just stop thinking. I've never been with a man who isn't bound to me. Just enjoy it. But, I was once a girl, raised in the proper sense, and old habits are hard to break. One side of my brain insists that if I keep going like this, I'll probably never see him again. The other side has a direct link to my body and reminds me how amazing this feels.

His kisses are soft and gentle, and again I start to lose myself in his strong embrace. I try and listen to my body and rationalize this will give me insight into how humans really live. It would help me relate better to what Charlotte and Samantha must deal with in their dating lives. And that's when the brakes in my mind squealed to a halt. I'm bound to them and not James. Their safety depends on my keeping a clear head.

Besides, the word "slut" kept coming to mind mixed with other niggling thoughts like "don't scare him off," "play it cool," "he's trying to get in your pants" and with that last one, I finally realized it was true, so I pushed gently against James and rolled out from under him.

"You alright?" he said, his eyes shining, his breath slightly ragged.

"Yeah. This has been a great night, but I think we should stop while we're still ahead."

"I get it. So, since you live here and I work here..." his voice trailed off.

Oh no, was he going to give me the "it's too complicated" talk? That we don't want to get into an uncomfortable situation? Darn, maybe I should've just slept with him while I had the chance. After all, as I've pointed out, I'm well overdue.

"Yes?" I said, the fear building.

"I just hope you're okay with seeing a lot of me because I'd really like to get to know you better."

I've learned that being a Genie means that images and premonitions can strike at the most inopportune times and at that precise moment, I suddenly had a flash image of Charlotte talking with Phineas. I had to leave, fast. "Oh no."

James looked at me bewildered. "Did you say no?"

"No. I meant yes. I'm just a bit light-headed from...us. Call me tomorrow?" I said while ushering James to the door and pulling my shoes on at the same time.

"Are you going somewhere?"

"No. I mean, yes."

"That's a funny little phrase you've got going there," he said chuckling.

"I'm going out, but not like *out* out. I have to help my...my...I forgot that I promised to check on a friend who was in trouble earlier."

How lame was that? Friend? What am I supposed to call them? If I start spending a lot of time with James, how do I explain why I hang out with two high school girls? Maybe they're my nieces? But that leads to questions about siblings. Or, maybe I'm a counselor of some sort? Think, please think, I willed my brain.

"Suki, you don't have to tell me everything tonight. We'll get to know each other and take this a bit slower next time." He leaned toward me and as our lips met, the blackness behind my closed eyes turned bright like snow falling all around me. James' arms were holding me close and my mind seemed to move in a million directions while I felt like I was being lifted although I had my two feet planted firmly on the ground. As we pulled away from each other, he kept his hands on my arms, somehow knowing that I needed to be steadied. He gave me a questioning look as if to ask if I was okay. His voice sounded so faint in my head, reassuring me about something that I couldn't quite hear. Finally, the reverie stopped and we returned to normal.

"You'll be okay?"

It was a question, but he said it with a smile on his lips as if also telling me what I needed to hear.

I nodded and with that, the elevator bell dinged, announcing the end of our date. James stepped inside and took a little piece of my heart with him.

"Why can't I hear anything?" Raven communicated telepathically to Phineas. They were perched on a tree just outside of my window although obviously I didn't know it at the time or I wouldn't have been making out with James with the blinds open. That type of show is so totally unladylike, at least that's what my old beau Charles Lasegue would say. He practically invented the term exhibitionism.

I met Charles in Paris in the mid-1800s when he was studying philosophy and was the first to believe that knowing a patient's history could tell you a great deal about a person's illness. Of course, some people believed Charles was just being nosy with all of his questions, but I quite liked how he took such an interest in people. We got along swimmingly until the

French government asked him to investigate an epidemic of cholera that had broken out in Southern Russia. I was having so much fun in Paris and Charles was more into his work than me, so we parted ways.

James' bar downstairs reminded me so much of the brasseries and cafes I went to in Paris with Charles. I found myself wondering what it would be like to return there with James, or some other romantic faraway place. Of course, the entire notion of flying off someplace with James was pure nonsense because for one thing, I had only just met him, and second, Charlotte and Samantha need me.

As if forgetting that the blinds were open wasn't bad enough, the movement of the branches caught my attention and I thought that I saw two blackbirds perching, but when I moved closer to the window for a better look, they were gone. The thought that perhaps Raven and Phineas had been hovering nearby when I was with James made my skin crawl. I hadn't thought carefully. Exposing my own vulnerabilities with them nearby was certainly not wise. I listened once again, feeling their presence. I concentrated on stirring the air, bringing up the wind so as to interfere with their energy frequencies and any ability they may have to detect mine.

Raven spoke in a hushed tone to Phineas. "I feel so cold, too. Do you?"

Phineas extended his wings, placing them around Raven. She noted that his temperature was normal, but he wasn't able to communicate.

"Something's wrong here. She's protected. But I

can't get a sense of what, or by whom. Perhaps the energies surrounding this place are too old to penetrate." Raven flew off suddenly with Phineas behind her. When they reached their beach house, both were breathing raggedly with exhaustion.

"You haven't said a word since we got here."

"I'm okay," Phineas answered. "I could hear every thought coming from you, but it was like in those horror films...I tried to talk, but nothing came out."

"It's so frustrating. Leave it to that Genie to be so secretive. She did this once before. I remember tracking her in Bermuda when she was on vacation in 1843 and she actually made her own boat disappear. I started courting the coast guard and pretended I actually cared about what happened to her. Nobody could even find a trace of the boat. There was no wreckage, no oil spill, nothing. She created some kind of wormhole that controls the laws of physics to actually hide away there and transport to and from the area undetected. The media started calling it the Bermuda Triangle. Maybe she's done the same thing here in L.A. Next thing you know, she'll be renting the place out to celebs who need to dodge the media."

"Listen, it wasn't reasonable to think we could extract information from Suzette. She's centuries old and from what you've said she's as smart and powerful as you are – just in a different way," Phineas added quickly when he saw Raven's brow furrow.

"You're right. It was always the plan to get to the girls, so that's what we'll do." "But, where they go, Suzette will follow," Phineas noted.

"You're right. We need to divide and conquer. Julius Caesar may have dreamt up that line, but my Ulysses S. Grant put it into practice, dividing those Southern states right up. It was an amazing victory. Not so much because I cared about the abolishment of slavery, I just wanted to beat Suki, Miss Southern Belle." Raven sighed, "Yes, Ulysses may have been a lousy kisser, but he knew his way around a battlefield."

"Must you talk about other men?"

"I said he was a lousy kisser. Phin, you're the only one for me now. Not only are you devilishly sexy, but you're also whip smart. We'll get the girls apart so that Suki's attention is divided."

"It seems her attention is already diverted. Who is that guy and why would she spend time with him?

"I'm sure he's nobody. Suki was always a bit soft when it came to good-looking men."

Phineas pulled her in close. "You see? You still share some commonalities with her."

Raven kissed him lightly, but pulled back. "Well, I wouldn't waste my time with a bartender. Maybe that's why she came to her senses. One minute she's going at it hot and heavy and then," Raven snapped her fingers, "she just stops? On second thought, maybe something happened with the girls to make her jump like that."

"Shall we find out?" Phineas asked.

"Yeah," Raven agreed. "Samantha is going to be discharged from the hospital tomorrow morning and I want to be there to find out where Suki is going to take them. She knows it's too dangerous to leave them in their own houses alone."

"And what about Charlotte?"

"She is a very pure soul. It's not going to be easy to tempt her. You think you can get her?"

Phineas appeared deep in thought, but his mind was unreadable to Raven. She chocked it up to his thoughts just working overtime with the tasks at hand, so that no one idea in particular jumped out at her. She took in his clear, green eyes, his perfect cheekbones that framed an even more beautiful face.

"On second thought, she probably doesn't stand a chance against you," Raven noted before placing a hand to the back of Phineas' head and pulling him in close for a kiss. "Just don't get carried away."

"Never," he spoke while layering kisses down her neck. But inside the depths of his mind, he knew that he was looking forward to seeing Charlotte. His biggest concern was not how to get Charlotte to want to be with him, but rather, how he would keep his own heart from getting attached to her.

"I don't see why we can't stay at our own places," Samantha pouted. "I'm not a child. I've been taking care of myself since I was sixteen."

"In a word, my place is – amazing," I assured her. "Besides, it's only until you get your strength back. It's not like anyone's going to miss you at home."

"Thanks a lot," Samantha said.

"Maybe it's a good idea," Charlotte chimed in and then whispered to Samantha, "Besides, don't you want to see what her place is like?"

I smiled at both girls. They may have been used to taking care of themselves, but I knew they would enjoy themselves at my place. I could keep watch over them and also give them some much needed tips. Like fashion for one thing; boys for another; and, some serious work in the hair and makeup department.

"Maybe we should pick up some essentials from your house and then when you're feeling up to it, we can go shopping for anything we've forgotten." The last thing I wanted to do was spend much time at their homes when Raven and Phineas were sure to have the places staked out.

Still, Samantha resisted. "Listen Suki, I appreciate the offer, but it's really not necessary. I feel embarrassed at the time you've both already spent sitting by my bedside."

"Samantha, I don't know why you've been put on Raven's radar, but something in your future points to her and she's after you. That's the simple truth. You and Charlotte are bound to me. You released me and I have an obligation to protect and to serve."

"We've got a regular police woman here," Charlotte mused.

"But in a cuter uniform!" I added. "So we have a deal? At least until you use up your last two wishes?"

"Deal," they said in unison.

"Great. Let's break you out of here and get ready for the party."

"What party?" Samantha asked.

"The one I'm throwing in your honor."

"I hate parties," Charlotte complained. "And Samantha's just getting out of the hospital. I thought you were supposed to be her guardian. Shouldn't she be taking it easy?"

"She will be. We're just having a few people to my place for dinner...like Josh and Ryan."

"And could I invite Phin?" Charlotte asked.

I sighed feeling the exasperation that comes with taking care of teenagers. "I thought you didn't think the party was a good idea."

"Well, I'm warming up to it."

"Charlotte, he's certainly not a good idea. Have you not listened to a thing I've said? He and Raven tried to kill your best friend."

"You don't really have proof of that," Charlotte reminded me.

"I know them. I've known them for three centuries."

"He's that old?" Samantha asked. "Gross Charlotte."

I looked across the room at a vase of flowers and my anger suddenly made it shatter. The girls jumped at the sound.

"Sorry. Too many neurons, so little control. I sometimes lose it when I've been sealed up for a spell. You weren't implying that *I'm* gross."

The girls suddenly realized their mistake. "Sorry Suki," Charlotte replied for the both of them.

"I never meant that you were gross."

"Totally. It's impossible to think of Phin being around that long," added Charlotte. "He's cute and says the right things and is one of the first guys to make me feel so alive."

"But Josh did that too," I reminded her.

"Not like this. I admired him from afar. And, I can't ignore that he has a girlfriend," she countered.

"I'm not inviting his girlfriend. So this will give you a chance to see if there's anything there without her always landing by his side."

"We're not going to talk you out of this, are we?" Charlotte noted.

"Nope."

Samantha looked to Charlotte and then back to myself. "Well, it looks like I'm getting a welcome home party."

"Ladies, after you," I said leaving the stark hospital room behind.

Over the years I've embraced hobbies made popular by the land in which I lived. While in France, I played baccarat. I rode in England chasing after the foxes and hounds. I even perfected a recipe for key lime pie while living in the south, but there's one thing that I find I can do no matter where I live. Shopping. If there's one thing this Genie knows, it's where the best stores are located.

During one trip to France, I bought the most adorable hat from a dear friend, Coco. I wore it to the

French Ambassadors's home and soon her hats were all the talk of the town. Absolutely everyone had to have one. She opened up the cutest boutique and later, when I first visited Los Angeles, I knew that it was the ideal location for her to expand her business. What with Hollywood booming and actresses in the spotlight, I told Coco that her name would become synonymous with grace and fashion. All we had to do was find the perfect actress to be seen around town in her fashions and she would be on her way. Coco thought the travel to the States and setting up shops seemed like a terrible amount of trouble. She thought certainly the French Ambassador's gatherings were sufficient publicity and that's when it hit me. An ambassador of fashion was what we needed. Someone who could be considered Hollywood royalty while also having ties to Europe and England. But who?

That's when I discovered the young and talented Audrey Hepburn, whose father was an English banker and whose mother was a Dutch baroness. But even more important, she had the perfect frame for Coco's petite dresses. Truth be told, Coco was great with hat designs, but her first dress design was a bit of a mistake in the fact that it was two sizes too small for the French Ambassador's wife. It was quite a debacle. Giselle came in for a fitting, determined to look chic, but couldn't get herself into the dress. It was a case of Cinderella's stepsisters trying to squeeze into the shoe. As hard as we tried, the zip just wouldn't budge. Giselle stormed out determined to ruin Coco's reputation. That's when we found perfect Audrey.

Sweet. Soft-spoken. And thin as a waif. The poor girl was bordering on unhealthy, but she did look beautiful in clothes.

It was the premiere of her first big film, "Roman Holiday," and she turned up on the red carpet in Coco's first dress design. The photographers went crazy. The journalists all wrote down Coco's name and the next day, her shop was overrun with new clients. At my urging, Coco developed her own fashion line, calling it House of Chanel and the Chanel label soon became the one to own. If I were to make over Samantha and Charlotte, I knew just where to take them. First stop...Chanel on Rodeo Drive.

"Suki, we can't afford this shop," Samantha whispered as we walked past the doorman.

"We can't even afford the parking," Charlotte added.

"We're just getting you some basics. Nothing fancy," I assured them. "Every girl needs a LBD in her closet. Chanel coined the phrase and Audrey wore one every chance she got, even insisted on wearing one in her film, 'Breakfast at Tiffany's'."

"Well, that's fine for movie stars, but we can't afford a little black dress. We'll be lucky if we have the cash for a little black t-shirt," Charlotte said nervously.

Samantha added her natural sarcasm to the conversation. "I'll probably have to settle for a little black handkerchief in this place."

"Relax. It's on me."

"Suki, how'd you get so much money?" Samantha

asked.

"Samantha, it's not lady-like to inquire about finances."

"It's also not lady-like to accept lavish gifts," she pointed out. "They come with strings attached."

I surveyed the girls and realized Samantha was right. There was a string attached to this gift. "You're right. Here's the quick answer. I've lived for over three hundred years. I've saved my money over the years. I've invested wisely. And, I've been blessed by many men who have chosen to give me some very lucrative gifts that I have also wisely saved and invested."

"And why do you want to share with us?" Charlotte repeated.

"Because Raven and Phineas want something from you. Something that isn't of pure intentions. I am responsible for you and when released from my bottle, a nurturing sense is also released within me. If something happens to you, a small piece of me dies inside. I know it's hard to understand because we've really just met, but it's a chemical reaction. I am tied to you now. Like a mother to a child."

Samantha and Charlotte looked me over. I stood before them in a black pencil skirt, white blouse and Christian Louboutin heels. My hair had been recently styled and I had gone on a bit of a shopping spree myself, treating myself to new makeup and other essentials to bring myself up to date with Los Angeles of present day.

"You are cooler than most moms," Samantha

noted.

"And our moms aren't around," Charlotte admitted sadly.

"But she doesn't look old enough to be our mom," Samantha added.

"Finally, I'm hearing some manners," I interjected and then whispered, "Actually, I don't look old enough to be any mom."

They looked at me, sizing me up and trying to figure out what to do next so I helped them make the logical decision. "Listen, I'm willing to do the job of looking after you and while I'm at it, you two need some help in the fashion department so stop arguing with me and let's get at it."

"Where do we start?" asked Charlotte.

"With the essentials, of course," I answered.

Essentials included a basic black wardrobe, which is definitely considered not only essential, but absolutely necessary at any Los Angeles party. So in addition to two little black dresses, we also picked up black pumps, trousers and white accent tops. The girls then headed to Guiseppe Franco Salon for eyebrow waxing, facials, manicures, makeup lessons, and hair styling. The expedition took over four hours, but worth every minute. When I saw them walk out in a whole new look from top to toe, I couldn't have been prouder if I was indeed their true birth mother. It was time to party.

Chapter Seven

℘he moment the kids from school arrived at my penthouse, the girls' popularity quotient went up about triple percent. Perhaps it was due to the doorman at Maison 360 having already been introduced to Samantha and Charlotte and being instructed to tell each arriving guest that they were "expected," or once they took the elevator up to the penthouse floor they realized that my suite was the only one on that floor. And, if that wasn't enough, a sushi chef preparing delicacies in one corner while penguin clad waiters, all of whom doubled as male models, passing out canapes throughout the rest of the room made them realize that this was no ordinary high school party.

Hundreds of twinkling tea candles lit the room seductively while black linens graced the tables. Silver napkins emblazoned with the initials "S" and "C" spelled out the message that the girls had style. And in case any naysayers dared complain that this was too high brow, a disc jockey, karaoke game as well as a pole dancing bar awaited for when the party really jumped into gear. The overall opinion was that this was the party of the year. But it wasn't just the ambiance that got noticed.

"Charlotte, you look…," Josh stumbled trying to find the right word. "You look amazing."

In response, a rose colored blush spread across Charlotte's cheeks. "Thank you."

"Do you want to dance?"

"Sure."

They moved to the dance floor that I had installed in the living room. It wasn't by accident that the next song that played was a slow one. Josh smoothly caught Charlotte by the wrist before she could slip off the dance floor.

"I don't mind a slow one, if you don't."

"What would Ashley think?"

"I'm not sure I care right now. In truth, she complains a lot and sometimes I'm not sure why we're together."

The answer took Charlotte by surprise. It was an about-face from her last conversation with Josh, and while she was pleased for the attention, she wasn't sure she liked the fact that it took getting a whole makeover to receive it.

"To tell you the truth, Charlotte, I've been thinking about ending it with Ashley."

Charlotte was aware of Josh's hand sliding lower down her back. Just a week ago, she would have been thrilled, but now not so much. It seemed that his interest in her was very superficially based.

"Really? I would never have guessed there was trouble in paradise."

"It's hardly paradise. This, on the other hand, comes close."

Without warning, Josh led Charlotte off the dance floor to a darkened corner. He maneuvered her so that her back was up against the wall, while he leaned in close.

"Charlotte, you even smell amazing," he said bending his face to her neck and inhaling her perfume.

"Josh...I don't feel right about this. You're with Ashley," she said trying to get out from his hold.

"I don't care. I want you."

A few weeks ago, experiencing this would have been a dream come true for Charlotte, but now she only felt confusion. Her heart no longer ached for Josh. In fact, she had spent the better part of the last week thinking of Phineas. And what's more, she didn't like the idea that Josh may have never approached her had Suki not given her the makeover.

"Let's go back to the party," she said more forcefully.

"What's the hurry?" Josh replied, until another voice boomed its disapproval.

"Charlotte, is everything alright?"

Surprised at hearing Charlotte's name called and by another boy nonetheless, Josh automatically pulled away, only to find Phineas had stopped him from landing his first kiss with her.

"Phin, what are you doing here?" Charlotte immediately started to smooth her hair, fidget her feet.

Phineas noticed and smiled to himself, knowing that just because he caught her alone with another guy didn't mean her heart wasn't still beating for him.

"I knew you were here, so I couldn't imagine a place that I would rather be as well."

Charlotte blushed again and this time it was Josh who noticed her behavior.

"Hey man, we were...you know, busy."

Phineas sized up Josh and since he was a demon gypsy with supernatural powers, decided that Josh's disapproval meant absolutely nothing to him. "Yeah, I saw what you were doing and I don't think Charlotte is the type of girl to be acting that way in public."

"You don't need to speak for her," Josh said as an attempt at chivalry.

"You're right. I wouldn't dream of it. It's better if Charlotte answer for herself. Charlotte, would you like to dance with me?" Phineas asked sweetly.

Charlotte looked between the two of them, unsure of how to proceed. Being interested in a guy was new for her to begin with, but having two guys appear to like her right back was certainly unchartered territory.

"You've got to be kidding," Josh answered back. "Take a hike, man. She's with me."

"I don't think she is," Phineas answered sternly. "Charlotte is too good for you. She doesn't need to play second fiddle to a guy who can't seem to decide if he has a girlfriend or not."

Josh stared down Phineas. "What's that supposed to mean?"

"It means you have a girlfriend, don't you? If you and your girlfriend actually break up then I suppose you're free to pursue a new relationship, but until that time, I can call you a two-timer and suggest to my friend, Charlotte, that she stay clear of trash like you."

It happened without warning. While Phineas' words were true indeed, Josh didn't take a liking to them and threw the first punch. But he soon quickly discovered the futility of taking such action against Phineas, who without even looking in the direction of the punch innately knew to duck out of harm's way. And when Josh immediately threw a second punch, this time Phineas allowed it to meet his jaw only to show everyone at the party that Josh was in the wrong. Phineas shook his head momentarily, much akin to the type of motion a surfer would do to his hair as he steps from the waves, and then gave Josh's torso a decided shove, which resulted in catapulting him across the room.

"He'll be fine," Phineas said to Charlotte. "I'll be right back."

Phineas walked over to where Josh landed, still dazed and confused over how he got there. "Look at me," Phineas said evenly as he took Josh's hand. The connection made between the mind and body -- Phineas' eyes boring into Josh's, his hand holding Josh's firmly provided Phineas with the ability to control him completely. "You'll walk over to Charlotte and tell her you had too much to drink tonight. You'll ask her to forgive you for anything that you might have said in your inebriated state. In fact, you'll tell her that you don't know what came over you and plead with her not to repeat it to Ashley." Within seconds of releasing Josh's hand, Phineas watched as Josh indeed crossed the room and spoke a few words to Charlotte, before leaving the party.

Charlotte was left alone, giving Phineas the opening he needed.

"He'll be okay. Just needs to sleep it off."

"I didn't even know he was drunk," Charlotte said quietly. "I thought he was…"

"What? What did you think, Charlotte?"

Phineas used the same trick on Charlotte, looking into her eyes, taking her hand in his own to read as well as control her thoughts. What he saw told him everything he needed to know. He knew that while Charlotte was flattered over Josh's attention, she was more interested in him.

"You know, Josh isn't all he's cracked up to be. Guys like him never are."

"What do you mean? Guys like him?"

"I've known guys like that, the kind who appear to be the big man on campus, but in reality, they're just insecure players. He has a girlfriend that's a trophy so he can look good to the other tools he hangs out with. If he had any real confidence about him, he would make decisions based on what he believes in, not what he thinks will help his popularity."

Charlotte thought about the timing of Josh's interest in her, the fact that she now looked like she was part of the in crowd. It didn't matter to her. In fact, she was relieved to have seen this side of Josh, and even more pleased that Phineas had taken an interest in her before tonight. She looked at him carefully. "You're really perceptive."

"I am. I know that you deserve to spend time with someone who has the time to give you. Come dance with me, Charlotte."

"Err, does Suki know you're here?" she said looking around.

"Let's dance. Nothing else matters."

And to Charlotte, no truer words could be spoken as Phineas led her onto the dance floor.

"What is he doing here?" I said more to myself than to Samantha, who was twirling a strand of her red hair between her fingers.

"It's your house. Didn't you invite him?" Samantha asked me.

"I can't believe the nerve he has. At least his evil sister didn't come along with him."

"He seems like he really likes her. Maybe you should give him a chance."

"You've got to be kidding. I wouldn't trust Phineas with Charlotte any more than I would trust a wolf to guard the henhouse."

"So are you going to throw him out?"

"Of course not."

It was Samantha's turn to look surprised. "But I thought you just said..."

"Exactly. I don't trust him. Keep your friends

closer and your enemies closer. There's been more than a few generals, leading some of the finest armies, who have taught me that lesson. And, if I didn't heed their advice, then I certainly would listen to Southern roots that taught me to always be a lady. For those reasons, he can stay--as long as he behaves himself."

"Are you going to talk to him?"

"I'll give Charlotte a chance to have some fun, and then I'll talk to him. What about you, sugar? Are you having any fun? Where is that cute Ryan boy?"

"Over by the food table," Samantha said wistfully.

"Why so sad?"

"He's not into me. He's got a girlfriend."

"That, as evidence of the way Josh was acting earlier, is not necessarily a permanent condition. Now scoot. Go talk to that boy before some other girl does. You don't get many opportunities to get him away from Jessica. He would be so much better off with you. That girl speaks about him as if he's her lap dog."

Samantha looked toward Ryan, took a deep breath to ready herself and smiled with new found confidence that comes from a day of shopping and primping. "Okay. You win."

"And hopefully you will as well." I said smiling back at Samantha as she left to find Ryan. I was hopeful that my being sent here wasn't in vain. As I watched Samantha chatting to Ryan across the room, I smiled to myself knowing that I had a bit of a hand at forming her new found confidence. But, a glance at the dance floor revealed Josh was a long forgotten memory in Charlotte's mind. It didn't come as a complete surprise that she should act this way. For all I knew, Phineas was compelling her.

I narrowed my eyes and focused on Phineas' thoughts. Like a static signal, the message I received was a jumble of positive and negative energy flows. He had gained more powers since the last time I encountered him, no doubt studying hard under Raven's tutelage. It was impossible to get a proper read on his intentions toward Charlotte. I quietly slipped among the party-goers, edging my way closer to where they were dancing.

Phineas was dancing a slow, sensual dance with one hand placed gently on the small of Charlotte's back while the other held tightly to her free hand, holding it closely against his strong chest. It was no wonder that Charlotte seemed to be in a dreamland. He only had to apply the slightest pressure for her to respond, moving left and then right, forward and back. It was a dance between two people who seemed to have been born with a connection to each other.

Suddenly, he stopped swaying and looked at her. "You really are sweet." His tone was more of surprise than a declaration of appreciation and Charlotte laughed in response. Phineas tried to recover, "You're different."

"That's a compliment, right?" Charlotte asked.

I trained my hearing to their conversation and realized that something was indeed different about Phineas as well. It worried me. I had no idea what he and Raven wanted with the girls, but he looked at Charlotte in pure astonishment as if even he found wonder in what he had discovered about her. I couldn't tell if Phineas was still commanding her thoughts, but just as soon as I tried to tap into his mind, he turned and saw me. No sooner, he dropped his hand from Charlotte's and excused himself.

"Charlotte, you're great and I could dance with you all night, but I promised my sister that I would help her with something. It's getting late and I need to go."

"Sure, I understand. Will I see you again?"

"Of course. I'll get in touch with you."

I didn't have to place too much stress on my intuitive powers to know Raven must be nearby for Phineas darted from the party as fast as a grunion running to lay its eggs before the tide carries him out to sea once again. I listened to the sound floating on the wind and sure as daylight, her angry caw rang out the moment Phineas left my penthouse. I went to the window and saw two black birds perched on the tree just outside my living room.

Chapter Eight

"You looked awfully cozy," she hissed once they had returned to human form and were driving down Pacific Coast Highway.

"I was doing what you instructed. Hey cool it," Phineas complained. Raven was driving the way she lived, fast and on the edge of destruction.

"What's the biggie? You're immortal."

"But everyone else on the road isn't."

"Collateral damage for pissing me off, dear brother."

"Why are you so mad? You're the one who wanted me to get close to Charlotte and Samantha, to find out why they would be chosen as Releasors. What's the problem?"

"You don't have to enjoy it so much. I read you, damn it!"

Phineas sat in silence, knowing it was futile to deny it. Finally he broke the silence. "I don't feel that way now, not when I'm with you. It was probably something that Suzette was doing. You know, some sort of defense for the girls, compelling me to actually think I liked her in order to keep them safe from me."

Raven seemed to mull over the possibility and nodded slightly to herself. As she calmed, her driving became less erratic and her anger subsided. "You just worried me."

"You have nothing to worry about." Phineas ran his hand along Raven's arm and she slowed the car even more and pulled over to the side of the road. Phineas knew in spite of Raven's tough side and powers, she was still a woman, and a jealous one at that. He hoped that his explanation would suffice because truth be told, he couldn't explain the way he had felt for Charlotte when he was with her and it scared him as much as it did Raven.

"I guess I have no choice," she admitted. "It's just that it's so easy for you to get close to them. I mean, really, right there in Suki's suite. Even that Genie is mesmerized by your good looks."

"That's not true. She just knows that I'm not going to harm her Releasors right under her nose at her own party. It was the perfect place to make a move."

Raven tensed with his words, until Phineas turned her to face him. "I don't mean that in the way you're thinking. I wanted into her mind, not her clothing. The only one that I'm going to make a move on is you," he said delivering a light kiss on her cheek.

Raven regarded the fact that Phineas' kiss was more brotherly than boyfriend like, but decided they had fought enough for one evening. "Okay, I believe you. You're a good actor."

"Exactly. That's all it is."

"Phin, when you got close to Suki, did you notice if she was wearing a necklace...a Celtic amulet?"

"I didn't notice," he said, absently twirling a lock of Raven's black hair between his fingers. "Why?"

Raven leaned her head against Phineas' shoulder. "I've seen its design through the ages, but only in relation to Suki's Releasors."

"That's an odd coincidence."

"It is. Every person released by Suki became great *because* of her. Like a muse, she directed them, inspired them and more importantly, she got the public to believe in them. Overindulgent parents will tell their children that greatness lives inside them, but without the adoration of the public, you're nothing. One of those girls will receive the Amulet and then...God, I've got to have it," she said with a look in her eye that even made Phineas uneasy.

"Why do you need it? You are already powerful."

"These girls seem like typical teenagers and maybe they are. But either because they released Suki or due to her tutelage, they will grow into so much more. Everyone near that damned Genie achieves fame and it seems to be greater with each passing generation. One of these girls will hold the world in their hand."

Phineas had never seen such determination in his sister. Her own words seemed to light a fury within her.

"Phin, stay close to Charlotte. I may not like it, but it's the only way of knowing if it's her. She'll begin to trust you and then, she'll tell you everything."

"And Samantha?"

"I don't think it's her. There's a prophecy associated with that symbol. It talks about a chosen one and calls them 'the white dove.' Charlotte is the first in centuries to even come close to that description."

Phineas thought to Charlotte's porcelain complexion, her high cheek bones, the sweep of blonde hair across her forehead, the lashes that were surprisingly dark considering her light hair and finally, her lips--full and red, lips that he desperately wanted to feel with his own.

"Are you with me?"

"Sorry. What did you say?"

"Phin, try and focus. I said, we have to eliminate Samantha. It will make Charlotte vulnerable, ripe for the picking. And it will entice Suki to hand over the Amulet. She's probably at a loss for which one to give it to. We'll just help make that decision for her."

"Isn't that a bit of a risk? What if you're wrong and its Samantha who has the power to unlock its secrets?"

"I've watched Suki for centuries; I don't think I am. Besides, I know things that she doesn't. When you have to earn your powers like I do, struggling to open one's mind to the possibility of other realms, rather than just being handed your powers on a silver platter, it makes you appreciate it more. Suki doesn't know about the prophecy because she's never had to study the relationship between Genies and their Releasors. She just accepts it as a part of her life."

"So what is this prophecy about?"

"It's a symbiotic relationship between herself and her Releasors. She needs them so that she can live in the real world, but they need her for inspiration -- except one, who will develop powers unto him or herself."

"The White Dove?"

"Yes. I get brief visions, but like a puff of smoke it quickly dissipates. You make sure to stay close to Charlotte. Just remember our rules, my sweet Phin."

"Not too close."

"Exactly."

Raven leaned into Phineas. Again, he kissed her on the cheek, a move designed to appease her and calm her mood, which he recognized as simmering danger. He knew he should have shown more passion toward her, but something -- or someone -- was holding him back. "Raven, can we go home now? I'm just beat," he said as way of an explanation.

Raven's dark eyes seemed to turn even blacker. "There's something I need to do. Can I meet you back there?"

Phineas looked outside the car window at the bluffs of Malibu on one side and the ocean on the other. About a mile in the distance the lights from homes in The Colony, the exclusive gated area where he and Raven shared a home, twinkled and shined. "Raven, it's cold and we're a good mile from home."

"So fly."

"I've shifted once tonight. Like I said, I'm really tired."

"Stop whining. It's not like you need your energy for me," she said and indicated the door of the car.

Phineas exhaled a defeated breath and got out of the car, took a minute to transform and flew off toward the homes. Satisfied that he wasn't going to come looking for her, Raven turned the car around to head back to my suite.

Raven may have initially started following me in and out through time to avenge John's death, but her reason for confronting me tonight was altogether different. As they say, I wasn't born yesterday and I quickly realized that the depths of her revenge had grown to include a desire to possess my powers and find the amulet that burns stronger each time it is given to one of my Releasors.

Desperate to talk about the party, the girls decided to go downstairs to the restaurant for dessert and hot chocolate while I took advantage of the quiet. I had just finished washing my hair and was about to retire for the night when I realized I hadn't locked the door after the last party-goer had left. I walked down the hallway from my bedroom to the sitting room, stopping to straighten a photo of the girls that was misaligned from its hook on the wall, almost as if someone had purposefully knocked it askew. That's when I heard her voice.

"Such lovely girls. Especially since your little makeover expedition."

I turned to see Raven languishing on my couch as if she were about to watch a movie. But I knew this wasn't a social call.

"That was a fun afternoon," I agreed. "You should really try some girl time. It would do you good to connect in a positive manner."

Raven laughed and approached me. "I'd rather spend time with them at their funeral. Looking forward to that."

I knew that the time for false civility had ended. "You weren't invited here. Please leave."

I summoned the elements and blew a frigid gust of wind against her, forcing her toward the door. She struggled against the wind, flailing backwards for a few feet, but swiftly recovered. Her strength to combat what I threw her way was remarkable. She had fallen down, but then simply held her hands up in front of her and shielded the onslaught of wind until it merely died down. And then to my utter surprise, she recovered swiftly enough to play dirty.

Raven redirected the element toward me and soon got the upper hand. I was thrown against the opposite wall of my suite. My back hit the wall at full force, and the impact of my collision caused a painting to become dislodged, tumbling over my head. I forced myself to stand as quickly as possible. That maneuver, along with a wound that caused a trickle of blood to drip from my temple, left me feeling dizzy.

"You made it so easy to visit," she said moving closer to me.

Although I've told the girls to be wary of Raven, and I've known of her quest for power, I was surprised nonetheless by the sheer hatred that I saw in her eyes. She took advantage of my state and with lightening speed she grabbed my wrist in one hand and with the other, pointed a finger at me that revealed a talon-like nail polished in crimson. I twisted the arm that she held and struck at her with my free hand, but she merely dodged her head out of harm's way and smiled knowing that her hold on me was more than just with her hand. "It's almost as if you wanted me here," she spoke. "Tell me, Suki, did you want me to come? Have you missed me that much?"

Her words had the desired effect. The pain that I felt over the loss of our friendship fueled her and she slowly ran one claw-like nail over my shoulder, causing the blood to immediately flow.

I gasped more from the shock of her action than the pain. She used my surprise to her advantage. Although she released my bound hand, she just as quickly used both of hers to swipe at my body again, gauging her nails from each hand through my skin, tearing at the flesh just under my collarbone and continuing down the length of my arms. There was no time to react. Pools of blood released from each line where her nails had made their mark. Raven's handiwork littered my body and left me reeling in pain.

A burning pain coursed through the scratches she had left on me and it took more energy than usual for me to command the elements. Raven observed me as if waiting for something. And then, it hit me. A wave of dizziness, ten times stronger than that caused by the bump on the head, flowed over me.

"Why are you here?" I asked her weakly.

"I want your amulet and I want you gone," she spoke serenely, having now taken out an emery board to repair any damage she had done to her nails.

"You know that I can't leave," I said with as much force as I could muster. With all that was left in me, I summoned the elements and sent a fireball toward Raven, but she easily dodged it. There was still a bit of fight left in me and with a burst of wind, Raven was thrown across the room into a full length mirror, shattering it with the impact. She fell to the ground only momentarily, before dusting herself off.

"Well done," she said clapping lightly. "I'm surprised you can do that in your condition."

"What do you mean? I'm in my own house. There's nothing you can do to me here," I said trying to sound much stronger than I felt as waves of nausea started to affect me.

"True," she said approaching me like prey, "that's why I had to resort to fighting like a girl. Just a little scratch, huh Suki?"

And with a sudden sharp pain that hit my temples, combined with the dizziness and nausea, I was brought to my knees. In addition to the pain, I felt something I hadn't in many years -- fear. It wasn't magic working against me here, but a natural poison found near my own home. Growing just outside the main doors to the building were white oleander, a beautiful, but deadly flower.

"What have you done?"

"You know," she said with a smile and then plucked a flower out of her pocket and took a long whiff.

"You couldn't have poisoned me. I haven't eaten a thing here all night," I said feeling increasingly weak in spite of my words. And that's when it hit me. She must have had the plant's extracts under her nails, transferring them directly into my blood stream when she scratched me so deeply.

"And there it is," Raven said satisfied, "your expression says it all. It's that miraculous moment when you actually figure something out. Too bad you haven't figured out that I'm also going to kill your Releasors and take your amulet."

I felt myself lapsing into unconsciousness while thoughts over my history with Raven flitted through my mind. "It's in the past," I whispered.

Before she began ransacking my house in search of the amulet, I could hear her last words. "The past, my ass. What you did will never be forgotten."

But as my world turned to black, I was at least reassured that Raven had no idea that I wasn't referring to our relationship, but the amulet itself.

I awoke to find James holding my head in his lap, gently pouring droplets of something sweet into my mouth.

"Welcome back," he said wearing a look of relief.

"What is this?"

"Quinine mixed with a trace of grenadine. You wouldn't like the taste of the Quinine alone," he said by way of explanation. "Just sip it. It'll take away the nausea."

My mind raced with questions of how long I was out, where were the girls, and naturally, the recourse that would befall all of us when Raven realized that the amulet wasn't in my possession.

"Slow down," James said as I attempted to pull myself up to a seated position. "Too many questions."

I gave him a funny look.

"I meant that you look like you're *about* to ask a million questions. Just lie still...there's no need to rush anything."

The way he spoke that line was so innately sexy, as if the words were a quiet purr on his lips. In spite of the blow to my head and the poison that miraculously seemed to have left my body, my thoughts were running wild with other activities that I wouldn't mind taking slowly with James.

For some reason, he appeared surprised. I chocked it up to thinking that he wasn't used to seeing a woman as strong as myself momentarily incapacitated. He looked me over and I noticed the corners of his mouth curve upwards slightly. "You seem to be feeling much better," he said repositioning himself so that he was on his side next to me.

His fingers were lightly running through my hair,

making me feel so relaxed and comforted that I no longer wanted to get up, although I knew that lying next to James could place me in a precarious state. "Your cure has made me feel right as rain, so I should probably…"

He spoke firmly. "Suki, enjoy the quiet for a few more minutes."

He adjusted a makeshift pillow under my head that was actually a t-shirt and presumably his since he was shirtless and gorgeous. I wondered what it would be like to run my hands over his chest, feeling the sinew of his muscles along my palm. Again, he chuckled. *"That can be arranged."*

Maybe I hit my head harder than I originally thought. Here I was now awake, but feeling like I was hallucinating, imagining the words I wanted James to speak. "What's so funny?"

He looked at me smugly. "Are you sure you're feeling up for that?"

"And what are you referring to?"

"I think you know."

His eyes…mouth, his entire being smiled back at me. I took a moment to intuitively read him, and to my relief discovered that he was of pure intentions. That knowledge and the fact that he looked simply amazing, placed my mind at ease…and made me ache for contact with him.

His mouth was tender at first as he whispered against my lips, "Suki, I was so worried when I found you."

His arms held his body prone over mine, but he

slowly lowered himself onto me. I could feel the hardness of his manhood press against me. I responded by wrapping my arms around his neck and arching my back toward him to feel him even closer.

"God, I want you."

He was in my head and it was freaking me out. In spite of how good he felt, I rolled out from under him. I had never felt anything like this with a man who wasn't my Releasor and for that matter, no past Releasor had ever invaded my thoughts.

"Are you okay?" he asked.

"Yes. I'm just feeling a bit light-headed." It was only a half lie. "So, how did you know about this?" I asked indicating the glass of red potion he gave me earlier.

"Being a bartender in this life has its advantages. And, it's the only thing I know that counteracts oleander."

"This life?"

"We'll talk more when you're feeling better."

As if to establish that point, he continued. "I bet you'll be back to your usual self very soon," he said, his eye wandering to the highest shelf where my bottle with its beautiful encrusted butterfly sat proud.

"How did you know to come up here?"

"Intuition?"

Hmm, interesting choice of words. "That's all the explanation I'm going to get?" I blushed and smiled up at him. My ordeal was long forgotten, now replaced with decidedly happier thoughts. He leaned into me, "I'm so glad you're okay."

I kept a hold on his blue eyes, so beautiful and clear, and relished in the feel of his strong arms holding me tightly. His chin had a bit of ragged stubble, darker than the hair on his head and in spite of still feeling woozy, I wanted him to kiss me again. I tipped my head ever so gently upward and waited...to hear a knock at the door.

James planted a kiss, way too sweet and far too platonic, on my cheek and then offered explanation to the next question in my mind.

"The girls returned home while you were still knocked out."

"Oh no."

"They're fine, but they were obviously worried about you. I told them that I knew how to help, but I needed them to stay downstairs."

The knock became more insistent and James went to open it. The look the two of them gave me was one of sheer relief.

"We were so worried, Suki," Charlotte said, throwing her arms around me.

"We were so worried," Samantha added, surveying my form that still rested on the floor.

James offered his hand to me and helped me up. When I was comfortably plopped onto my couch, he said, "I should leave you all alone."

"Wait. You haven't explained how you knew...We should talk, don't you think?"

"Tomorrow. I promise," he said as he walked out the door.

I nodded and smiled to myself as I closed the

door.

"Tomorrow?" Samantha teased. "Suki has a boyfriend," she said in a sing-song voice.

"Don't be so immature. I'm over three centuries old. I'm entitled."

They both smirked at me, but then the mood grew more somber again.

"How could this happen? It's because of us," added Samantha.

"Don't blame yourself," I insisted. "Raven, would have come looking for the amulet one day, with or without me being Released by you. But this means that you two have to be on high alert."

"What amulet?" Charlotte said picking up on my words.

I took a deep breath and explained that the stone held extreme power to its wearer -- the ability to look into the minds of those who have previously worn it.

"But we don't have it," Samantha stated the obvious.

"I know. It's hidden," I explained. "Raven believes that the amulet alone is what gives my Releasors their power or talent, but that's not true. It does bring power, but my Releasors all have something within them first. Some people may need a bit of a confidence boost, perhaps a push in the right direction, which is where I come in. The amulet merely intensifies what I bring out in a person. Power isn't something that one adjusts to in an afternoon. The amulet helps channel one's powers; it brings focus and clarity, and when you have that, in turn you become more powerful. But remember, I only grant wishes that are derived from an unselfish desire. This keeps the power of the amulet from falling into the wrong hands as well"

They nodded their understanding. "But Raven is so power hungry. What would happen if she got a hold of it?"

"She would use it and see the work of the great minds and I'm afraid she wouldn't use that knowledge for the greater good, but for herself, which is why it has to remain hidden for now. You must believe that it will be there for you, if and when you need it."

I walked to the kitchen to put the kettle on for a cup of much needed tea. When I returned, it was obvious that the girls were in deep thought.

"What's wrong," I asked, putting the kettle on for a cup of much needed tea.

"You're so different from Raven and yet you were friends with her once," Charlotte noted. "We heard the phrase in school, 'Power corrupts and absolute power corrupts absolutely.'"

"That pretty much sums up Raven," I admitted.

"Will you tell us about her?" Samantha asked. "You know, it would be good to know more, for our own protection."

I knew that she was playing me somewhat, but it was probably time that she heard more about Raven's background. "Okay, but you'll have to be patient because I've been lying on that floor with nobody to talk to and I'm just not used to keeping quiet for so long."

"Great, I feel a story coming on," Samantha teased.

I grabbed a plate of cookies, poured tea for the three of us and then deposited myself between them.

Chapter Nine

"Raven was born from a mortal mother and a father who was a practicing warlock, which meant that Raven possessed dormant powers. Her parents foolishly believed that if they never told her about her true lineage, then perhaps she wouldn't discover her powers on her own. And so, they attempted to keep this a secret, believing that they were protecting her and giving her a chance at a normal life. "

"It's hard to imagine Raven doing 'normal'," Samantha said, rolling her eyes.

"Quite," I agreed. "But Raven figured it out after hearing them argue. Not long after she learned the truth, her mother became very ill and suffered greatly. Watching her mother lose weight and become weakened from the typhus scared Raven, as it would any child. But her reaction to her death was also childlike and her father didn't have the sense or perhaps the fortitude to stop it. She was determined to never experience anything like that herself and so she worked to cross-over, offering herself along with her mother as a sacrifice."

"How old were you when you became friends?" Charlotte asked.

"We were both 21 during the witch trials--young and foolish, but obviously not totally innocent."

I sat quietly for a moment, reflecting on how things may have turned out differently had Raven never developed her powers or if she had used them to influence others back then.

"Ironically, she never used her powers for selfish reasons back then," I added. I involuntarily shook my head, thinking back to the way we were.

"Imagine what she would have been like if she had *two* witches for parents," Charlotte said while curling her long legs underneath her.

"Well, in the case of full-blooded witches, their powers automatically kick in when they hit the age of maturity. But for Raven, who was a half-blood witch, the powers must be cultivated. It's a bit like a farmer tending his crops. In fact, that is just the sort of advice I told my darling Grant Wood, an exceptional artist I met while traveling through Iowa in 1929."

"Here we go," Samantha said with a hearty laugh.

"Well, it's true. He had so much talent, but it was always simmering below the surface, until I came along." I stared at both girls, neither of which seemed convinced of the role I played as muse to my Releasors over the years. "Don't you want to hear about him?"

"Of course we do," Charlotte spoke and nudged Samantha.

"Yes, go ahead," she replied dutifully.

I clapped my hands and smiled at them, settling into my spot between them. "I was living with Grant who was 38 years old at the time. Let me think...I was 268, but of course, I didn't look a day over 19."

"Of course," the girls teased me.

"I'll ignore your sarcasm," I said and continued. "So, when Grant asked if he could paint me, I readily agreed knowing that it's not every day a handsome painter asks to immortalize a Genie of my age. The request was so complimentary that to me, refusing seemed as unheard of as dumping gators into a watering hole. But to my utter surprise, his painting was anything, but complimentary. I had disrobed for the occasion and yet when I looked at his work I noticed that my bosom seemed to grow outside my head, and where it should've been was instead my arm protruding from my chest like an elephant's trunk."

The girls stared at me, their mouths agape. I'm not sure if it was from hearing that I had posed in the nude or the shock of the outcome, at any rate, I kept going with the tale. "I tried to look on the bright side."

"There was one?" Samantha asked.

"Well, it's true that in the painting, I had only one breast and one arm, but at least his artistic license allowed me two eyes...even if they did sit one on top of the other."

"It sounds more like a fruit salad, all tossed around, rather than a portrait of you," Charlotte noted.

"Indeed," I agreed. "I took one look at Grant and

said it was no wonder he was still undiscovered."

"What'd he say?" Samantha asked.

I rolled my eyes at the memory. "I can still recall his words today. He said, 'But it's real. It's your essence -- two eyes so beautiful they should be front and center of your face, your arms so sensual I want them to wrap around my heart center and your breast'..."

"Stop. Don't go on explaining," Samantha begged."

"Very well. I told him, 'Grant, you have talent, but it needs to be redirected. Leave this crazy style for the loons like Van Gogh. What you need is realism. I should know, I've lived long enough.' And then I told him to grab his coat because we we're taking a drive. So we grabbed a picnic and blanket, popped into the car, and headed for Eldon, a quiet town in the country, to discover some inspiration."

"And? Did you find it?" Charlotte asked.

"Sort of," I admitted. "We had an intense make out session right under the branches of an old oak tree. There was something so bohemian about Grant that I couldn't resist," I smiled. "An hour and a half later...,"

"An hour and a half?!" Samantha said in mock horror.

Charlotte teased right along with her, putting the back of her hand against her forehead and throwing her head back. "Where was your sense of Southern gentility?"

"Anyway," I said ignoring the implication. "I

finally asked him if the breeze from that oak had blown any inspiration into him. Grant looked down the lane, spotted a trim white cottage and took my hand in his own.

"Can you imagine if we had a house like that one?" he asked. "We could wake up together every morning, live a simple life just living off the land."

"Even farmers have it hard," I reminded him. "They have to bargain with the sun to shine and the rain to pour. Their wives wear a perpetual frown because one year it's a bumper season of apples, but they can't bear to eat one more pie. They complain so much that the next year the apple trees don't produce enough and they're stuck eating nothing, but beet root."

I took a breather from my story to refill my tea. "Grant laughed and called me his funny little minx." He said, 'I feel guilty having you all to myself. I should paint the most sullen farmer and dour wife so that everyone who sees the painting can imagine a story like the one you just told.' And that's just what he did."

"Wait a minute." Charlotte, who was obviously well-versed in art history, imagined the image.

I nodded. "That's right. Using the carpenter Gothic style, he painted the little cottage at the end of the lane along with the kind of people he fancied should live in that house. Grant wanted me to pose once again, but I simply couldn't be portrayed in that light. I suggested his sister, Nan, would be better as she had a closet full of prim clothing. And who better than to portray her frown-faced husband than a man who is used to seeing many a frown -- Grant's dentist, Byron McKeeby, from Cedar Rapids. Grant had recently visited the dentist for a tooth ache and left complaining that the treatment must have been something that Dr. McKeeby picked up from the devil himself. Grant decided to paint a pitchfork into the painting as tribute to the stern doctor. When the painting was complete, I declared it Grant's finest work."

"And that was it?" Samantha asked.

"Well, he didn't know it, but I felt that my work with him would not be complete until I ensured that he got the notoriety he deserved. I entered the painting into a competition at the Art Institute of Chicago, but the judges dismissed it. That's when I was forced to go above their heads and enter the dreams of one of their most powerful patrons. He woke up the next morning and low and behold, urged the judges to reconsider. They awarded Grant a third-place bronze medal and $300 to appease the patron, but still I was not satisfied."

"Big surprise there," Charlotte said with a wry smile, and as if to prove her point, she stood up and twirled in a circle, showing off another new outfit that I had insisted she buy.

"The next night, I entered this man's dreams yet again," I explained. "And he woke to convince the Art Institute to acquire the painting for its collection!"

"Where it remains today and is known as *American Gothic*," Charlotte added.

"Of course, at the time the *Chicago Evening Post* reprinted it with the caption *An Iowa Farmer and His Wife.* Naturally, real Iowa farmers and their wives were not amused. A horrible woman by the name of Jemima Thump told my dear Grant that he should have his head bashed in. Another threatened to bite off his ear. And then there was the backlash by Grant's own sister, who was upset about being depicted as the wife of a man twice her age. Grant was terribly depressed."

"Suki, something about the help you give your Releasors always seems to backfire," Samantha noted.

I felt a sudden chill from her words, but shook it off as my tea having gone cold. "The only way out of the problem was to put it in perspective for people. If my dear Grant was to be depressed, then so would the nation, so I launched the Great Depression."

"You did what?!" Charlotte exclaimed.

"Well, it worked...at least for Grant. Let me tell you, he was in high cotton -- popular as all get out. His painting was no longer seen as criticism, but as an expression of the farmers' pioneering spirit to stare bravely in the face of difficult times. It was a testament to our pioneering spirit. I encouraged Grant to play down the Paris-influenced bohemianism of his youth and redefine himself as America's overall clad artist."

"Oh my god," Samantha said putting her head in her hands.

"Wait, it gets better," I insisted. "Thanks to my plan, America embraced Grant, but my sweet artist died just one day before his 51st birthday on a cold day in February."

"How is that 'better'?" Charlotte asked.

"Because, his admirers sent hundreds of cards, flowers and chocolates, most of which arrived on February 14th. I encouraged the public to continue this tradition of sharing their love. There was a brief blip in my plan in 1969 when Pope Paul VI tried to revoke the tradition, but little ol' me persevered and you can imagine how tickled I am to know that it continues even today."

"Suki, that was a beautiful story, but we were talking about Raven," Charlotte reminded me.

"Oh yes, we were. Well, you know that itty bit of time when Valentine's Day was nearly revoked? I later learned that the Pope was momentarily under Raven's influence. That girl would do anything to prevent messages of love from being spread. She even turned her back on her own father simply because he didn't earlier reveal the truth about Raven's lineage to her."

A sudden gust of wind caused a tree branch to scratch menacingly against the window, making all of us jump.

I took each of the girls' hands in my own and felt more than ever before the need to guide my Releasors. "It's important for you to understand your enemies in order to protect yourself from them," I said carefully. "When Raven learned the truth she was furious and believed that she had lost valuable time in which she could have become stronger. Time is the only true gift that anyone can receive and for gypsies, cultivating one's powers into proper usage can take years of practice. Raven also believed that if she had known about her powers earlier she may have been powerful enough to stop the witch trials altogether. She thought that just maybe she would have been able to be with John and Pixie. Her anger sprouted a desire to learn dark magic and the more powerful she became, the more she turned her back on the physical world and anything remotely associated with humanity."

"After landing in a hospital because of her it's hard to believe she ever had any humanity," Samantha noted.

"That's not very far from the truth," I admitted. "She took the knowledge she had learned about crossing over into the Realms to went to New Orleans. She brought a lock from her dead mother's hair to a voodoo queen. But she learned that offering was considered child's play. The voodoo queen agreed to help her, but only if Raven would trust and agree to have the life drained from her.

Charlotte shuddered. "How could she survive that?"

Raven told me about it when we met. "She was revived with a drink of her own blood as well as that of an innocent child."

"Wouldn't people around wonder what happened to her?" Samantha astutely asked.

"Raven had no problem saying goodbye to the people in her life; she said that the only good human was one who could serve a purpose and only they would be acceptable company to Raven. She never spent time trying to bring out the best in a person's potential as I did and for the most part, people were a disappointment to Raven. Ever since her own heartbreak, she came to abhor shows of emotion and since humans were prone to them, she felt that was their ultimate weakness. It has been the one struggle she has experienced with Phineas."

"Wait, the blood part...Phineas didn't..." Charlotte asked.

"Charlotte, I know you're er...intrigued by him, but once and for all, you must listen to me. I think there's only one way to explain this and that's to show you," I said moving to the shelf to remove my bottle. I placed a hand over its slender neck and instructed the girls to do the same. "My bottle is more than just a vessel to transport me forward in time. It is a window into the past as well." I said and closed my eyes, visualizing the world as it was in London in 1865. "Now relax and keep a hold of my hand."

A cold wind rushed through my penthouse and a loud snap like that of thunder cracking occurred all around us. Mere seconds passed before our vision was limited, and our reality shifted. Although our bodies remained safely in my suite, our minds would be shown the past. The journey started with the clanging and turning of gears and wheels. The girls' nails dug into my hands out of fear for the unknown, but I held on tightly to them, knowing that the key to being brought out of this hallucination was to remain calm while in it.

The back alleys of the London streets in 1865 were not the safest place to be, but it was here that our minds arrived making us believe that we were there as well. Charlotte rolled her neck from side to side to get her bearings and like a young fawn, got to her feet within just moments of the transition into this other Realm.

Charlotte ran her hands down her sides, pressing unseen wrinkles of her dress away. It was as if she was meant for this time. Her naturally thin body, which she was self-conscious of back home for its lack of curves, looked perfect in the black and white stripes of the Edwardian styled dress she wore. Her normally straight, long blonde hair was pulled up in a loose bun, a few strands were allowed to be free, their ends curled and falling luxuriously. She stood up now looking perfectly regal.

She took in my own appearance. Like her, my hair had been curled into ringlets, but mine flowed down my back, with a diamond butterfly hair comb providing just the right touch of drama.

"What is that on your bottom?" Charlotte asked. I twirled for her revealing small pearl buttons that traced down my back, ending at a bustle that completed the high-necked, cream colored dress.

"Cute, isn't it?"

"The dress or your behind?" Charlotte asked rhetorically. "I guess we're not in Kansas anymore."

"Well, technically we are still in Beverly Hills, but you have been given a glimpse of London. It's quite remarkable how well you've adjusted to the change. Come here and help me with Samantha, and I'll explain the where and how of it all."

It was only then that Charlotte noticed that Samantha was still lying on the pavement just down from where she and I landed. "What happened?!"

"Her grip on my hand must have slipped. I've never shown two people the past before," I said by way of an apology.

"Never mind that," Charlotte scolded. "Will she be alright?"

With Charlotte it was sometimes difficult to remember that she was in her first life as her maturity and composure was beyond compare. "I should've warned you about the effects, but I feared it would only make you focus on the possibilities. Sometimes it's best to just believe in the other Realms, allowing one to see the possibilities and then return safely. She'll be fine," I said referring to Samantha. "It can feel a bit like the bends, you know after diving, but it doesn't last."

In my mind's eye I was reaching into my pocket book to retrieve the smelling salts that I carried back in the day for such occasions. As I waved them under Samantha's nose, I heard Charlotte's voice sounding a wee bit anxious and realized that her mind was placing new thoughts into it faster than I could control them.

"Suki, you might hurry up with your reviving."

I turned to see what she imagined to be occurring -- a tramp approaching her with a menacing and determined walk. He reached into his pocket for what I didn't know, but I wasn't in the mood to be delayed anymore. I harnessed the power of my bottle and released hundreds of butterflies into the air. I shut my eyes and allowed them to stir the wind, their delicate wings working in unison. Leaves circled the ground slowly at first and then gained strength and force as a full blown storm thrust its glory against the tramp throwing him backwards and causing him to lose his sight from dirt and sand that accosted his eyes. I rotated my finger in a counter-clockwise motion, careful to keep the wind away from myself and the girls. We were dressed too well to risk a wind storm messing up our hair or clothes.

The tramp tried to shield his eyes as he continued to stumble forward toward Charlotte, determined to reach her as if drawn to her beauty. I would have none of that today.

"Charlotte, you must send him away," I ordered. "Do not think of him. I will help you."

It was an easy fix on my part. I narrowed my eyes, puckered my lips slightly and gave one firm blow. The wind raged a bit harder, now forcing him to give up his mission, whatever that may have been, and turn and run away down the alley.

I let the wind subside and returned to Samantha. The smelling salts did the trick and she awoke having missed all of the action.

"Wake up, sleepy head. How do you feel and don't say, 'where am I?' It's too much of a cliche," I said offering my hand and helping her to her feet.

My experience with showing Releasors the past is that it tends to bring out a person's true nature. In Charlotte's case, her natural refinement was heightened. For Samantha, it was like asking a fish to leave the water. "Why am I dressed in this uncomfortable outfit?" she complained, tugging at the high neckline of her dress, and twisting at the waist in an effort to stretch the too tight fabric away from her figure.

"You look lovely, and appropriate for the time," I answered. "London, 1865."

"Why are we here, Suki?" Charlotte asked, stepping next to Samantha's side. The two of them faced me, standing as one, but not with me.

"Well technically, we're not here. My bottle has given you a view into this world, including its inhabitants. There's someone that I want you to meet."

"Whatever for?" Charlotte asked.

"Because Charlotte, I know this is hard for you to hear, but as I've explained, Phineas is not what he appears. And if I can't convince you, then perhaps the person inside here will."

I indicated my mind's memory of a grey stone building next to where we stood. I led them out of the alley to the front where the passersby of the high street were plentiful. We walked inside a shop whose rounded sign simply read, "Apothecary" in scrolling letters. An older man whose skin was the color of chocolate and mannerisms just as sweet approached me.

"Miss Suzette, you are a sight. It's been far too long since you last channeled us."

"Clive, I've missed you," I said taking his hand in my gloved one. Then leaning into his ear, I whispered, "You don't look a day over a century."

He laughed a hearty guffaw. "Are you here for Madame Ruby?

"I am -- for her *private* counsel," I emphasized.

Charlotte and Samantha watched our interchange and when Clive went into the back room of the shop, they hurried by my side.

"Is he like you?" Samantha asked.

"Is he with us or are we with him?" Charlotte asked.

"It's like I said, we are given a view into this world, but Clive and the person you are about to meet, can transcend time."

"I don't understand," Samantha said.

"They're not quite like me, but blessed," I admitted.

"With what?" Charlotte asked suspiciously.

"With extra life," I said simply. "It lets me visit those who I miss from the past. Come, she's ready for us." Clive was holding a red velvet curtain back, indicating we should walk through to the area it shielded.

"Thank you, Clive," a voice from behind the curtain called out. I smiled my own appreciation to Clive and led the girls to Madame Ruby, an elegant woman whose mere presence made one want to stand up just a bit straighter.

"Madame Ruby it's been far too long," I spoke.

"Suki, my child, the fact that I haven't seen you means you have been well, so I'm not unhappy about the length of your absence. What can I help you with?"

"These are my wards," I said indicating Charlotte and Samantha, "and I fear for their safety."

"Is their fate the effect of ill health, accident or human deliberation?"

"We've already had one accident befall Samantha. I fear the next incident will be one that is pre-meditated, but not by a human."

"I see," Madame Ruby replied, and then indicated that Samantha and Charlotte should come closer. The girls each took a step forward and when Madame Ruby held out her hands, they each knew to take one. Even Samantha felt compelled to comply.

Madame Ruby sat with eyes closed and when she finally opened them, she looked at me and simply nodded, an acceptance of the truth behind my words. "They must see for themselves," she said and the candles that lit the quiet room blew out with a gust of wind. Images of Raven flashed across the wall behind her. They came too rapidly to track, but they were paired with the acceleration of our hearts beating faster and louder as the pictures of Raven became more vivid. When they finally stopped, the girls both collapsed into chairs, panting and breathing as if they had just ran for their lives.

"Why am I feeling so out of breath?" Samantha asked. "What did you do to us?"

"Samantha, mind your manners," I warned. As a Genie, I had already recovered, but I knew that Samantha's weak heart wouldn't be able to withstand another stress test at the hands of Madame Ruby.

"Perhaps she'd like another go?" Madame Ruby asked.

"That won't be necessary," Charlotte spoke up, one hand still on her chest as if to steady her own heart. "But if I may ask, there wasn't any image of Phineas. Does that mean he is okay?"

Clive had come in with two cups of tea. I raised an eyebrow to Madame Ruby as if to ask whether they were laced.

She met my gaze and waved her hand dismissively at me. "It's only what your own mind would allow them to have -- it's just Elderflower, to calm the nerves."

I handed the first cup to Charlotte, and answered her question, "But Charlotte, there were images of Phineas."

"Interesting. She is powerful," Madame Ruby said to me. "It's a defense mechanism. She only sees what she's open to seeing," Madame Ruby added.

"Then that makes him all the more dangerous to her," I added.

Madame Ruby nodded.

For once, Samantha took my side. "I saw him Charlotte. You need to listen to Suki. He and Raven...they're together." And then she leaned closer to Charlotte and whispered, "In every way."

Charlotte shook her head. "I don't need to hear

about this."

"Perhaps you'd like to know a little history considering you've come so far, or at least your mind has," Madame Ruby replied. "I understand your inability to see the truth," she spoke to Charlotte. "Phineas still has a hold on his humanity, but that's only because he is a fairly young gypsy. Raven is carving it away. You did see her images, did you not?"

We all looked to Charlotte, who lowered her eyes, remembering the vivid details of destruction and pain that Raven has caused over the years, and nodded.

Madame Ruby continued, "Like Raven, he was born under the sign of Gemini and with her tutelage they combined to form the bond of Gemini's twins. But in contrast to Suzette's life as a Genie, where powers grow with each passing year, demon gypsies can only grow their power from capturing the wisdom of others and learning to harness their secrets. I've known Suzette throughout the ages," she said turning her eyes toward me, but continuing to speak to the girls. "You would be wise to listen to her. She has lived for centuries yearning to meet the other two who would form the Triad."

Madame Ruby then chuckled, "Suzette, remember when you feared that you were destined to form it with Raven and Phineas?"

I smiled in spite of myself. The time when I could see myself living as best buds with Raven was long gone and the very idea of living through the ages in such close proximity to her and Phineas was so horrifying that it made me roll my eyes and shake my head.

Madame Ruby continued. "You may have sensed that these girls have something to do with unleashing the Triad's power. You are correct in that assumption. But, I fear that you will all go through some harrowing times before reaching that destiny. It may even involve the other Realms."

"Thank you, Madame Ruby." I rose and indicated to the girls that they should do the same.

"You'll be careful, Suzette?"

"Of course," I said and hugged her hard. For years I had taken care of others. It was nice to feel the comfort of knowing that someone was looking after me. And then, as if she could read my thoughts, which I always suspected she could, she gave me one final word.

"Raven found Phineas, which may seem like her way to build on her own evil by teaching him to do the same, but it's also a remnant of her fleeting humanity. She wanted someone by her side. There's someone watching out for you as well, Suzette. You won't always be searching."

I nodded, amused that she felt I needed someone, but I remembered my manners nonetheless. "Thank you, Madame Ruby." I took Charlotte and Samantha each by the hand, and felt the wind lift us back to the Realms of our own reality.

Chapter Ten

The first trip into other Realms can take a lot out of a human; and, Charlotte and Samantha, although clearly destined for something great, were no exception on this front. When our minds passed through, the grinding of gears and clocks signaling the passage of time were loud and monotonous. Although the constant ticking and humming blocked out all other noise so that Charlotte and Samantha wouldn't hear the struggles of generations as they passed through time, it did little to ease their transition back into the present. The loud gears sounded like a metronome that lulled them into a deep sleep.

I locked the doors to my apartment, ensured that the curtains were drawn and the building was protected, and then I also retreated into my bottle for some much needed rest and the chance to figure out what was expected of me. Neither girl had made any further wish requests. They asked nothing beyond the initial waste of a request to prove my powers. Fortunately, they took the responsibility seriously and hadn't wished for anything frivolous.

The fact that they were young meant that they had yet to choose their path in life and therefore, had no idea of what to ask from me. It also put me at a loss on how to lead them. I needed to change the game. Up until now, we had been focused on defense, merely keeping Raven and Phineas at arm's length. It was time to play a bit of offense. I needed time to figure out what Raven and Phineas could want from the girls and how their lives were meant to intersect with mine.

Prior to Samantha and Charlotte releasing me, Raven and Phineas had been more like stealth wolves surrounding their prey, patiently awaiting the kill. They had never exacted revenge on any of my Releasors, instead choosing to wait until my presence would trigger the Triad.

I had been warned of the Triad's eruption by my father, but still couldn't believe that my mere presence could set off a trail of events that would lead to the world's changing course and possibly affect the balance between good and evil. Each time, I wondered if one of the men who had Released me would unleash a stronger bond of magic. But thus far, neither heads of state, nor men who influenced generations to come, had been chosen.

But the very name of this event -- Triad -- implied that three would be involved. Perhaps that is why Raven never struck one of my Releasors until now. This was the first time that I had been released by not one, but two people. Combining with myself, formed three, although I knew that Raven hoped to separate the bond and keep the magic of one girl for her use with Phineas. She was certainly not one to go through a lifetime, and perhaps more than one, with someone she considered below her stature. Living an endless life was an exception reserved for Phineas alone, and I couldn't see her using her dark magic for anyone's benefit except for the two of them.

Unlike her, I had never had a problem with being tied to new people. It was the basic difference between those with natural gifts of magic and the others who had to cultivate dark magic on their own. I saw every person who released me as an opportunity to spread my knowledge, serve as their muse, and somehow better their generation. Each life who released me and was therefore, tied to me, presented an opportunity to gather knowledge that would be captured by the Amulet. Raven saw most people as being beneath her. But I understood that there was knowledge to be gathered from every soul as every person has a purpose. Sometimes, one just has to search for it.

Within the comfort and safety of my bottle, I sensed Raven's enthusiasm and desire to unleash some horrible deed. Although my powers were stronger than hers and Phineas' combined, she played dirty and with that, could get the upper hand as she had when she tricked me with the oleander poison earlier. She was obviously growing impatient and therefore, more reckless. I needed to figure out what powers lie dormant inside of Charlotte and Samantha, and quickly figure out how to harness it.

The exclusive, gated community of The Colony in Malibu was quiet as usual. When Raven and Phineas first purchased their home, the only neighbors were a few rock stars and celebrities. It was the perfect choice of a home base for these sorts of neighbors had the means to travel frequently, the snobbery to not want to get involved in neighborhood bake sales, and the arrogance to not notice anything beyond their own front door. Therefore, when Raven and Phineas disappeared for decades on end, there was nobody to report them missing.

Tonight was like many on the street. With the exception of Colony Patrol, the private security company that monitored the virtually non-existent comings and goings of the street, there was no traffic about. Nobody around to notice Raven instructing Phineas on his lessons.

"No, like this," Raven concentrated and a hefty branch that had been lying on the ground suddenly flew up, nearly hitting Phineas across the cheek, had he not ducked in time.

"Like that, huh?"

"I'm just trying to wake you up. Now do it," she said motioning to the branch.

Phineas narrowed his eyes, repeated the incantation that helped him focus his thoughts, but only succeeded in causing a small twig to rotate in its spot.

"Well done," Raven noted sarcastically.

"Do you think shifting and flying for the better part of an hour has anything to do with my being so tired?"

Raven contemplated him for a moment. "Maybe you would wake up if I were to do something more interesting." She moved toward him, her hips swinging seductively in a clingy black dress that was simple only in its design. When she stood directly in front of Phineas, she took each of his hands and proceeded to place them directly on her breasts and then guided them downward and across her backside. Phineas instantly knew that she wasn't wearing anything underneath. Then, in spite of being outdoors, she slowly and seductively peeled the dress off, leaving her standing in front of him in just her high heels.

"Maybe we should go inside," Phineas noted.

"Is that because you want me or you just don't want anyone else to want me?"

Phineas swallowed hard. It was near impossible not to want Raven, whose shiny black hair all but covered each perfectly round breast, her stomach flat and toned. But unexplainably, his thoughts went to Charlotte. He didn't know why he felt suddenly guilty for standing with Raven in her current state. He hadn't even kissed Charlotte, certainly there was no bond between them, and yet, somehow he felt that he owed her. He felt, oddly enough, that they belonged together.

Raven seemed to sense his thoughts waning from

her and she took control of the situation. As quickly as the thought of Charlotte came to him, it left, again replaced by a mounting desire for Raven. He was sure that Raven was compelling his thoughts now as he reached out to cup her rear and pull her hips into his sudden hardness. He also knew that he didn't stand a chance against her, given the circumstances.

"That's not very brotherly," she teased, leading him up the walk and into their home. The door had just barely closed and already their mouths found each other.

Phineas pulled away first and noted, "We have a somewhat complicated relationship now, don't we? It's rather difficult to form lasting attachments when the average person has a nasty habit of dying eventually. You're the most consistent girlfriend I can find."

"Wow, you really know how to win a girl over," Raven teased, flipping her black hair over her shoulder.

"I wish you could be like this more of the time. You know, light-hearted?"

"That implies that I have a heart."

"It gets buried a lot, but it's there," Phineas said, twirling her hair between his fingers.

"Don't forget that fact when you're seducing Charlotte." Raven's tone changed to cold again, angry at herself for sending Phineas toward Charlotte in the first place. She brushed a lock of his sandy brown hair from his eyes. You could get lost in those eyes and at that moment, Raven took in Phin's. "About my heart..." she started cautiously, "does it own yours?"

Phineas exhaled deeply. There was no point in lying just to tell her what she wanted to hear, and since he had regained control of his mind, he focused on the truth. "Raven, you waited for me and gave me this life. I will always be eternally grateful to you. I was so young when I lost my parents, and then you came along. You are my family."

"That's all you feel for me? I'm *family*?"

The answer didn't please Raven. "Look at me, Phin," she commanded. He knew Raven had the power to influence, hell, he could do it as well, but he had never experienced anything like what she was doing to him at that moment. He felt his resolve melting away, and suddenly his body felt like it was on fire, burning with a desire for Raven that would kill him unless it was satiated. Without even thinking, he grabbed her by the shoulders and pulled her close to him. His mouth sought out hers, his tongue immediately intertwining with hers. His hands roamed over her breasts and then downward between her legs.

And although he was taking everything he could from Raven, she was the one in control. "Stop," she said and instantly he was at attention, his breathing ragged, his heart pounding.

"What are you doing?" he asked angrily.

"Aren't you having fun?"

"Is this how you want it?!"

"What I don't want is you forgetting what we have while you're trying to get information out of

Charlotte," she said running a finger down the front of his throat, slowly edging her way down his chest and to his stomach and then strategically stopping just before the naughty bit.

Phineas' voice took on a bitter quality. "I've lived with you for 250 years. I think I know what's waiting for me at home."

"Enough!"

Raven stared at him, her anger bubbling over until the wind blew against the window with sudden and extreme force. She allowed the wind to die down slowly, but as the gale force trickled into a light breeze, its energy was channeled into Phineas stronger than any he had ever felt take hold. He looked at Raven no longer angry, but hungry with desire.

"That's better," she said noting the change in the way he looked at her. "How do I look for a 250-year old gypsy?" she said bringing his hands back up to her breasts again while hers roamed his body.

He couldn't help himself. He closed his eyes and felt the need rising within him. His breath caught as Raven undid the zipper on his pants, allowing her hands access to his manhood. "Touch me, Phin," she commanded. Again, his mind strayed to Charlotte, but he felt powerless not to obey Raven. He bent his head toward her perfectly shaped breasts and led each pale pink bud into his mouth, letting his tongue tease the tips. "I don't have reason to worry about the assignment I've given you, do I?"

Phineas looked up and met Raven's glance. Her

black eyes glowed brightly in the darkness, her pupils larger than usual, forcing him to fall deeper into her spell. She held his chin in her hand, forcing him to stare into her eyes.

"No, I want you," he said with urgency and then he held Raven against him, so he could press his hips against hers. He picked her up and carried her to the bedroom, where he laid her across the enormous bed. He grabbed each of her ankles, spreading her legs and then cupped her hips and pulled her into his mouth so his tongue could explore deep within her wetness. She didn't care that he was being rough. It was raw and evidence of the power she wielded upon him. She thrust her hips upward, pushing herself against his mouth.

He stopped only to position himself over her and then in one swift motion, he thrust himself inside her. Raven wrapped her legs around his waist, holding on tightly as he pushed deeper inside her until she drained everything out of him.

"Well, that was fun. I'm going to take a bath now," she announced and walked into the bathroom leaving Phineas alone with his thoughts.

Raven finally emerged from her bath and went downstairs to find Phineas brooding, sitting on the couch and mindlessly flipping through channels on the television.

"Whatcha watching?"

When he ignored her, she grabbed the controls and flipped off the T.V. "Phin, give it a rest. It's not like you didn't enjoy yourself."

"Jeez Raven, it was like rape. What was the point?"

She continued to stand, blocking the television. "You are so overly dramatic. The point, dear Phin, was to remind you that we're a team and long after all of these girls are gone and that Genie is cooped up in her bottle again, you and I will still be here, stronger than ever...if you help me."

Phineas sighed loudly. "Maybe you should just keep me under your spell 24-7. I would be much more pliable, don't you think?"

Raven stood there silent for a moment in her thoughts. Finally, she sat next to him, nuzzled her head in the crook of his neck and wrapped her arms around his waist. For once, she didn't take anything from him. Instead, he felt her give what actually felt like love, a pure energy flowed into him.

"Come on, Phin. Don't stay mad at me. I've got news that I'm bursting to tell you..."

"Okay, okay. Tell me, but I have to warn you, I'm not in the mood for any plan that involves sending someone back to the hospital."

Raven repositioned herself so that her head rested in Phineas' lap. She looked up at him and smiled gleefully. "I read Ryan's thoughts recently and he's been having some for Road Kill Girl."

"First off, 'road kill' is a little insensitive, even for you. And second, I thought you told me she wasn't part of the A-crowd. Why is the perfect Ryan Mills having thoughts for a lesser girl when he's with Miss Popularity?"

"The human heart is a stupid facility completely void of reason or logic."

"That must be why you keep yours all but dormant."

"Cute. What I meant was that watching their school crush dramas makes an otherwise dull trip more interesting. It's like live television," she said tossing the controls and catching them one-handed.

"You'd think they would keep control of their heart, particularly since doing otherwise can be social suicide at this place," Phineas astutely noted.

"I think Suki was brought to this place and time, not just for her Releasors, but for what they will encounter here. Finding the Amulet will ensure that those girls don't get to it first, but equally important is finding out who they are meant to be with."

Phineas was silent in thought for a moment. He shook his head, trying to make sense out of Raven's words. "But to imply that they need to end up with one of those guys is craziness. You've got two average girls, although perhaps a bit smarter than most. Throw in two more average guys, even if they are above in the looks department. It still equates to four *humans*. What kind of supernatural phenomenon could that lot possibly create?"

"That's it, Phin! The answer lies in their creation--a child who will break the mold and be extraordinary."

"You've got to be kidding."

"It makes sense. Suki gives them a makeover and it leads them closer to their destiny."

"That's a bit superficial, isn't it? Also, you really think Suki was Released just to play matchmaker?"

"It's not that simple. The prophecy...the White Dove...it is Charlotte and she will not only learn the secrets of every Releasor before her, but will prove to be the most powerful yet. It talks about a Triad making that so."

"So you don't think that Suki forms the Triad with the girls?"

"I admit that it's a possibility, but then again, Suki can't remain in this Realm once they use up their wishes. Charlotte and Samantha are only two. Therefore, a more realistic combination would be Charlotte, her mate, and their unborn child."

"And the Amulet will force these powers to come to fruition."

Raven nodded. "It could be hidden anywhere, in any time. If they receive it before we find it, then we use collateral to get what should be rightfully ours."

"And what would that be?" Phineas asked, not liking where her thoughts were leading.

"Taking a baby..." Raven shrugged her shoulders... "it would be easy. You're living proof that I can do that," she said nuzzling Phineas' neck.

He moved aside, not happy to be thought of as a toy to be taken.

"Yep, Josh and Ryan will have no problem being with those girls now that they're actually dipping a toe into the hot tub. Don't you think?"

Phineas was having none of this and decided to play along. "Totally. Charlotte is way hot."

"Don't sugar coat it, darling."

"Keep your jealousy in check, Raven. You asked the question."

"And now you can provide the answer."

Phineas sat down next to Raven and stretched his legs over the coffee table, he let his feet fall onto the glass in the manner that always bothered her. "Do tell. I love hearing the extent of your mind's depravity."

"Ryan can keep Samantha occupied, and then, with all of the attention you're giving to Charlotte, Josh is bound to get jealous and Ashley will notice. No guy likes a clingy girl. He'll eventually break up and then you can just skedaddle," she said making a scooting motion with her hand.

"Just like that? Let me ask you something, Raven. Did you ever consider that I might get used to hanging out with Charlotte?"

The second he said it, he knew it was a mistake, but Phineas was never power hungry or vindictive like Raven. He was along for the ride and feeling lately that he wanted to get off.

"Take that back. After all I've done for you...I saved your life." Suddenly, Raven took Phineas' hand in her own and stared into his eyes. The wind began to blow as she channeled the elements.

"Raven, what are you doing?" Phineas asked, a feeling of cold and then extreme heat surrounded his heart.

"Humans think there's no worse feeling than a broken heart and you know what? They're right. You never get over it. I lost my one love, but I was lucky enough to build a life with you. Phin, I made sure you would never hurt for someone like I did, and still you make comments like that one."

"Raven, I'm sorry for upsetting you, but stop what you're doing, whatever it is, it's...it's uncomfortable."

"I bet. What you're feeling is centuries of emotion that were hidden away from you, but no longer. I give you permission to feel."

And with that, the wind calmed and with it, Phineas' own heart rate returned to normal. He rested his hand on his chest, taking deep breaths and testing his own reality.

"What have you done?"

"You won't be able to truly connect to Charlotte if you can't feel. She's too guarded with her own emotions. Your human emotions were all but shriveled up, much like a grape in the sunshine. It happens slowly so as not to land you in a total depression. Gypsies with our abilities chalk it up to living so many years that you've seen it all. We learn to tune into them and then just as quickly, shut off that faucet when the feelings affect our judgement. You always managed to hold onto a bit of humanity within you, but mainly everything you thought you were feeling was just learned responses to social situations."

"How could you do that to me? Allow me to be human with feelings, and then just shut it down?"

"You have eternal life and you want to live with emotions? Really?"

Phineas thought about the truth in her words. She was right. He considered the atrocities he had witnessed humans bear upon each other and wondered why he was always able to regard them in such a removed manner, as if analyzing humans and their actions from a point of superiority.

Raven touched his cheek gently, teasing him with the emotion of being cared for. "The ability to tune out was a gift I shared with you. Maybe you'll be lucky and you won't feel anything for Charlotte, after all, she'll end up with Josh and you'll end up broken hearted."

Phineas sat in silence, already beginning to feel an unfamiliar emotion -- dread.

"Oh, and in case you're wondering, I never turn off my feelings when I'm with you." Raven moved closer to Phin, pressing herself against his chest and turning her face upward toward him. "Now you'll be able to respond emotionally when it serves you, but don't worry, you'll still remember how to tune it out. It's just that it takes years to really achieve that balance."

Phineas was still processing the news. "So everything I think that I've felt before..."

"Learned responses, like from the media. You know how you're supposed to feel without the danger of actually feeling it."

Phineas nodded his head slowly, wrapping his mind around the new abilities that were ironically the most basic of instincts for humans. It was a gift, but Raven could never know that.

"It's probably best this way," he said simply.

"Let's try something." Raven tilted her head upward toward Phineas. "Kiss me?"

He bent his head to kiss her mouth, wondering if it would be different. He noted that Raven was uncharacteristically gentle and he returned her kiss just as tentatively, as if he were trying to ride a bicycle for the first time. But as if to prove her point, Raven took the moment and shifted the response from thought toward instinct. The sensation didn't last and the kiss quickly heated. Raven pressed her body against his. Her tongue weaved into his mouth and soon Phineas allowed his hands to roam over her body.

But an image of Charlotte suddenly flashed in his mind, and along with it, something else that was new to him. It was a feeling that Raven hadn't taken into account. Guilt. He felt terrible over what she was asking him to do.

"What's wrong with you?" Raven demanded, shaking him from his thoughts.

"Nothing."

"You seem distant. I don't like it. I can change you back," she warned.

"Don't be ridiculous. I'm here, with you," he said nuzzling her neck. "I'm just wondering how you expect me to get close to Charlotte...especially with

Suki as her guardian."

"Because you will prove yourself to be trustworthy. That girl hasn't had anyone to open up to since her parents died."

The new nagging feeling returned with sudden force. Raven was right that Phineas would have to learn how to keep these feelings in check. "Raven, don't you see how wrong it is to prey on someone that is so obviously incapable of harming you?" he said hoping that he could appeal to the humanity that was dormant inside of her.

Raven considered him. "You're right. It's child's play. Let's forget about hurting her, for now. Just tap into that pretty little head of hers and find out why in the world she became a Releasor. Or...she's going to prove completely useless to me anyway, and then..." she let her voice trail off, the implication clear. "Ironically, you getting close to her is about all that's going to save her."

Phineas and Raven's long history could be described as sizzling whereas in the last two years, Josh and Ashley's relationship had barely reached a level above simmer. At Malibu High School what you know is not nearly as important as who you know. And, nobody knew this fact better than the girls who had all but written it down in a popularity code book.

But Jessica and Ashley had been sitting atop the mountain for so long they never imagined anyone could cause them to tumble down it, let alone two ordinary girls like Charlotte and Samantha. And perhaps they would have been correct had Raven not found the perfect moment to set in motion her plan.

She arrived at school, positively glowing at her good fortune. Jessica was comforting Ashley, who was in tears after a fight with Josh.

"I can't believe that he even went to the hospital to be with Charlotte," Ashley wailed.

"Did he tell you he was going?" Jessica asked.

"No, I just found out. I wouldn't have cared if he talked to me about it."

Jessica raised her eyebrows in question.

"Alright," Ashley agreed, "maybe I would've cared, but that's what makes this so lame. He kept it a secret and I found out from overhearing *them*."

"No way."

"Yes way, Charlotte was totally bragging about how he came to make sure she wasn't lonely, sitting by sick ol' Samantha's bedside all day. Why would he care so much about a lab partner? It's not like they're friends."

"You know what Ash? Maybe if you kept Josh a bit happier he wouldn't have found the need to go in the first place," Jessica chimed in. "It's even affecting Ryan and I. Thank you very much."

"What do you mean?"

"Ryan keeps going on about Samantha's near miss and how great it was to see her at some party that we weren't even invited to. I had to actually comfort him about her. It was so annoying. If you had given Josh a little bit of what he's been waiting for then he would be happily occupied."

"Jessica, only you would tell me to sleep with Josh so he doesn't go off with other girls. If that's the type of guy he is, then I don't need him."

"But you know he's not like that and you do need him. He's been beyond patient with you. So what's the hold up?"

"I'm not ready. Enough said."

Overhearing their argument was just what Raven needed to set things into action as she strode purposefully toward Ashley. "I heard you talking. You know that Samantha's near miss will probably change Charlotte's attitude and that could be really bad news for you."

"What are you talking about? Do I look like a care one hoot about Charlotte?"

Raven took a deep breath as if gathering the patience to explain something to a child. "You should care. My brother works at the hospital. He said that people change after going through a near death experience; it affects those around them too. I bet she'll just go for it -- all of it.

"Go for what?" Ashley asked.

Raven took a minute to adjust the thigh-high stockings that had dared edge below her skirt. Jessica and Ashley may have been considered the popular girls at school, but compared to Raven's sophistication they were out of their league and knew it. After a sufficient number of boys had snuck a glance at Raven's exposed thigh, she smiled and continued her lesson. "Don't you see? She thinks she has nothing to lose. That includes embarrassment, which is an emotion that typically keeps us from acting on impulses. But in the case of Charlotte, who obviously has the hots for your boyfriend..." she said pointedly at Ashley, "she'll let him know how she's feeling."

"So what? Josh wouldn't go for someone like her."

"Just trying to help," Raven said holding up her hands. "I'd keep him on a very short leash." The bell rang as if punctuating her last sentiment, giving Raven an excuse to let her warning hang in the air.

Chapter Eleven

$\mathcal{T}$he more time I spent with Charlotte and Samantha the more I could sense an energy about them, something undiscovered, but brewing beneath the surface. It was my destiny to protect them, but without fully understanding why they were targets -- two girls of their young age with seemingly insignificant contributions to the world -- it was difficult to foresee what possessed the biggest threat.

It was their first day back at school, and therefore, the first time I would have them out of my sight. I felt like I was sending two lambs out into the wild, but I knew that the best way to instigate their powers was to welcome danger.

The moment they got to school, a crowd gathered to wish Samantha well. Caught up in the middle of new found popularity, Samantha took in the attention. But in the midst of the crowds, Charlotte looked up and saw Phineas at the opposite end of the hallway, as if a beacon shined a spotlight right on him. Immediately, they locked eyes, and he approached.

"It's good to see you, Charlotte."

Charlotte's heart was pounding in her head. In spite of what Madame Ruby had foreshadowed she couldn't help wanting to be with him...in every way. She stared at his perfect face, took in his strong physique, and racked her brain for something...anything clever to say back. "Thanks, um, it's good to be back.."

"Hey, I wanted to ask you something at the party, but...it didn't seem like the right time."

"What is it?

Phineas recalled the well rehearsed line that Raven had prepared for him. For a moment, he wanted to back out, to leave Charlotte in peace with her life. If only he could lie to Raven and say that she just wasn't interested in him. But that would never work. He had been over this a million times in his head. Making matters worse was his bad fortune that he was wildly attracted to Charlotte. The same irony entered his mind. Just maybe he could keep her safe by being close to her. At least he would know Raven's plans and he could try to manipulate them from his end.

"Well, it's none of my business except that I do like you. I'm just wondering if there's something between you and Josh. I wouldn't want to, you know..."

"God no. We're just friends," Charlotte said a bit quicker than necessary. "He's with Ashley." And in spite of her best efforts to sound casual, her voice caught in her throat with the admission that someone she had once liked was with somebody else.

The bell sounding the beginning of first period rang and the throngs of students dispersed, but Phineas didn't make a move to leave.

"Come here," Phineas said cocking his finger toward Charlotte. She wouldn't have been able to turn away if she had wanted. Phineas' power of persuasion was overwhelming. Who could say no to a gorgeous, gypsy demon? Charlotte edged closer to him and in turn, Phineas leaned in to whisper in her ear, although the hallway was now empty and silent.

"Ashley has nothing over you. And for what it's worth, you're too good for Josh. Go out with me?"

Charlotte stared into Phineas' clear, green eyes and he back into hers. Suddenly the air shifted in the hallway, but it wasn't the result of black magic. Even Phineas hadn't expected it. He felt a true desire to connect with her, even before Raven had restored his emotions. But now, it was more intense than anything he could imagine. He tried to get a grip as he stared at her, again regretting the mission that Raven had sent him on.

"If you really wanted him, you could get him," Phineas said, taking in her eyes, the fullness of her lips.

"Why would you say that?"

"Because you're beautiful," he said leaning in even closer to her.

Charlotte quickly licked her lips. Her breath held in her throat for she didn't dare inhale. Phineas was mesmerized by her, his eyes took in her face, and he started to slowly move in to kiss her. How he wanted to kiss her.

"Charlotte! You're supposed to be in class," Samantha said with an edge in her voice that Charlotte had never heard before.

"Alright...I'll be there."

"Now. This isn't like you."

"Okaay," Charlotte answered back, and then turned back to Phineas. "Sorry, maybe I'll see you at lunch?"

"Definitely. Bye."

Charlotte practically skipped down the hall to where Samantha was waiting outside of their chem lab. Although Charlotte appeared happier than I had yet to see her, filled with hope and anticipation, it was at that exact moment that Samantha's powers were surprisingly triggered.

"Charlotte, I saw the images of him when Suki showed us the past, but now, I know things as well...things about him."

"Things?" Charlotte teased. "Like what he eats for breakfast."

"I mean, I can see people for what they are now. Take Ashley and Jessica...we've always thought they were stuck-up snobs, but now when I look at them, I see into their soul and it's filled with selfishness. When I focus on someone, it's as if there's a spotlight on their soul and I can tell if they are innately good or bad."

Charlotte didn't seem to be in any overt danger, and yet, sensing that her friend was nearing it, had caused Samantha's powers to kick in. Phineas hadn't made his way to his class yet and he remained just down the hall, seemingly sorting out something in his locker.

"He's listening," Samantha whispered back.

"He's across the building, Sam."

At that moment, Phineas looked up and waved to Charlotte, who beamed a smile back at him. Samantha merely glared at Phineas, and then grabbed Charlotte by the arm to lead her in the opposite direction.

"What is bothering you?" Charlotte asked.

"I told you. He has evil within him. What were you doing out here with him?"

"Gosh, this is reminiscent to the time my mother caught me making out in my room with my first boyfriend."

Samantha shivered involuntarily, closed her eyes and put her fingertips to her temples as if to quell a headache.

"Are you going to tell me what's wrong?" Charlotte asked. "Are you okay?"

"I'm fine, but you're not. You need to stay away from him."

"You were fine with him before. You even admitted that he was gorgeous."

"I know it's an about-face, Charlotte. It's crazy -- like Suki crazy, but I think she's right. You should stay away from him, and ever farther away from that psycho sister of his."

"I don't want to talk about this. Phineas isn't like Raven."

That was my cue to appear before this turned into a BFF knock-down, drag-out. It's not that I wanted to interfere, although I have been known to be a tad bit nosy, but mainly I couldn't bear to have two best friends fight over two evils like Raven and Phineas. It was bad enough that my friendship with Raven came to such a permanent end. I wasn't going to let her accomplish the same result with Charlotte and Samantha.

"Did someone mention crazy and my name together in the same sentence? You know that I'm not the least bit offended. Crazy is just a term applied to people who are ingenious and misunderstood by the masses."

Charlotte and Samantha gave me a look of doubt, which coming from them I was becoming accustomed to.

Charlotte spoke up first, "She's being totally unreasonable and you won't understand. There's no point in talking about it."

"You forget that I'm a Genie, released by you two. That means I see what you experience. So Charlotte, I already know that Samantha behaved with a little less decorum than is appropriate for a lady."

"Hey, do you have any idea what she was about to do?" Samantha interjected.

I ignored the interruption and raising of her voice, which only validated my previous point. "And Samantha, I also know that Charlotte may have nearly succumbed to Phineas' charm, regardless of how repulsive that idea is to me."

"Oh come on, he's gorgeous and sweet and..."

"And he's a gypsy demon who wants something from you and Samantha." I tried a different tact. "Listen, we may disagree about Phin, but at least we have accomplished something with you, dear one," I said looking at Samantha. "You recognized it, didn't you?"

She merely nodded. It wasn't a happy omission, but rather an acceptance of something latent that had emerged whether she wanted it to or not.

Samantha took my hand. "It was like I could see the real him, not what's on the outside, but what's on the inside."

"And?" I asked.

"It was like a warning to me that something is dangerous there, but to be honest, I'm not sure the danger totally lies within him. It was all muddled images and they just came too fast."

Samantha leaned against the wall, looking exhausted.

"It's okay," I said wrapping an arm around her. "You'll get better at this."

"I don't want to do it again. I feel nauseous now."

"It won't always affect you so much. It's your first time going within someone."

Charlotte looked like she might cry. "Samantha, how could you? I think I could really like this boy."

"You are so frustrating. I didn't do anything. It's him. That's what we keep saying," she said motioning her head in my direction. You shouldn't like him and for all we know, he's doing some sort of hocus pocus to make you like him. And, it's not like I wanted to be inside his head. Eww."

Charlotte sat in silence for a minute as if processing the fact that she couldn't be sure that her feelings were actually her own and not manufactured by someone who didn't have her best interests at heart.

We walked toward the school exit. "You know, it probably was silly to return to school on a Friday. Teachers never do much before the weekend."

Charlotte and Samantha eyed me up and down.

"I mean, what's one more day? Maybe we should figure out what Raven and Phineas are up to."

"Let's do it," Samantha agreed. "You in?" she said turning to Charlotte.

"Well, I'm not going to stay here alone."

Samantha exited the building first. I gently tugged on Charlotte's arm. "It's not just the fact that she could read Phineas' essence that's bothering you, is it?" She shook her head. "Don't worry. There's something special about you, too. You wouldn't have both released me if it was just about Samantha's powers. Your time will come, Charlotte. Magic isn't something to rush. You need to be ready for the power."

I put my arm around her and we followed Samantha out to my car, but I suddenly got a nasty chill up my spine and turned back to the building to see Raven watching us from a window on the second floor. She smiled menacingly and her message was clear: I wasn't able to be with the girls all the time, and when I'm not, they better be able to protect themselves.

Chapter Twelve

We spent the afternoon at my place where I ordered pizza and spinach salad, and we passed the time with a continuous stream of romantic comedies. By nightfall, I had hoped the girls would be too tired to leave as I still feared for them to be left alone, but I could also understand their need for a good night's sleep in their own beds. My place wasn't home to them -- yet. I argued that I wasn't as effective in protecting them if I wasn't near them, but it was no use.

"You're more vulnerable when you're alone," I argued.

"Suki, I've been on my own for a year now. I'm used to it and sometimes, I even like it better that way," Charlotte said.

"Hey!" Samantha interjected.

Charlotte threw her arm around Samantha's neck. "Present company not included."

I surveyed both of them, took into consideration that I was exhausted from the day's activities and reluctantly agreed to let them leave, as long as they stayed at Charlotte's place together. "Promise you'll stay in."

"We're going home and straight to sleep," Charlotte agreed.

I smiled at the two of them, peas in a pod, and said my goodnights.

After they left, I felt quite simply that a glass of merlot would hit the spot. They may have wanted some alone time, but I wasn't ready to be in solitude with my thoughts, which would naturally go to Raven and worry. I checked my makeup, changed into a cute little black dress and strolled downstairs to the building's bar. It was time I got that bit of an explanation from James.

When I walked into the bar, he had his back to me, but he noticed my reflection in the mirror that covered the wall behind the bar and turned around wearing a big smile that made me feel like the only girl in the place.

Truth be told, the place was packed, but for one moment in time when he stared at me before speaking, it felt like everything had slowed down and we were the only two people in the bar...er, well one Genie and whatever he may be. I still hadn't been able to figure out how he was able to hear my thoughts when Raven had attacked. One thing was for sure, no human had ever been able to pull that off before.

He placed a napkin down on the bar in front of me. "You're feeling better, I trust? I was hoping you'd be here last night, but..." he let his voice trail off.

I merely smiled, pleased that he sincerely sounded both disappointed that he hadn't seen me and happy that I was with him now. "What would the neighbors say if they saw me hanging out at the bar every night?

"Oh, let 'em talk. So, have you had dinner?"

He took my hands in his own. They felt warm and strong, and for the first time since the girls had released me I allowed myself to relax. There was something about the energy he possessed that made me feel somehow more...human. My stomach suddenly growled and my cheeks blushed red in response.

He smiled a sexy look at me as if he knew that my body was having a reaction to his proximity rather than a lack of food.

"I haven't eaten lately," I admitted and hoped that he would believe that was the only hunger I was experiencing. I may be a Genie, but having been human once meant I was still able to feel human emotions as well as pain and pleasure. Living as a Genie was like finally being able to tap into more brain power. I could read people's pasts, influence their futures, and had power over the elements, but try as I might, I couldn't escape my own need for love and there was something electric happening between James and I.

"How about I order you something and you eat it here to keep me company? My shift ends in half an hour and I'm pretty sure it'll go faster if you're around."

"I'd like that," I said.

Fifteen minutes later, a sampling plate was

placed in front of me with all of my favorites. I looked at it in alarm, but not because it wasn't mouth-watering. On the contrary, I couldn't wait to dig in. But the selection was indeed bizarre. The foods didn't even go together. There was no regional theme behind the selections, no rhyme or reason for how he decided to include such a mishmash of dishes. The only thing they had in common was the simple fact that these were my favorites, hand-selected by James.

"Brie in puffed pastry with cranberry relish, chicken satay with peanut dipping sauce, vegetables in a madras curry, and I've got a flourless chocolate cake with raspberry sauce waiting for when you've finished this," he said indicating the plate in front of me.

"How could you possibly know?"

"Just eat. We'll talk later."

Sure, bartenders are supposed to be insightful, but this was ridiculous. James was not all he appeared. Like Samantha and Charlotte, this trip out of my bottle was bringing surprises at every turn. Just as Samantha and Charlotte were not ordinary, James was certainly not your everyday man. I shook my head ever so slightly. The minute I first laid eyes on his chiseled features, strong torso and killer smile, I could've told anyone who asked that he was beyond average, but I never meant it so literally.

I watched James move about the bar, easily filling his customers needs while shooting the breeze and yet, always keeping a watchful eye over me. The food was delicious and went down easily. It was the first time anyone had ever done something that was solely for me, and I felt giddy from the attention.

"Wait here," James said as he cleared my now empty plate away. "I'm going to get rid of this, along with the last table over there in the corner."

I looked over my shoulder and indeed, the place was empty albeit for one couple who looked more than ready to get on with the rest of their date. They left arm in arm, the woman nuzzling her date's neck, and her date in return allowing his hand to wander up the back of her blouse completely unashamed.

James noticed their public display as well and my blush returned when he looked at me at that precise moment, presumably to check if I was also watching. He raised his eyebrows comically in my direction as if to imply that he had similar intentions toward me. I felt so happy that the sudden shift in the air took me completely by surprise.

The crack of the lightening in a formerly still sky shook me to my core. I looked up and saw the enormous mirror shake from the force that was hitting our world. Part electrical storm, part earthquake, and certainly partly supernatural. The lights flickered from the strain the generators were taking from the storm before another massive crack sent them out completely.

I closed my eyes to connect with Samantha and Charlotte, but nothing out of the ordinary faced them. Whatever was coming was here for me, and I wouldn't have an easy time explaining it to James. I had to get him out of here, not only for his safety, but for the sake of this pseudo first date.

Telling a guy that you're a year or two older than he is might be awkward. Letting him know that you're a few centuries older and being chased through time by demons was an altogether more serious conversation. It had been a ridiculously long time since I had been with a man, and just my luck, it seemed that period was going to be extended indefinitely. If I were ever to end up with James, I better return my concentration to the more immediate issue at hand, getting him out of here safely. However, it turned out that I might have been wasting my worry.

He appeared at my side, full of bravado. His blue eyes looked determined, his brown hair was slightly ruffled. He looked all man and it just melted my heart. It had been centuries since a man actually thought he could take care of me in the manner that I had grown accustomed to while living in the South. I had spent so many years in and out of my bottle, being released by men who looked to me for guidance, that I had forgotten how nice it was to return to the more civilized ways of courtship. In spite of the sound of the storm and the feeling that outside forces were at work, my heart swelled for how cute James was in trying to be chivalrous.

"Are you ready?" he said taking my hand.

"Ready for what, sugar?"

"You'll see," he said grimly. He squeezed my hand. "Just don't let go."

Suddenly another flash of lightening occurred

and with its bright beam illuminating the otherwise darkened room, I could see the horror in front of me. I opened my eyes wide unbelieving what was happening. The mirror was rippling and moving, strained faces were captured within the glass and the more the mirror moved, looking as if it were about to shatter, the more the souls trapped within it suffered, their mouths open wide in fear. It was a vision of people trapped between Realms, struggling to find a foothold in a permanent place of being.

"James, you have to get down," I said trying to pull him under the bar, a chair, anything that could protect him from the pending explosion of glass and the captured souls within it. But the more I tried to protect him, the more he pulled on me.

"Suki, you need to listen to me. Now."

Bless his heart. He was acting as nervous as a long-tailed cat in a room full of rocking chairs. And through it all, he was trying to protect me.

"Really, honey. I'm quite capable of taking care of this situation," I said trying desperately to lead him away. "It's very gallant of you and I do appreciate it, but you're going to have to trust me now."

"You're a bit out of your depth here. Suki, I don't mean to worry you, but your powers are going to be slightly impaired where we're going."

The lightening beams and resulting thunder grew too loud to hear him. The storm was completely upon us. It was so loud that I obviously couldn't hear him correctly. Funny, I had thought he mentioned my powers. Now I knew for sure...there was no way an ordinary human could recognize something like that within me. My heart had been doing a little dance for James since I set eyes on him. I only hoped it wasn't misplaced. Just as soon as that thought entered my mind, the mirror cracked and shattered with impossible force sending shards of glass flying at us with bullet-like strength.

A stabbing pain suddenly hit my chest, just below the collar bone. I didn't dare look down, I was too entranced in what was happening to that mirror. Most of it had fallen away, the glass flying across the room. But there in the very center, the reflection shimmered and rippled, beckoning me not to turn away.

"Hold on," James commanded as he pulled me toward an opening in the glass that spread wider and wider into complete darkness.

I dug my heels into the ground and pulled against him. There was something outside of normal human forces at work here and he was pulling me toward it! Trails and clouds of dark black smoke swirled throughout the room. The center of the mirror opened into a black hole that looked like a gaping mouth about to swallow us both. The more I resisted, the more it seemed to swell open as if laughing at my resistance.

"You just need to trust me," James said turning toward me. "Look at me," he commanded.

I looked into his eyes, blue as my bottle, and suddenly felt the fight drain out of me. He grabbed my arm and pulled me into the mirror's blackness where the air shifted into a gentle, cool breeze rather than the torrent that was wreaking havoc inside the bar. I felt so terribly tired. I just wanted to close my eyes, and yet I also felt I shouldn't.

"What's happening?"

"Sleep," he commanded. And I did.

I awoke to a light tapping at the door. Before I had a chance to say, "come in," a large black woman wearing a simple blue-checked housecoat and a kindly smile entered with a basket of first aid materials.

"Time to change them bandages," she said in a Southern accent that was thick as honey. It was like music to my ears.

"Oh, I'm alright. No need to fuss over me."

"Miss Suzette, you've been through quite an ordeal from what Mr. James tells me. I'm Maebeline, his maid. Now yous just relax and let me tend to you."

Her words had the desired effect. James. Ordeal. His maid?! I had completely forgotten the last day. I must have slept longer than I've ever done in my life and looking around, it was no wonder.

I was lying on the most beautiful bed made with cream colored satin sheets, matching bed skirt, the softest feather down pillows, and an impossibly plush duvet in an elegant shade of charcoal grey. I sat up and stretched, taking in my surroundings -- an elegantly decorated Victorian bedroom. The magnificent bed with its ornately carved headboard and footboard featuring delicate curves and cherubs was angled into the middle of the room and because I was luxuriating within its cozy confines, I also appeared front and center when James, who just like Maebeline, simply walked right in after providing a delicate, but brief knock at the door.

"Oh good, you're awake. You've been out for awhile. You must be starving so I've arranged for breakfast...after Maebeline attends to your injuries."

"It's busier than Grand Central Station in here," I said feeling a bit miffed that he was now my host and obviously had the upper hand at what was going on. Not to mention, I was wearing a rather flimsy nightie that was now completely on display due to Maebeline's fastidious efforts to check me for injury.

"I'm fine," I said trying to pull the covers over myself. "It's impossible for me to get hurt."

"And what about this?" she said holding up my wrist triumphantly.

I looked down at myself and sure enough there was a nasty gash that ran from the inside of my wrist clear up halfway between it and my elbow.

"That's impossible," I said suddenly forgetting my whereabouts, the fact that James was staring at me in a state of undress, and that this Southern woman, who reminded me a scary deal of my own nanny, was now waving some sort of shaman healing tool over my body.

"There. That part's done."

I looked over at James wondering if he believed

this stuff. It was actually quite ironic considering that I had spent the better part of three centuries having to explain my powers to humans. One would think that I could accept powers in others, but the pain in my arm remained and frankly, Maebeline seemed just a tad bit off her rocker.

"Just go with it," James whispered.

Maebeline took that cue to continue whatever she thought she had started. "Now, just a little bit of witch hazel combined with my words and you'll be good to go. Lie back and close your eyes, Suzette."

"Please, call me Suki."

"Suki, lie down," Maebeline ordered.

I looked from her to James, both of whom raised their eyebrows as if to say, "What are you waiting for?"

"Alright, fine," I said with a huff and did as I was told.

Maebeline closed her eyes and breathed deeply for a moment or two, and then seemingly more relaxed in a hypnotic state, she began to recite: "I call on Tuatha Dé Danann, the gods of light and order for healing; to the Formorians, gods of darkness and chaos, to take away pain; and to the Sidhe, to shield you from the mischievous spirits."

"Miss Suki, it's been a pleasure to serve you. Just holler if you need anything else." And with that, Maebeline walked out the door.

"That's it?"

"Don't be so dubious. Her powers are intense. She is human, but has learned how to convene with the Realm of the Otherworld. Her incantation does not protect forever. It heals you...for now."

"So, something was powerful enough to cause me injury, an occurrence that has never before happened, and now I'm healed? Just like that?"

"You're used to going forward in time. We just traveled through an extremely strong portal--going backwards. You're not used to it, and neither is your body."

I wrinkled my nose slightly, trying to wrap my head around the how and what of my new situation.

James walked to the side of my bed and took my hand, placing it over his forearm. With his other hand, he moved my hand slowly upward. "Think of moving through that portal as if you were gripping an arrow. You can slide your hand one way and it passes over it easily, but try moving the opposite direction and the jagged edge will dig into you." He had made his point verbally, but the analogy with our hands hardly seemed to demonstrate discomfort. With his hand over mine, his eyes staring into mine, he continued to move my hand up and then down, moving sensually and slowly along his muscular forearm--as if I were sliding my hand along something altogether different. My heart started to beat wildly, a tingling sensation building within me.

"I get it," I said quickly and pulled my hand away, but James easily caught it in his own. Gently, he held my hand below my injury and slowly unwrapped the bandage that Maebeline had so carefully put on just minutes earlier.

"You're actually checking it?" I said with annoyance.

He didn't acknowledge my implied annoyance, simply turned my wrist over to expose the inner side where the deep cut had just moments before blushed with crimson and gently brought it to his mouth and kissed it, letting his lips linger on the place. Instantly, my pulse quickened once again.

Another momentary knock sounded at the door, making me jump. I moved my hand away quickly to which James smirked and laughed.

"Serves you right. I guess Maebeline does know how to keep me safe." But unlike every time before, the knock wasn't followed by a person entering. Instead, James opened the door to find a tray had been left.

"Ahh, here it is. Maebeline brought your breakfast," he said simply. "Now that you're healed."

"About that?" I said examining my own wrist, which I was furious to admit showed no sign of injury and still left me tingling from James' kiss.

"It's time I explained myself -- and Maebeline. She is like me -- a Shade," he explained. "It's like I have a veil that shields me from the dangers that may lie between the different Realms. Traveling through time is one thing, but add a few trapped souls into the mix, and well...it gets nasty."

"Hold on. You're a what?"

"You know how the Realms are divided?"

"Heaven, Earth and...the Otherworld," I recited like a good schoolgirl.

"It's the Otherworld that is typically shielded from our world. Those two realities are separated by a Veil. And as that word implies, this separation can be at times very thin or even lifted entirely."

"Like when gypsies take on demon form," I said realizing that James knew a lot more about me than I had realized.

"Yes. And even Genies need a protective shield, which is where I come in."

"Oh please. You are not my knight in shining armor."

"No, I'm your Shade. And make no mistake, if I weren't needed, I wouldn't be here. It seems this is the second time I've come to your rescue."

I regarded James for a moment. I couldn't deny anything he said. There were far too many coincidences to name. There was nothing typical of this releasing. It started with Samantha and Charlotte themselves and the fact that both released me. Add to that the uncanny connection I felt toward James, someone who wasn't even involved in my release, how he was the one who found me after Raven's attack, and finally, the fact that I had not only been transported through time without my doing, but also injured during the occurrence.

"I don't understand," I said simply. "How is this all possible?" And then, I admitted the truth: "James, I'm over three centuries old and this kind of thing has never happened to me."

He gently took my hands in his own and kissed each one lightly. "Suki, you forget that you were human. Somewhere deep within you there is a vulnerability."

"And you and Maebeline?"

"We're more human than you in the fact that we can perish. However, our deaths are not permanent as long as one of us remains. It's a Celtic thing," he said offhandedly.

I took in what James was saying. "I've heard of it. Let me guess...your Mammie was a Celtic Shaman, you were raised from the dead, and now the two of you keep each other alive so that you can play superhero to wayward Genies. Have I missed anything?"

"I'm glad you're taking this so calmly. Some might think we were an abomination. And yet," he said, thoughtfully massaging the cleft at his chin, "others would probably be quite impressed. I suppose if you wake the dead enough, a certain reverence beholds oneself."

I rolled my eyes in spite of myself. James being revered! No wonder he was so damned arrogant. But then again, look at him. He was so handsome it wasn't a complete surprise that people throughout the years wouldn't be tempted to feel something supernatural toward him.

"May I continue?" he said with mock hurt.

"Please do, oh revered one."

"Maebeline had once been a slave, sold to a man whose ancestry was based in the ancient Celts. Their world was very different to Western society. No science, no technology. It couldn't be more different from the Industrial Revolution, where we've returned to right now."

"I can't leave the girls unattended."

"Your time here is a mere blip in their world. We'll stay only long enough to ensure that you are healed."

I took an involuntary glance out the window, and sure enough saw what appeared to be a coal manufacturing plant in the distance. My thoughts drifted to the peculiarity of my present circumstance, but James' voice brought me back.

"Maebeline was a smart cookie and knew that in order to survive she would have to play into their fears. And as it turned out, some of those fears weren't without merit. Call it Gods, or Genies," he said with intention, "but something powerful was at play to save her. She has the power to know spells and incantations. The Celts of that time were at the mercy of the land, sea and sky...the elements." He let that last part settle before continuing. "Maebeline formed a relationship, so to speak, with the denizens of the Other Realm. She could heal; she could harm; and she could bring people back from the dead if she attended to them before their heart became cemented in its new state."

"How do you know about me?" I asked realizing that he stressed Maebeline's relationship with the elements for a reason.

He didn't answer, but instead moved to a decorative side table that stood next to the bed, and casually thumbed the pages of two books that were placed there, Jane Austen's "Pride and Prejudice" along with "Persuasion."

"Interesting choices," I said referring to the books, as if after being transported back in time I would simply wallow in bed reading.

"I thought you'd appreciate the irony. Now, I'll tell you more after I heal your other wound," he said indicating the gash that hovered just above my breast. "It's started to bleed again."

I looked down and saw that he was correct, but there was no way in...well, any Realm, that I was going to let James touch me there until he started to explain more. I was feeling decidedly out of my element. "No way."

"Suki, let me explain this in a way you might relate to better. You and injuries...it's like the preacher's wife starring in a Vegas strip show. It doesn't happen everyday. Now let me help you."

The pain along my chest was great and I couldn't very well argue with his point. As if sensing my acceptance, he leaned toward me.

"Wait. Aren't you going to do the mumbo jumbo that Maebeline did?"

"Nah, she's better at incantations than I am. Just relax. Trust me, my way is just as effective...it's also more fun."

And before I could argue, he leaned toward me and kissed me. In spite of myself and almost instantly, I responded. His lips were warm and soft, his hands cradled my face making me feel so loved...and then filled with passion. Sensing the growing desire within me, he moved one hand underneath my back and pulled me closer to him. With his other hand, he traced delicate lines across my collarbone, down my chest, around my breast and back again. It was intoxicating and not only was I filled with a desire for him to continue, even more remarkable was that I couldn't feel any pain from where the shards of glass had spiked my chest. I moaned in spite of myself and tried to press myself to seating, wrapping my arms around James' neck, but that's when he stopped.

"There. I'd say you're better," he said looking down at my chest and admiring his work. "See? No more injury. Now, you should eat. Maebeline's an excellent cook."

"Of course she is, she's been around since Celtic times," I said, my voice rising at the embarrassment that he could so easily turn everything on and then off again.

James set down a silver domed tray and then accidentally bumped his foot against the lion clawed legs of the table and gave out a small yelp. I found it amusing that he could stub his toe in a manner so commonly human and yet somehow he had the power to transport me to Victorian times and then do what he just did to me.

"James, why are we here?" I asked while peaking underneath the tray. I took a sip of my tea, made perfectly to my liking in spite of the fact that I had never spent a morning with James prior.

He ignored my question and instead replied, "It's

Earl Grey."

Alright. Two could play this game. I was determined to be equally nonchalant. I took a sip. "Hmm, it even has milk and sugar. Just the way I like it. I wonder how you knew that?" I smiled sweetly. I would not to be outdone by his demeanor. If he was going to act like everything was perfectly normal, then so would I. After all, I was the Genie. So what if he was a Shade? Up until now, I had never even met such a thing.

Yes, I had heard of Shades, but I thought of them as fictitious, almost like Santa Claus. The one person who had showed me the way when I first got my powers had said they were the only ones who could ever come to my aid if I were in trouble. And since I had traveled for over three hundred years without seeing one, I came to believe that it was an entity that was simply too good to be true. Not that I could ever think of James in that way. No, I would not give him the satisfaction of having the upper hand over this situation.

"Are you with me?" he said waving a hand in front of me.

"Yes, I'm here. Tell me more."

"Maebeline's words had the power to bring people back from the dead as well. But there was one caveat. If their heart was like stone, meaning if they were too cold having been dead for longer than an hour, her words would be ineffective. And of course, she knew that there would be nobody to use words on her should she ever need it, so she trained the only person she could trust.

"You?!"

"Don't be so surprised? What have I ever done to you?" he asked.

I raised my eyebrows as if to say, 'look what you just did' and thought of the way I felt whenever he looked at me. The tingle that ran through my very being and made me feel like a school girl. The way he seemed to have a secret that he could use to make me a babbling idiot. The chill that I got when he placed even a finger on my hand. I had tried to ignore it, had wondered how it could be possible that a mere mortal could make a Genie feel so much desire for him, and now I knew. James wasn't mortal at all. Had I really fallen for him because of who he was or was it due to *what* he was? I had to admit that the idea of him being the one entity that could offer me protection was a powerful aphrodisiac.

"You misled me, that's what. I feel like a fool, James. Like when we left during the storm. I thought you needed my protection and then I find out that I'm the damsel in distress?"

He didn't answer, but instead his eyes took in every inch of me, making me feel even more vulnerable than I already was feeling. I didn't need to tell him the other obvious thing he had done. What could I say? 'James, you've made me want to jump you?' Certainly not the type of thing a lady would admit to and since it seemed I was back in the time when ladies didn't even think such thoughts, I had to do something to ensure that mine were kept to myself. It might have been a futile endeavor, but I did my best to redirect my thoughts to more appropriate subjects.

"Why did she pick you?" I asked, returning the conversation to him.

"I was just a child and therefore, still innocent."

"Hmmphf," I let escape, in spite of myself. Somehow, James and the word "innocent" just didn't go together. Quite frankly, he was all man and the sexiest one I had ever laid eyes on.

He raised his eyebrows at me, knowing perfectly well where my thoughts lay, and continued. "She was Mammie to me. My father had been a confederate soldier and she took care of our household. But when the blacks were being rounded up...," his voice trailed off. "Well, suffice it to say that she didn't like it. But she was pragmatic and knew the war would come to an end, but much of the hatred would remain. I loved her like a mother and promised to always take care of her the way she took care of me, especially when I saw what she could do."

"Like what?"

"A few words from her and a skinned knee would be healed, a stomach ache diminished, and things even more remarkable. The crops grew faster than our neighbors; our horses worked longer. At the time, she never brought back a dead man because there would be too many questions; and frankly, none of the dead were wanted. But she told me she could do it and I'd be damned if I didn't believe her."

I blushed from his tone. You can take a girl out of

the days of civility, but civility never is taken from a proper lady, which reminded me of my current state of lying in bed in his presence. "Do you have a robe for me? After all, you are in my bedroom," I said with extreme calm.

"Oh certainly," he said walking to a six-foot armoire that, like the other pieces in the room, was painted the warmest possible shade of cream and accented with intricate carvings and footed legs. "Here you are. May I sit down," he said indicating a lady's chair that faced a makeup table.

I nodded and he turned the chair around and sat with the back facing his chest, his legs astride it in a most 21st century mannerism. It was quite out of place, but who was I to comment? I was allowing a man that I've barely begun to see, sit in my bedroom while I lay in bed wearing a nightie.

"So you see, we made a pact that if anything happened to the other, we would bring them back. I knew that chances were that she would go first, simply because of her age, but I was wrong."

"You died as a child?" Just hearing this news made my heart ache for him.

He nodded. "Worse than just that. It was at the hands of my own father."

My breath caught from the sheer horror of the knowledge.

"My father was angry at one of our farmhands, really angry. But this man was Maebeline's first cousin and I wanted to protect him. So when my daddy got his shotgun and aimed that barrel, I jumped in front of it."

"Oh James, no." My heart went out to him and in that instant of emotion on my part, I felt something odd, a connection to be certain, but one that was different from the type I share with my Releasors. James must have felt it too, for he stopped his story and simply stared into my eyes. And then I felt my heart quicken again under the gaze of his magnificent, blue eyes.

He reached for me and kissed me hard. I arched my back and this time, he didn't stop when I sat up, wrapped my arms around his neck and gave into that kiss with the very soul of my being. His hands roamed my body, making me ache for him, for love that I hadn't felt in centuries. But, as our passion increased, my head started to spin either from the wave of emotions that flooded me or something else.

James pulled away from me. "I'm sorry. You're still weak from going back in time. Easy for me, but not so much for a Genie."

"Please...I'm perfectly capable."

He raised his eyebrow as if to say 'oh really?' before sitting himself back a safe distance from me and continuing.

"I didn't think twice about saving Maebeline's cousin. I guess I knew that she would hear the shot ring out and come to investigate. My father couldn't live with his own guilt, and since my mother had died a year earlier from cholera, he didn't see any reason to not shove that same shotgun down his own throat."

James had a faraway look in his eyes as if

remembering the day that he lost both parents. I couldn't bear to see his pain. I wanted so desperately to hold him and take away the hurt, but I just couldn't bring myself to make a move like that again, particularly not while in Victorian England. I just met his gaze and nodded, encouraging him to go on.

"It was easy for Maebeline to take my body away and work her magic," he said. "You can see why we ran, using the Underground Railroad to escape into the northern territories. We've been saving each other throughout the centuries. And now, we can be here to save others who need us."

I nodded, understanding the bond he had with her now.

"So, you want to know 'why we're here'? Not how we got here or the usual..." he put the back of his hand to his forehead and through his head back with flourish, "where am I? Or...the most obvious question."

Our eyes met each other and I nodded my consent. "Alright, tell me. Tell me how you became my Shade."

"It's not unlike the deal you make with your Releasors. They must wish for unselfish desires. When Maebeline brought me back to life the same sort of rule applied. I must live my life by giving to one deserving soul whose path crosses mine at the exact moment of my return. And that was you."

I looked at him questioningly. "I've lived so many lives before the time period of your death. Who was looking after me before that point?"

"I don't know. Perhaps there wasn't one. Perhaps you didn't need the protection. But you do now. So, why don't you continue to rest up, read a bit, just relax," he said getting up from his chair.

"James, while those are my favorite titles, I'm afraid that I won't have much time for them. I should get back to Samantha and Charlotte, so if you don't mind," I did a little scoot motion with my hands and indicated the door.

"I thought we could do a little sight-seeing after you have breakfast."

"That's really not necessary. As I said, I have plans today."

He looked amused. "Do you?"

"I'll have you know that I'm busier than a moth in a mitten. I promised the girls..." I searched my mind for an adequate reason, but only managed to come up with, "that we would have our nails done."

"You'll be back in time for that."

For the first time, my expression gave me away. I wasn't particularly put off by the fact that I had traveled back to Victorian times. I quite liked this period with all of its booming business. The inventions of the day provided well for the people. But, I was used to traveling forward in time, not backwards.

I weighed the desire to stay with James in my mind. "It will seem as if I've only been missing for a wee bit?"

"Precisely."

"And what about their safety?"

"They are connected to you now. If they are in danger, you'll feel it and we'll return. If all is well, then we can enjoy ourselves. My greatest gift is being able to travel forward as well as backward. It's how I'm able to fully protect you. Things would be different, however, if you or your Releasors went into the past alone. That would be tricky and potentially very dangerous."

"Do you think it was Raven who unleashed the storm?

"It's probable," he said. "She doesn't know that I would be there to protect you. At any rate, it all worked out well. Maebeline has been wanting to meet you -- to approve of you," he said with a wry smile.

My eyes widened in surprise. "What do you mean?"

"The elements have aligned. Your 'assignment,' he said using quote marks with his fingers, "is not typical of those of your past and apparently, you will be needing my help."

"That's ridiculous. So you can say a few spells, big deal. I am gifted with foresight, the ability to read into someone's mind and did I mention that I've got a handle on the elements all by myself?"

"I have seen you work the wind," he said. "But have you ever seen anyone who can do it as well?" He closed his eyes and the wind shifted, swirling around and blowing the sheets back so that my legs were exposed.

I grabbed at them and then just as suddenly, it stopped. "Not funny," I said trying to retain my dignity.

"You can't blame a guy for wanting to check out your legs. I've got a few other tricks as well...I'll let you in on them later."

"We'll see about that. So, do I have suitable clothing here?" I said pulling open the curtain just a tad and taking note of the weather outside. "A vision of the past lets me dress in whatever my mind can imagine, but actually being in the past..."

"Don't worry. You have everything you could need."

I nodded, more to myself than to him.

"You realize, by suitable I don't just mean that they fit me."

"You will find dresses becoming a lady of this period." As if to demonstrate this point, James opened the armoire to reveal a myriad of dresses, some even with matching parasols. The fact that most were in my favorite colors -- from light lavender and deep plum to delicate shades of cream and crisp whites -- wasn't lost on me. I pointed to one that featured white satin with a tint of ice blue coloring. The dress almost looked ethereal with a cinched waist and a billowing petticoat in contrast. The off-the-shoulder bodice featured a delicate lace, which perfectly accented the dress' otherwise simple design.

"Excellent choice," he said removing it from the high-hanging bar of the armoire and hanging it over a cream-colored dressing screen that folded into thirds and featured beautiful filigree carvings that surrounded three separate mirrors. I eyed the screen, adjusted the partitions to ensure more privacy, and although I wasn't thrilled with the dressing arrangements, I realized I had little choice so I took my dress and moved behind the partition. It wasn't until I was already half-way undressed that I thought I heard his voice in my head, *"Love the neckline on that one."*

I gasped out of fear that he actually saw me and stole a quick peek out from behind the partition to ensure his back was still turned. So help me, I thought I could see his shoulders shake slightly, as if he were holding in a laugh at my expense.

"You nearly ready?" he called to me.

I looked down at myself and indeed, the front was rather plunging. I took a deep breath as I walked out from behind the divider, but that only seemed to cause my bosom to heave further.

James smiled his approval and for the life of me I thought I heard his voice once again speaking inside my own mind. His whisper was ever so faint: *"very nice."* I took a double take, knowing it was an impossibility, but feeling a bit disconcerted nonetheless. I glanced at James and he smiled, and suddenly I wasn't so sure that the impossible hadn't occurred. I now knew that as my Shade, he could sense when I was in danger, but was that instinctive ability or could he really hear my thoughts?

I gave him a questioning glance, but in response, James merely held his hand toward the door. "Shall we?"

It was a beautiful day in London. There was a

chill in the air, but the sun was shining. As we walked down the high street, I felt a peacefulness that I hadn't experienced in a long time. All around us, elegantly dressed men and women window shopped and browsed the wares from street vendors.

"Why are we here?" I asked again.

"Truthfully, I think it was just timing. Maebeline hasn't seen me in ages and wanted to know what I was up to. I needed to check in on my business..."

"You have a business here?"

"I'm more than a bartender," he said smugly. "Let's just say that I dabble in advanced steam power."

"James, what's your surname?"

"Watt."

"*The* James Watt?"

"Well, I'm actually James Watt, the second. I share the name with my father, but hopefully that's our only similarity."

My knowledge of history didn't fail me. I looked at James a bit in awe, just the knowledge that he was part of the famed partnership of Boulton and Watt -- creative geniuses behind much of the Industrial Revolution's new designs -- was intoxicating to say the least. James was known to have created a double-acting rotative version of the early steam engine that improved its power tremendously.

"But how is that possible?"

"Once Matthew...Boulton," he said by way of explanation, "and I developed the centrifugal governor, parallel motion, and flywheel, it was quite simple to directly drive the rotary machinery of a factory or mill. We constructed just shy of 500 engines."

He leaned toward me and whispered in my ear conspiratorially, "We were very successful. You, my dear, are strolling with quite a catch."

I elbowed him in the ribs. "That's not what I meant," I said trying to wrap my head around the story. How were you a young boy living in the Southern United States during the early 1800s if you were already a man here at the same time?"

"Maebeline," he said simply. "She brought me back in more ways than one. She woke me from the dead and then retrieved me to an earlier time. Suki, you go forward, but as I mentioned, one of my greatest gifts is the ability to go backwards in time as well as other Realms."

I didn't very much like the fact that James had powers that I didn't. Somehow, I felt vulnerable around him. It was a feeling that I wasn't used to having around men. I was used to being the one in control. This was foreign and unexpected, and I hated to admit it, but I liked James all the more because of it. His hand gently rested against the small of my back as we walked, and between the knowledge of who he was, his inherent powers, and simply the way he made me feel, I realized that never had a man made me believe that he was so...capable.

"So, Maebeline took care of you?"

"She was a mother to me. She knew that a black woman in the South during those times couldn't keep a young, white boy as her own, so she moved us to England where people were more accepting of differences. She taught me what I needed to know about the world and allowed me to age more rapidly than normal, while keeping herself preserved."

James leaned in close again. "Show me a woman who isn't vain about growing old and I'll show you an apparition if there ever was one."

I rolled me eyes, knowing full well that he linked me into that category and darn it, he was correct. "Do go on with your story."

"Nobody would recognize me from that Atlanta school boy. For that matter, I had no family left that would come looking for me. When I reached this age," he said fanning his hand from his head and then downward, "I asked Maebeline to halt me and I did the same for her. Life has been good for us here."

"Alright, Maebeline was gifted with an innate knowledge of Celtic healing and protection. You've learned a few things here and there. Sure, you can control the wind, but all the elements?"

"Not like you," he admitted.

"Score one for team Genie," I smiled.

"I can travel backwards. You're only on fast-forward. Score one for the Shade."

I fumed with that one for a moment. "Go on, what's your other trick?"

"What makes you think there's more. Isn't that enough?"

"I control the elements *and* I'm a muse. By its very nature, you can't have someone capable of controlling opposing systems unless they have other powers at play. I wouldn't be able to accomplish these tasks if I couldn't also influence. So dish. What's yours."

"It's personal," he said looking away from me.

"Now you're being modest? That's a first."

"It has to do with the healing that I learned from Maebeline. It's just not something a gentleman speaks of."

"You are not that much of a gentleman. I can tell."

James stopped walking and turned to stare at me. "Okay, just remember, you asked. I tried to hold back earlier, but well...ah, hell with it. It's better if I just show you," he said and took my hand in his. With his other hand, he lightly ran his finger over the inside of my wrist where it previously was sliced from the broken glass. He lightly traced small circles over the area that was injured, instantly making my mind forget that we were standing in the midst of a busy street. My legs felt weak, my heart started pounding, and more than anything my thoughts went to wishing we were once again in the bedroom back home.

"I have a talent for pleasure," he said still holding my hand. "It's particularly strong in areas previously experiencing pain."

I caught my breath and pulled away quickly, causing James to laugh at me. The nerve.

"That's...that's ridiculous. I'm sure your charms won't work on me," I said proudly and continued walking.

I could hear James in my head once again, whispering to me: *"But yours have worked their magic on me."*

I whisked back around. "What was that?"

"What?" he said innocently.

"That thing you're doing." I lowered my voice so not to be overheard by passersby. "You're in my head."

"Have you ever been around someone else who can control the elements? It's a talent we share and so we can also communicate -- intimately. The more you let me into your heart, the more I get into your head. That's what happens with supernaturals...and those who are meant for each other."

I composed myself. I couldn't let myself fall for James. It would be too painful. Whenever my assignment ended with Charlotte and Samantha, when their three wishes were over, or I hated to think of it, when their lives ended, whichever came first, I would be back inside my bottle and who knows where it would take me next.

"Now I know you're insane. I can hear you because...well, it's just like being with my Releasors. That's all."

"Okay, I'm guessing that Charlotte and Samantha probably wanted you to prove yourself to them, so you did your thing -- read their past, and you'll inspire their future. But you can't read me the way you can your Releasors. In short, I am a closed book."

In spite of myself, I stomped my foot. He was right. I didn't know a thing about him; I was at a distinct disadvantage.

"Hey, don't take it so hard. It's sort of a two-way street. My voice is faint to you because you haven't really let me in. You can hear me quite clearly, but I only hear the tiniest iota of your thoughts...for now."

I looked up at him, somewhat relieved by his words, while also wondering just when and under what circumstances the situation would change. I did want to let him in.

"So, it's like Raven and Phineas...they share the same powers; I've seen the way they communicate."

He reached for my wrist again, tried his little trick on me, but I pulled away. "Oh no you don't."

He held on to me tightly. "Suki, this is so much more than communication -- it's *connection,*" he smirked. "Oh, and as our kisses become more intense, so does our connection to each other's thoughts."

Getting close to James was what I craved and feared all in the same moment. Centuries had passed since Raven and I had the argument that ended our friendship and yet, her warning rang out in my head as if it were yesterday. I had taken her one true love away from her. Could it be that was why I had never found anyone for myself? I couldn't imagine that Raven would work her magic against me so personally. She seemed more determined to harm those around me. And that's when a panic struck me deep within my soul. Spending time with James could put Samantha and Charlotte in danger. It now seemed highly probable that Raven was in favor of this dalliance as it placed my Releasors directly in harm's way.

He seemed to instinctively know that my mind was a bundle of nerves and working overtime. He relaxed his hold on my hand and gently traced back and forth against the inside of my wrist with his thumb. Jumpin' catfish...how can the touch of his thumb render me completely mindless? All I could think of was the delicate tingling sensation that started at his touch and sent chills throughout my body.

"Better?"

"Much," I admitted.

We stopped walking and he took my hand in both of his. They were strong and I felt safe. He smiled down at me. "Close your eyes for a minute. Take some deep breaths." He applied a bit more pressure with his thumb to the inside of my wrist and proceeded to massage the palm of my hand, hitting every pulse point, nerve ending and chakra until the simple act of touching my hand seemed highly erotic. "Opposable thumbs...who knew they could bring so much pleasure?"

I opened my eyes. "That will be enough of that," I said and took a distinct step backwards. But it wasn't just my movement that caused a shift in the mood. The wind picked up and suddenly, James was on high alert.

"Something's wrong," he said.

"I feel it too."

James reached for me and this time, it was a protective stance.

"James, Raven opened up that portal to bring us here, but there's no harm coming to either of us. The only reason for the portal opening was to get me to go through it..."

"We need to leave. Are you feeling better?"

"I'm fine."

"Let's go," he said leading me down the nearest alley.

"What about Maebeline? Don't you need to say goodbye?"

"We have an understanding. She knows I'll be back in due time."

He held my body tightly next to his as the wind shuffled around us. My heart beat wildly from being so close as well as filled with a fear of not being close enough to Charlotte and Samantha.

"You'll get there," he reassured me. And the reality of the situation hit me like a thunderbolt. He wasn't only in my head. He was already finding his way into my heart. I swallowed hard as the air seemed to lift us higher. Again, the gears and engines of time rumbled around us as we moved through a black mist and then were deposited just outside my hotel in Beverly Hills.

"Are you okay?" James asked again.

"I feel fine."

He turned my wrist over to inspect the previous injury. "Sometimes it returns when you reenter the Realm where it occurred, but it's like you said, you're fine." He looked up to the sky and I could see a worried frown cross his face.

"What's wrong?"

"It's unusual for the wind to follow me," he noted.

And that's when panic struck me. "It's not just wind. It's advanced neuron activity causing the energy in the air. Something's happened or happening to them."

I focused my mind's eye on Samantha and Charlotte. I could see both of them. The trouble was they weren't together. The question in front of me was who to go to first. I prayed we hadn't stayed away too long and Raven's plan hadn't taken its course.

Chapter Thirteen

As Phineas drove his car along Pacific Coast Highway, his conversation with Charlotte replayed in his mind. Everything he had told her was true. She could get Josh if she really wanted to and he felt ill at ease wondering if a girl so pure of heart could even want him -- a boy turned demon gypsy. But the way she looked at him gave him hope in himself. He knew I must have warned her off against him, and yet Charlotte seemed approachable. What was more remarkable to him was that it wasn't because he had willed it to be. It made him feel there was a chance for his own redemption. If only she could fall for him without any interference of his powers.

He had started out the conversation just as Raven had instructed him to. He was to convince Charlotte to approach Josh and get this romance between the two of them started. They were the ones whose destiny were intertwined, and yet, it was inexplicable to him why he wanted to kiss her...why he was so drawn to her. He wanted her. It was the first time he had ever felt this way and he knew if Raven got wind of this she would be deadly furious. He had already seen enough drama at Malibu High to know how jealous girls could become over each other. Add to that a girl as powerful as Raven, and you had a seriously bad combination.

He took his time coming home, stopping at Dukes in Malibu to admire the ocean view and marvel at the simplicity of the lives of those who ate on the patio overlooking the Pacific. He looked at the tables that were primarily taken over by couples whose attention was only on each other and knew that he was in trouble. His mind was totally and utterly preoccupied by Charlotte. He needed to get his head back to reality. He and Raven had traveled throughout time together and would continue to do so. There was no place for a modern girl in his life. He needed to get back in touch with his powers to eliminate these human thoughts from his mind. He could fight the emotions that Raven had allowed him to feel. He just needed to get his mind off Charlotte and back onto his powers.

He cocked his head and focused on a couple across the crowded room. Concentrating only on them, he used his heightened sensory powers, those cultivated by Raven and taken from their animal form, to force his hearing to tune out all other noise and decipher only their conversation.

"I want to get out of here. Now," the girl said in a husky voice to her date.

"What about dessert?" he asked.

"I'll be your dessert...at your place."

"Check!" the guy shouted immediately afterward.

Phineas shook his head. The couple's advances toward each other only caused him to think of Charlotte more. Again, he forced himself to focus on his powers, concentrating this time on his heightened sense of smell, but even that seemed to play tricks on him. He could remember her perfume as if she were standing right next to him.

"Hey, what are you doing here? Would you like some company?"

Charlotte. Here. Now. His brain seemed to be on pause, only registering basic thoughts. How was it possible that just her presence made his heart quicken? She wasn't in danger, he was.

"You shouldn't be here."

"It's nice to see you too. I guess I'll be going."

She turned to leave the bar area and inexplicably he caught her arm. "I'm sorry. I didn't mean that the way it sounded. I just assumed that Suki would want you to stay close to Samantha -- considering..."

"She's at home. Duke's has her favorite fish tacos so I'm bringing them home."

"Home?"

"Well, Suki's home. We've been spending so much time there..." Her voice trailed off, but he knew what was on her mind. For some reason, he always knew.

"I would never hurt you."

Somehow saying the sentiment aloud made it sound more ominous rather than appease Charlotte's guilt for wanting to be near Phineas. "She doesn't like you."

"She really has no reason not to," Phineas reasoned. "Sure, she has a long history with Raven, but I've done nothing to her, or to you."

"What about Samantha?"

She stared at him, but he couldn't respond.

"Please, Phin. Tell me you didn't cause that accident."

Phineas raked his fingers through his hair. "I don't know, Charlotte. Sometimes I don't know what is me and what's Raven controlling me, like a puppeteer. But I do know that I don't want to cause you pain." He reached out to brush her cheek.

"Don't," she said, putting distance between them before any further contact could be made.

"Please don't pull away from me, Charlotte. You're the first person I've felt a connection to in, well you wouldn't believe me if I told you how long."

"Try me."

"Will you trust me?"

"I don't know..."

Phineas took both of Charlotte's hands in his own and looked at her beautiful face. "Kiss me," he said simply. "Kiss me and then tell me that you can't feel how much I care."

Charlotte looked to Phin, his pleading eyes, his face raw with emotion, and she closed her eyes. He looked at her standing in front of him, so trusting with her eyes closed, so vulnerable. He could have done anything to her at that moment, but all he wanted to do was what he did, lean in ever so slowly and then he gently pressed his lips to hers. The kiss was soft and sweet, just like Charlotte, he thought to himself. When he stopped, she opened her eyes and smiled.

"Do you trust me now?"

"I want to."

"Then come with me."

He took her hand and walked to the restaurant's coat closet, a small dark space where he could concentrate. Still holding tightly to her hand, Phineas closed his eyes and focused on the time when he was alive with hope and the world seemed to be his for the taking. It was merely a period of three years, but it was the best years of his life. Raven had already taught him the power to influence. She was on a mission to search for the Amulet and so she had given him the freedom to remain in the past, at least for a brief period before she summoned him back.

The air seemed to shift and Charlotte shivered involuntarily. Phineas instinctively put a protective arm around her. "When I give the word, I want you to take a deep breath and then continue to breathe evenly, and whatever you do, don't let go of my hand. Are you ready?"

Charlotte didn't know what she was in for, but she nodded nonetheless. They may have been in a small dark closet, but suddenly a cold breeze hit her full force in the face as if she were flying through the night skies. She felt Phineas' hand close in on hers, providing the only warmth through her otherwise shivering body. The air seemed to pull out of her body and she recalled Phineas telling her to keep breathing. But she felt like she was being pulled underwater. It was cold and dark and the air was leaving her.

"Charlotte, breathe!" Phineas commanded her. She could hear his voice, but it seemed so far away. He willed it to be and so it was. She opened her eyes, finding herself lying on the floor, her head resting gently in Phineas' lap. He looked slightly younger, but his clothes suggested another time. He wore a smart white shirt with a slightly ruffled front and a grey striped ascot under a black waistcoat. His trousers appeared to be custom made for him, again of a dark shade of grey with a slight pinstripe. And on his beautiful head was a top hat with a ribbon of black silk snaking its way around the brim.

"You, you're so elegant."

"You should see yourself," Phineas said taking her hand and helping her to her feet. As she stood, she noticed for the first time the change in her own appearance. Gone were her jeans and plain white tee, now replaced with a pale blue dress with a full petticoat that begged to be twirled in. Delicate white ribbons zig-zagged at her waist, cinching it in and accenting her thin frame. As she went to take his hand, she noticed that her own were encased in white lace gloves.

"This is different from before. With Suki, we were merely given a glimpse into the past. But, we're actually here. How did this happen?"

"Gypsies know how to harness the power of the mind. It can be used as a portal. I've been here before and so, I can return."

"Time portals don't exist," said Charlotte more strongly than she actually felt given her current circumstance.

"They do. It's just that most people have no idea what they're dealing with, but Raven does and she taught me."

"How does she know about it?"

"Because she's traveled, and frankly, because she's deeply opportunistic. She will align herself with anyone who has knowledge that may later benefit her. Mainly heads of state, scientists, and people who have something she wants," said Phineas.

Charlotte sat down again and looked around. "That doesn't explain to me how we are here."

"Raven once met a plasma physicist. Leave it to her to find someone with that expertise," Phineas continued. "He told her about X-points."

"What's that?"

"They're electron diffusion regions. It's places where the magnetic field of Earth connects to the magnetic field of the Sun, and the result is a direct passage through the atmosphere."

Charlotte looked at him dubiously, but Phineas continued nonetheless. "Charlotte, these portals open and close throughout the day."

"It sounds perfectly impossible, and yet we're here," she said starting to come around.

"It will make more sense to you if you understand that evidence of this is all around you. When the geomagnetic field meets the onrushing solar wind, it ignites the openings. Some are short-lived, others are sustained. But in every case, tons of energetic particles flow through the openings. This is how Earth is heated, why we have storms, and even the most beautiful of polar auroras."

"You know a lot about it. Why?"

Phineas took Charlotte's hand and he instantly felt her purity and warmth. He stared into her eyes, wishing with his entire being that Raven had not paired him against her. "I have to learn as much as I can about my abilities if I live with Raven. Someday, it will be needed. Raven knows that with knowledge comes power. I do as well, only our motivations are different."

"It's a lot to take in, you realize."

"It's that resistance to believe in things unbelievable that keeps people from learning more, or at least from being open to learn," Phineas continued. "Raven has taught me to not only rely on my instincts and senses, but to develop them. Visualization leads to transformation, on more levels than one," he said, not daring to mention his ability to shift into bird form.

"You make her sound like she's not all bad," Charlotte said confused.

"She's not," Phineas concurred. "But it's back to what I said about knowledge. You get power and then the power corrupts. She isn't satisfied until she gets it all."

"So what could she possibly gain from me? I doubt it's my uncanny algebraic skills or the way I can recall trivia better than anyone I know."

"I don't know, but I want you to believe that I'm not like her. Come. I want you to see a different me. I willed it and so we've returned to that time."

Charlotte looked weary. "What time, Phin? Where and when are we?"

"London, 1850. The tail end of the Industrial Revolution. It's the most glorious time and there's something I want you to see."

Charlotte didn't initially move. She was too busy taking it all in. The people walking on the street in similar, if not even grander Victorian garb to what Charlotte and Phineas wore. Vendors called out to them to buy their wares. The bustle of the street, alive with activity and promise of riches. Charlotte finally came back to set her gaze on Phineas.

"This is a lot to take in, Phin. You're right about the energy. I feel it."

"Come on."

"There's more?"

"There," he said pointing in the distance to a tower that extended from a cloudy mist of swirling steam spewing high above the city. Every passerby could see the outcome of a textile plant run entirely on newly-developed, refined coal. "That's where it started."

They walked toward the city center and stopped for a moment as a crowd gathered to listen to a man standing on a podium. "This factory represents our country's continued success. For the first time in history, the living standards of the masses of ordinary people have begun to undergo sustained growth. Nothing remotely like this economic behavior has happened before."

"Who is that?" Charlotte asked.

"That's Robert E. Lucas, Jr., the Nobel Prize winner. But there's someone else I want you to see, or at least, see what he started. I want you to know what I was, before I became this amalgamation of a man -- some sort of freak that lives throughout times. Everyone hopes to make an impression or affect change, but I wanted that in the way that most men do. I wanted to create something great through my work, not by forcing nature and people the way that Raven does. Come with me. Let me show you."

Phineas led her to an office building adjacent to the textiles plant. The place was closed with the door locked, but a window above it was just the tiniest bit ajar. "Charles was always forgetting his key. We regularly let ourselves in this way. I'll be right back," he said as he hoisted himself up and climbed through. Within minutes he was back having unlocked the front door to the building.

"Is this where you worked?"

"Yes, it's where Charles developed the Analytical Engine in 1837."

"Who?"

"Charles Babbage. He was amazing. The machine you are about to see changed the future and I worked on it alongside him."

Phineas took Charlotte down a corridor, past two other offices and finally, into a large room in the back full of machines, whirring and purring with life. There, in the center of the room, proudly placed as if on a stage, was Charles' crowning glory and the machine that would lead to riches for generations to come.

"It's like a computer."

"Charles was credited with inventing the first one. Each one of his designs became more complex than the last with one mechanical engine leading way to the next. Charles was thought of as a mathematician, but he was so much more -- a mechanical engineer and philosopher, and most important, an inventor.

Charlotte walked around the massive machine, taking in the rows of gleaming columns, thousands of sector gears with their shiny gold teeth that interlock and turn, connecting metal cranks that attach to a series of spinning wheels.

"As a mathematician first and foremost, Charles dreamed of a machine that could make his tabulations error proof."

"What a difference it must have made."

Phineas chuckled slightly. "He called it the Difference Engine, using logarithms and trigonometry functions to help navigators and scientists with their calculations. The problem occurred when he developed it even further and that machine, his Analytical Engine, became another success."

"If it was a success, then why was that a problem."

"Because he was relying on government funds to

build these machines and support his staff and research. When he created something farther down the line from the Difference Engine and it worked even better, the government then deemed the Difference Engine obsolete. Even though the Analytical Engine incorporated more computing, specifically conditional branching and loops as well as memory, they lost confidence in the need for a machine that simply computed."

"Okay, so he lost his funding, but obviously his inventions went on. So it couldn't be all bad. What does this have to do with all of us?"

"What he knew, I now know. I was his apprentice so I learned everything there was about the development of these machines as well as the ones that would come afterwards."

"Raven taught me to harness the power of the mind, only mine works slightly differently than hers. I can turn on my mind, much like a machine. I've used my mind to bring us to this place. It's possible because I've been here before. Raven's powers are slightly different. Hers come from other people's knowledge. She *takes* what she needs."

"I don't understand."

"By just holding my hand, I brought you here. With just a look into her eyes, and she'll know all of your secrets."

"But I don't have any."

"You do. You just don't know it yet. She's waiting for something to happen. It's why I'm here too."

"You've been with her for centuries. You told me

yourself."

"Yeah, but I've basically been her apprentice as well. A companion--or more like a pet that she has trained. She has a plan, Charlotte. And you're in the center of it. As much as I hate to admit it," he said taking her hand in his own, "probably Josh too."

Charlotte looked at Phineas, seemingly so lost in his desire for her. She felt the connection between them, or was it that he was willing her to feel it? It was confusing for her to both fear someone and want them.

"There's nothing between Josh and I," Charlotte said more to herself than Phineas.

"But you would like there to be?" he pressed.

Charlotte looked up and saw Phineas staring at her closely. She barely dared to breathe as his gaze on her was so intent. She shook her head rapidly. "I had a crush on him before I met him. But now that I know him…"

"Boring, thick as two logs…stop me if I get close," Phineas said easily, moving closer to Charlotte.

Her breath hitched at his approach. "That's right," she said slowly. "He has no spine. He'll do anything Ashley says, and he's more concerned with his image than following his heart."

Phineas suddenly turned away from Charlotte. "So you think 'following his heart' would be to date you? Ashley is just a means to his popularity?"

"No! That's not what I meant. He only sees me as a friend, and that's all I want as well. It's just that he's not a very good friend because the minute Ashley is around, he takes off." Charlotte reached out to touch Phineas' sleeve and tugged gently, willing him not to walk away. "I'm not interested in Josh."

Phineas whirled around, the look in his eyes daring Charlotte to change her story, to alter the course of what her words implied. He closed the distance between them and stared at her with his magnetic, green eyes. He looked angry and the air started to shift and whir around them. She didn't dare exhale for fear of what could happen if Phineas grew more agitated.

The answer came when he suddenly grabbed Charlotte's arms and pulled her into his embrace. He didn't even blink, almost daring her to pull away, and when she didn't, he met her mouth with his own and released her arms only to place both of his hands on her waist and pull her in closer to him. Their kiss was electric, the wind stirring Charlotte's hair before it settled as Phineas' emotions changed from anger to passion. His mouth moved from hers and traveled down her neck, leaving gentle kisses along every beautiful inch of her delicate throat, making up for the sudden force that he displayed just moments before.

A sigh escaped Charlotte and at the same time, Phineas released her, and she took a slight stumble backwards, light-headed from his attention. He easily steadied her and gave her a sideways smile, knowing the effect he had on her and that she had never been kissed like that before.

Before any words could be exchanged, voices

were heard just outside the door. Phineas looked at Charlotte, and calmly placed a finger to his lips while brushing a wayward curl out of her face.

"What do we do?" Charlotte asked, panicked.

"Just follow my lead," he said moving toward the door.

"Wait. What are you doing?"

"I'm going to invite them in. Going through that window was a real bitch."

Phineas opened the door with his signature charm, his bright smile beaming. "Gentlemen, can I be of assistance?"

"I say, young man, what are you doing in here?"

Phineas couldn't resist turning over his shoulder to look at Charlotte, whose cheeks were still flushed. He raised his eyebrows to her devilishly, and just as quickly turned back to the men. A quick appraisal of them reassured him that neither was his former boss. He couldn't be quite sure just how far back in time he had brought Charlotte. There's always a bit of room for miscalculations when jumping through time, not unlike driving on an English motorway and missing the exit only to realize the next one won't appear for another two miles. Phineas had jumped long enough to know that it really doesn't make any sense to fret about a wrong turn here or a few decades there. One has to just make the best of an otherwise less than perfect situation, and because these minor inconveniences, as he liked to refer to them, arose from time to time he had learned the gift of gab out of necessity.

"Phineas Rambaldi," he said holding out his hand to the men. It was the first time that Charlotte had heard his surname and being a romantic and a teenage girl, she automatically started rolling it around in her head, connecting it to her own name. "And this is Miss Charlotte Bloom. How can I help you?"

The men looked at Phineas with a bit more relax in their foreheads, but they weren't about to lose all semblance of suspicion. "Why are you here on the weekend?"

"Oh, just a bit keen, really. I'm completing my fellowship from Oxford. Just one more week and after that, I've promised Miss Charlotte to marry her."

The three men turned to look at Charlotte, who now looked more surprised than ever, but quickly recovered herself upon seeing Phineas' easy grin and returned one that was just as radiant. He crossed the room to place an arm around her waist. "Yes, she's finally gone and made me the happiest man in London, or probably all of England. Isn't that right, Sugar?"

The men regarded Charlotte, waiting for her affirmation of true love. "Yes...being with you is magical," she said and for a moment, she and Phineas looked at each other as if they were alone once again.

"So, I'm clerking on the weekends now," Phineas continued. "Sooner I save up, the sooner we can be hitched."

"Hmmf, young love," one man chuckled to the next.

"Indeed!" the other returned with a hearty guffaw. "Alright, young man, do you know where Miss Ada may have placed our report that we presented last week? Just need to add this section to it," he said handing over a series of papers to Phineas. We would like her to have the full package for the morning."

"Let's see if we can't find it together. Shall we?" Phineas said showing them down the corridor. Charlotte remained in her place until she heard their voices disappear down the dank corridor. She stared down at her feet, now encased in old-fashioned black leather shoes that laced half-way up her leg, tugged at similar laces that cinched her waist into an impossibly small circle, and then, as if the reality of this truly surreal moment hit her, she began to pace the room, trying to busy herself or at least appear busy in case someone else turned up.

"What have I done?" she asked herself, and stared out a magnificent stained glass window. "Suki warned me; Samantha warned me, but I can't help myself."

Without Phineas' calming voice, the whir of the machines sounded as if they were mocking her. The turning of the gears made a thumping getout getout getout getout. She moved into the hallway if only to appease their insistent, albeit imagined demands. She sought out the quiet from the next office, located even farther down into the building's basement. Above her, the ceiling showed the exposed wooden beams, criss-crossed into Victorian arches. Charlotte inhaled the musty cold air and sat down at a nearby roll-top desk that was closed for the weekend along with the rest of the place. Except one small paper had another idea in mind as its corner peaked through the corrugated wood. Charlotte would have ignored it, leaving it for its owner to push back into place except a name at the tip of it had caught her eye. Written in a raised, gold lettering was the name Augusta Ada King, the same name mentioned by the men who had arrived, and below it in a scrolling hand appeared a name she certainly recognized -- Phineas Rambaldi. How curious was that? Phineas' time here was centuries ago, and yet it was as if he hadn't even left.

Careful to not tear the page, Charlotte pulled gently, easing it out from underneath the desk's massive top. At the bottom of the page, in the same raised lettering were words that informed her of Ada's station in life -- Countess of Lovelace. Charlotte stole a quick look down the hall to ensure that Phineas was still occupied. With no sight of him, she read on.

August 20, 1842
Dear Charles,
I will be in London again on the 9th and I look forward to seeing your Analytical Engine. I'm pleased that my algorithm was of use to you.
I spoke with a young man from your office by telephone, a Mr. Phineas Rambaldi. He mentioned an idea to calculate a sequence of Bernoulli numbers using the algorithm. Quite resourceful, he is. Although he was rather vague with his reason for doing so. At any rate, I look forward to seeing you

once more so that we can continue with our research. I believe that our numeric calculations are only the beginning of what these magnificent machines can do.

Truly Yours,

Ada

Curiosity got the best of Charlotte and she pushed open the massive roll-top. The cover had hidden a work station that included the typical piles of papers on the desk's surface, square cubbies containing pencils and other necessities of the time, and pasted onto the corner cubby were three photographs, each featuring Raven and one showing Phineas with her. Charlotte reached for it and lightly tugged it off its resting place. Phineas had his eyes closed, his lips pressed against Raven's cheek. She looked at the camera wearing a haughty expression, as if she were staring right at Charlotte mocking her and letting her know that she held Phineas' heart. Charlotte turned the image over and her heart dropped when she read the scrolled writing on the back -- 1841 with my one love.

Charlotte could hear the footsteps of the men moving about on the floor above her. She quickly pasted the photo back into place and closed the desk's top. She jumped when it squeaked and dropped its massive top onto her fingertips, causing her to drop the note mentioning Phineas. She bent as quickly as she could in the full skirted petticoat she wore and stretched her arm to retrieve the note, which had come to rest farther underneath the desk.

"Damn it, I'm even clumsy in the 1800s," she muttered to herself, trying desperately to reach the note, but it was no use unless she crawled way underneath the desk.

She thought she must look quite a sight what with her legs splayed out behind her, massive skirt floating around as if she were the center of a jelly donut, and feeling a bit like a turtle that has been uprighted and struggling upside down on its own shell. Still reeling from the shock of finding photographs of Phineas and Raven, she wasn't expecting another surprise and yet, as she crawled further underneath the desk something most mysterious caught her eye -- a small, yellowed envelope that had been taped to the underside of the desk and beckoned her with the words scrolled upon it -- *For the Companion to Mr. Phineas Rambaldi.*

Sliding her fingernail underneath the envelope, she pried back the tape that had become even stickier with age. Still hidden underneath the desk, she removed the yellowed paper from its envelope and read in horror the warning that was obviously meant for her.

Take what is rightfully mine and your heart will live heavy forever.

Charlotte's heart pounded and her throat felt dry. A note left for her centuries earlier? It must be a mistake. She hadn't even been a dream in her parents' minds. For that matter, even her own parents hadn't been around. Her head tried to make sense of the foreshadowing, but she was getting nowhere. The note may have been written centuries earlier, and in a formal tongue, but there's one thing that time doesn't change -- the nature of emotion -- and this was certainly written by a girl who had every intention of keeping another one away from her man. Raven.

Charlotte tried to compose her thoughts and calm her mind. She reread the note and then, feeling weary from the knowledge that Raven was a certain and formidable enemy, she felt defeated and took a moment to lie down on the cold stone floor. Curled in the fetal position, her mind processed everything she had learned in the last day with surprising accuracy.

As if she were a computer, Charlotte's brain ticked off the information Phineas had provided about the Analytical Engine, its predecessor the Difference Engine. She closed her eyes and saw logarithms and algebraic configurations. She recalled names that he mentioned only in passing: Charles Babbage and Ada Lovelace. But that wasn't all.

The facts that Phineas ticked off about time travel, his relationship with Raven, even the pull of the elements raced through her brain at lightening speed.

It was then that Charlotte had an inkling as to what might be the reason she was a Releasor. Samantha had developed a new skill, the power to tune into a person's true essence. Charlotte had always had something remarkable about her--an uncanny ability to remember any fact presented to her.

Beyond a photographic memory, Charlotte's mind would remember anything presented to it. Up until now, she chocked it up to lessons that were too easy to challenge her. But Phineas' descriptions of electronic neurons and portals were anything, but simple and still, Charlotte recalled it all.

Feeling exhausted from the realization, she opened her eyes and that's when she saw it. A small, blue velvet pouch was wedged on the inside surface of one of the desk's massive legs. Instinctively, Charlotte sat up and listened for any sign that Phineas was returning with the men. And then, she reached for the pouch and released it from its hiding place of the last century. Within the pouch was a silver chain on which an oval-shaped stone of a pale lavender set within a delicate silver filigree was hung. It was wrapped in a yellowed paper, which indicated that it was clearly meant for her.

If you're reading this note, you are perhaps my final Releasor. With this stone, the Amulet of Pollux, insight into the brightest minds that I have had the privilege to influence are now beholden to you. Keep it safe and it will do the same for you.

Suzette --

Phineas' voice echoed down the hallway. Charlotte quickly slipped the silver chain and amulet over her neck, and took care in folding up both notes -- the one from Suki and the other from Raven -- before crawling out from under the desk on all fours, moving with the heavy petticoat as if wading through butter. It was most unladylike, but that was the least of her concerns.

Charlotte pulled herself to standing and tucked both notes into her brassiere as it seemed to be the only part of her outfit that had traveled with her from the 20th century. She hurried back down the corridor just as Phineas returned to the same room with the men in tow.

As he closed the door leading to the street, he turned toward Charlotte, who was trying her best not to look guilty. Phineas' words from earlier weighed heavily on her own mind at that moment. With Raven's training, certainly he could sense her unease and wonder what was afoot. When he had left, he was jovial and warm, but now a look of menace shone in his eyes that she had seen just earlier when his jealousy of Josh had gotten the better of him. Charlotte looked upon him innocently, trying to display the behavior she wanted Phineas to see. He narrowed his eyes, seemingly trying to get inside her head, and then when satisfied, he smiled, took her hand, and the tension dissipated. Whatever danger she had seen in Phineas earlier seemed to always simmer just below the surface.

"Where were you in there? It's not a good idea for you to just wander off," he mentioned casually.

And just as sweetly, Charlotte replied, "You left me. Remember?"

"Momentarily. But you weren't supposed to go snooping around. What if someone else had arrived and seen you?"

Charlotte twirled in front of him, the skirt of her petticoat blooming upward. "I look like I belong."

"But you don't, so we better get what I came here for and then get you back before Samantha or Suki wonder about you."

"Not to mention Raven," Charlotte said pointedly. "Wouldn't want to keep her waiting."

The moment the sentence escaped her, Charlotte knew it was a mistake. Just half an hour earlier, Phineas and she had been wrapped in each other's arms and now she was all but accusing him of being involved with Raven. She saw him narrow his eyes, the threatening look returning to his demeanor. Charlotte instinctively regretted speaking out of turn.

Phineas remained silent for a moment, observing Charlotte like a wolf contemplating the best way to attack its lunch. He stood in front of her, again a bit closer than one would consider a polite distance for a man and woman to be, particularly during Victorian times. "She is my step-sister," he said evenly. "What exactly are you implying?"

Charlotte shifted uncomfortably, but answered nevertheless. "Something about the way she looks at you is more possessive than sisterly, more like a girlfriend."

Phineas smiled at Charlotte in spite of the fact that he didn't particularly care for the reality of her words. He wished she hadn't seen through their hoax. Everyone else believed his relationship with Raven to be platonic, but not Charlotte. Something was certainly different about this girl. Raven was right for being interested in her. She was whip smart and observant of human nature like nobody he had ever met. But that didn't mean he was going to admit to any truth behind her words. Even if technically he and Raven weren't related, their relationship could be categorized as just plain old wrong.

Moving even closer to her, his head poised just above hers, Phineas looked down into Charlotte's eyes. "Suzette doesn't know you're here."

"What are you saying?" her voice catching in her throat, nerves jangling from the proximity of him.

"Are you afraid of me, Charlotte?"

"Should I be?" she said, taking a step back in spite of herself.

"Suzette thinks you should, but how do you feel?" he said, taking her hand in his own. It felt cold and his eyes matched the feeling.

Charlotte knew that she was on dangerous ground. Phin had made his point. There was nobody here to help her. She needed to help herself. Charlotte steeled herself and looked into Phineas' transparent green eyes as clear as looking into a rambling stream, and at that moment, she felt as if it flowed straight to her heart. There was nothing she could think of to say, no comeback, no explanation, just one plaguing thought. Phineas wasn't a boy. He was all man and she was sunk, done for and totally without reason falling for him. And damn it, she couldn't trust him worth a darn.

"I came here willingly. I trust you. And if that

proves to be a mistake, then you are the one who will have to live an eternity with the consequences of your actions."

He shook his head in amazement. "You're something else."

She didn't know the extent of Phineas' powers. She didn't realize that while some gypsies could read thoughts, he could place them and with the simple power of suggestion, just like that, the image of man and woman -- their carnal need for each other -- was placed in her head. But not wanting to take advantage of the situation, just as quickly, he removed it. Although he was capable of influencing her, he wanted to prove to himself that she would be his willingly.

He closed the small distance between them, and then with curiosity waited for Charlotte's natural reaction. Seeing no fear in her eyes, but more a look of dare, he placed his hand gently behind her head and pulled her in toward his lips, soft and inviting. And when she didn't resist, he allowed his other hand to find the small of her back. Charlotte willingly pressed against him, his manhood making itself known.

A small moan of surprise coupled with passion escaped her lips, which he again covered with his own.

"Forget everyone else, Charlotte. Be mine."

She pulled away from Phineas suddenly, which surprised herself as much as Phineas. He was amused by her inner strength, the capabilities that he saw shining below the surface.

"Do you think that I would kiss you if I'm into someone else? There's a saying...'If you're not with the one you love, then love the one you're with.' Is that what you think this is?"

Although Charlotte had placed a more respectable distance between them, Phineas held up his hand and then ever so gently took hers as if trying not to frighten off a small kitten. "Charlotte, I just want to know that when you're with me, you're here willingly. I'm worried that I wouldn't know."

"Well why else would I be here? It's not like you kidnapped me."

Phineas smirked at the absurdity of her remark because in reality he had kidnapped her and took her over two centuries back in time with him.

"You know what I mean," Charlotte said easily, a bond having now been formed between them. "I don't believe those things about you."

"And Josh?"

"He's not the one for me."

Phineas looked at her, wondering if her words were spoken simply as a way for her to placate him, something she uttered for her own protection, or if he could be fortunate enough for it to be the truth. It was probably too much to hope for as he had never known Raven to be wrong, and she believed that Charlotte's destiny pointed toward Josh.

He kissed Charlotte again, not wanting to put too much thought into it. There was something innocent about Charlotte, and he hoped with any heart that he still possessed that being with her could be possible. He couldn't deny the fact that he wanted love and a part of him was even coming to believe that he deserved that bit of happiness in his life. Except that he couldn't be sure that his own desire for Charlotte hadn't influenced the same thoughts within her mind.

"Do you know of Kahlil Gibran, the literary rebel from Lebanon?"

"I don't think so."

"You've probably heard of one of his most famous romantic phrases: 'If you love somebody, let them go, for if they return, they were always yours. If they don't, they never were.'"

"I remember now. Is that a reference to me and Josh...or you and Raven."

Again, Charlotte's perceptiveness took him off-guard. He was of course, referring to Josh, who he saw toying with Charlotte's emotions, leading her on and then returning to Ashley's side, but of course, Charlotte was right. Raven had control over Phineas as well.

"Gibran died in 1931. People said his writings were among the most romantic of the time," he said almost wistfully."

Charlotte followed his gaze outside the window where couples strolled arm in arm down the high street. "My relationship with Raven is complicated. She gave me my life, my powers." Phineas turned back toward Charlotte. "I needed her to teach me how to develop my powers, and to comfort me when everyone around us eventually dies off."

Charlotte felt a sick drop in her stomach as her mind went to the photographs she had found. There was no doubt in her mind at this point that anything she had felt toward Josh was simply a school-girl crush. Her feelings for Phineas were primal and strong. She was both drawn to him and feared what she was feeling.

"What would Raven say about this," Charlotte asked.

Phineas shook his head. "As my powers grow, I gain control and perspective. Humans are fragile...their lives can be snatched away from them. And with that knowledge, I've realized that it's imperative that I hold onto my humanity, whatever scrap is left within me. That would be the ultimate show of power."

"And Raven?"

"Power and control fuel her. The more she has, the more she wants."

"Then why would she possibly be interested in me? I have no power. What could she possibly want in me?"

"There's something so strong within you. Your perception is unparalleled. I'm willing to bet that you have the power to change your destiny. So be with me."

Charlotte sucked in her breath, knowing that it was impossible to hide her thoughts from someone like Phineas. "But, I've seen you together. You share so much history with her. I can't forget what I know."

The moment the words were out of her mouth, a

light switch went on and Phineas knew what was so special about Charlotte. He held her in his arms once more. "Charlotte, your knowledge is your power...and your curse. For just a moment, forget what you know and tell me how you feel. Right now, with me."

"I want you, but I've been warned away from you by people I trust," she said.

"Suzette and Samantha."

Charlotte nodded. "That's not easy to ignore...but, I don't have to tell them," she said with a devilish glint in her eye.

Phineas smiled and pulled her in close. "She'll know. She's a Genie and you're her Releasor. You're connected. Do as she says for awhile. It will keep you safe and if we're meant to be..." his voice trailed off.

"Just like Gibran wrote," Charlotte muttered. She knew he was right. Involuntarily, her hand went to her neck and touched the amulet that felt as if it were heating up against her skin.

"Is that new? I hadn't noticed it before," Phineas said staring at the stone.

Instinctively, Charlotte didn't want to tell him anything about the note or how she came in possession of the stone. "Phineas, kiss me again. If we're returning, it may be a very long time before we're together."

And with that simple request, his thoughts left the amulet and he leaned in toward Charlotte. His lips found hers. He kissed her gently with a longing for love. It was so different from the heated passion that Raven insisted on. With Charlotte, he felt hope. When they finally pulled apart, Phineas took her hand in his own. "Are you ready?"

"What do I have to do?"

"It's slightly more tricky returning so just hold on, trust me, and don't let go. When the air swirls around you, just imagine yourself running. Don't stop until your back. See yourself running like the wind." The look of concern in Charlotte's eyes was undeniable. "Charlotte, everything will be fine," Phineas promised.

She wanted with all her heart to trust him and as those warm thoughts entered her mind, just as quickly the room seemed to spin, the forces of wind took over and all sound and sight disappeared as she was transported through the continuum of time, moving swiftly and feeling as if she were being tossed this way and that. She did as Phineas said and while holding his hand, imagined herself running a marathon, fast and hard, as she moved toward the Realm of the present.

Chapter Fourteen

If we had arrived five minutes earlier or Charlotte just five minutes later then our paths may have intersected, but as Raven's plot would have it, the timing worked against us.

Raven's temper flared after seeing the way Phineas looked at Charlotte. It was one thing for him to pretend to like her at school, but this was altogether different. He wasn't that good of an actor. She never expected that giving him insight into his humanity would have such dramatic effects. He was falling for Charlotte, which was a dangerous betrayal of his heart. If Phineas felt temptation toward Charlotte or even worse, love for this girl, then Raven would ensure that he also got a sense of what it felt like to experience sorrow and regret.

She soared higher and higher in bird form, trying to calm her mood. Her only solace came in the ridiculous irony that Phineas staying away longer than he should have with Charlotte had provided Raven with more time to put her plan into action.

James and I moved through time at precisely the same moment that Phineas had taken Charlotte back, allowing the portal to grow more than usual. It was like a road being widened to accommodate more traffic. With its mouth open wide, Raven was able to pull even more of the elements through for her own devices. Wind caused the tides to rise; static electricity pumped energy into the air; and through it all, the humans became more vulnerable.

Raven soared overhead, her emotions no longer focused on Phineas' betrayal. If he were going to run around behind her back, then she would use it to her advantage. One thing was for certain, she would deal with him later. Now was the time for more important business. Samantha was alone and therefore, vulnerable.

Raven planted the image in Samantha's mind with such suddenness that she was totally caught off-guard. One moment she was taking her run in P.E., the next her mind's eye saw Charlotte running, showing intense fear in her eyes with Phineas trailing right behind her. Raven had manipulated the image of Charlotte and Phineas running through time. Instead, it appeared that Charlotte was running from Phineas or at the very least the dark trail of smoke that plumed into the air behind him as if he were propelled toward her faster than humanly possible, like an evil-steaming machine.

Samantha ran faster, feeling the same fear that Charlotte felt as she entered the other Realm. As if in a waking nightmare, Samantha ran without seeing. She ran through the cross-country track at her fastest speed never slowing for the section the kids had dubbed break-a-leg bend, a part of the track that was littered with pebbles and rocks and even limbs of trees that grew at odd angles across the track. It was only a small stretch of land that included a steep incline that typically served as the point where the students would naturally slow down and take it easy, catch their breath and grab a water break before continuing on for the last mile. But Samantha was having none of that. She was taking advantage of the incline, running from something unseen, but more frightening than she could ever imagine.

"You have to help her." Raven planted the command of pure genius in Samantha's mind. Raven had taken this tactic from observing Genie practices over the years. Unlike the type of action that was typical of gypsies, this was a selfless plea. It was the kind of suggestion that would cause Samantha to use up one of her wishes and it propelled Samantha faster.

The edge of her foot landed on a rock, causing her ankle to twist, but her leg to remain straight. She went down hard landing on her knee and outstretched hands. A trickle of blood dripped from her knee. Samantha wiped her dirty hands on her gym shorts and stood up slowly, testing her weight.

A few of the other runners, including Ryan, had caught up to her by now and stopped momentarily.

"Sam, you okay? It looked like you went down hard," Ryan had come to her side.

"It's not sprained. I'm fine," she insisted. "I just rolled it." He offered his hand and pulled her up to standing.

"I just need to walk it out for a minute. You keep going; I'll be there in a minute." She watched Ryan run off and walked in circles for a moment, frustrated with herself, but safer than she was before. The images that Raven had planted in her mind had actually subsided. In Raven's quest to bring harm to Samantha, the mind's spell had actually been broken when she fell. But she wasn't going to give up.

Samantha was still a target. Raven spotted the trail ahead and noted the incline, rocks in the path and then the straight shot before the kids got out of school grounds to continue the cross-country course through the neighboring streets and along the bluffs of Malibu.

In her blackbird form, she cawed loudly and stirred the air so that a cold wind blew, making Samantha feel sufficiently awkward and vulnerable standing at this point of the run alone. She looked to where her friends were running up ahead and continued onward again, immediately restarting at break neck speed when Raven replanted the image of Charlotte's face frozen in fear, in her mind.

"Hey, take it easy Samantha," the coach called when she passed him just before the incline. His words startled her and she stumbled for a second time when her foot tripped over an old oak whose branches extended toward the track like talons reaching for her. She looked up at the coach, more annoyed than anything. His words brought her back to reality for a moment, but only caused her to veer a bit into the branch causing her hair to catch on a twig. She stopped angrily to free her hair. "Samantha," the coach repeated in warning. "Did you hear me?"

She nodded at the coach. "I'm okay. Going for my best time yet," she called back. "Damn," she whispered under her breath as she struggled to untangle a few strands of her hair that had wrapped around a wayward branch. And still the image of Charlotte played in her mind. She gave up trying and simply pulled her head back, causing a clump of hair to pull out and stay attached to the branch so she could take off running again. She rubbed her head where she had pulled out her own hair and then looked up in surprise when the caw of a blackbird sitting on a branch above her seemed to mock her pain.

"Take it easy on the streets," her coach reminded her and she nodded in the affirmative, never breaking stride.

She kept a more moderate pace so as not to be called out again by her coach, but the moment she got the thumb's up from him, she rounded the next bend and started running faster again. The gate of the school came into view, her coach's watchful eye disappeared, and she couldn't be stopped. Her mind temporarily cleared by her own pain, but Raven wouldn't put an end to her game just yet. A few tendrils of her flaming red hair were now freed and blowing behind her like fire lighting her on in her quest.

"Help her." Raven's command was a soft hush on

the wind. The thought propelled Samantha onward, into the busy streets without regard for the course her classmates had taken.

"Sam, it's this way," Ryan shouted after her, but she paid him no attention.

"What is she doing?" Jessica said taking the distraction of Samantha as an excuse to stop jogging for a moment. "Is my hair okay?" she asked Ashley.

Ashley scrutinized her for a minute, and then tucked one wayward strand that dared come out of Jessica's barrette back into place. "You're fine. Me?"

"Perfect."

By this time, Josh had caught up to them as well. "What's the hold up?"

"Samantha has gone AWOL," Ryan explained pointing in the general direction she had run.

Josh stared up the street "Why?"

"Oh for heaven's sake," Ashley pouted, "because she's a freak. Can we finish up this run already so we can all get out of here?"

Josh shrugged and then took off after Ashley and Jessica. Ryan looked over his shoulder once more, but when he couldn't catch sight of Samantha, he too turned back toward the runners' course.

Raven's hold over Samantha's thoughts was growing stronger. I had never needed anyone else's help where my Releasors were concerned, but I knew now that James was brought to me for a reason.

Although we were safely back in this Realm, I needed him now more than ever.

"What is it?" he asked taking in my expression.

"I said that I didn't need your help, but I do. There are boundaries to my powers and Raven has found a way...she's going to do something terrible and I fear that I can't stop it."

James wrapped his arms around me. They felt strong and with my head resting against his chest, it felt like home. I sobbed and let myself go. I had never expected to feel the emotions that I did, but this was an experience that was new to me. Being reliant on someone. Fear of not protecting my Releasors. Failure.

"Just breathe," he said stroking my hair.

I exhaled and felt my former strong self returning.

"Good," he said. "Now tell me, what do you see?"

I explained that once Raven got a foothold into someone's mind, her ability to influence it knew no bounds. "I see them both in danger. I don't know who to help."

"Describe the vision," he said calmly, taking my hands in his.

I closed my eyes and recounted the image of Charlotte and Samantha both running for their lives.

"They're both running? Together?"

"No, it seems they're apart, which is why I don't know where to go, what to do."

"Suki, just concentrate. Whose fear is stronger?"

I stopped for a moment and took a deep breath.

There was no doubt in my mind that Samantha was more tormented. I felt what she felt. Initially, it was just a seed of doubt about Charlotte's safety, but it soon grew into panic. The irony of the situation wasn't lost on me. Here I was her Genie, but I was helpless to do anything.

"Why can't you influence her yourself?" James asked. "You're strong."

"I'm able to influence my Releasors in order to benefit their lives, but if their wish takes precedence, then I am bound to uphold that first and foremost. Samantha's concern is for Charlotte. She wishes for her safety."

"And Charlotte?"

"She seems more nervous than fearful."

"Then you follow your heart and fulfill Samantha's request. Help her by guaranteeing Charlotte's safety."

There couldn't be any more noble Releasors in my past than Samantha and Charlotte proved to be now. Neither had ever asked for anything for themselves, but instead chose to help each other. BFFs to the end, I shook my head with remorse. Together they had used up one wish at the hospital when I was first released. For the other two, they had decided that each would get one, but it must be used to benefit the other. That way, they could be assured to give it adequate thought and not make any rash decisions. It was also the perfect way to remain selfless, by granting a wish unto the other person.

Only neither Samantha, nor Charlotte had yet to

verbalize their wishes. I had an inkling as to what each wanted -- the happiness and wellbeing of the other. They each had pain in their past that shaped who they had become as young women, and this made it easy for each of them to want for only simple things such as the happiness of their best friend.

"So I'm powerless to warn Samantha if she is running into danger?"

James nodded his head sadly. "The very nature of your wish granting is being used against your Releasors."

It was a terrible truth. Samantha's thoughts ran wild for Charlotte's safety, and it killed me that the very thing that filled her with goodness could take her away. It was her Achilles Heel, a story that Raven had first-hand knowledge of and the power to distort.

Once again, James and I stood in front of the massive mirror of his bar. Not a splinter of glass was missing, not a crack marred its finish. It was as if the accident never occurred, and yet here we were, tempting it to open once again.

"We go in and search for Charlotte, and just as quickly we get back out and find Samantha," James said.

I nodded. "Let's do it."

I had never seen James like this before. His eyes were focused on the mirror, willing it to open before us. His resolve and fortitude were undeniable. I could see the muscles in his arms tense and bulge as he squeezed his hands into fists. He closed his eyes and the wind shifted. We were pulled into the portal once again, but this time our travel took place in slow motion, giving us time to search for any signs of Charlotte and Samantha's most recent activities. The air swirled around us, carrying us on the winds of time and allowing us to survey the Realms, both past and present, for my Releasors.

Riding between the Realms was a new sensation for me and not one that I readily enjoyed. All at once I would feel the air speeding past me faster than a hot knife through butter, and then just as suddenly it would grow slower than a Sunday afternoon. A feeling of sea sickness was beginning to overtake me.

"Talk to me, Suki," James instructed. "Stay with me. Try to tell me a story."

I did as he said and recounted the story that had most likely given Raven the idea to use Samantha and Charlotte's friendship against them. "She obviously remembered the story of Thetis, a mother who inadvertently caused her own son's death by holding onto his heel as she dipped him into the River Styx as a wash of protection."

Telling the story helped me focus my mind. Greek mythology recounted how her baby Achilles was foretold that he would die in battle, and Raven understood too well a mother's desire to try anything in her power to protect her child, as she had done with Pixie.

But the magical and healing waters never touched Achilles' heel, where he was being held by Thetis, and later a poisoned arrow shot him in that very spot and he was killed. In those early days,

Raven had yet to convert into a demon gypsy, but it was she who recounted the story to one Samuel Taylor Coleridge, a British poet. Samuel had founded the Romantic Movement with his friend, William Wordsworth, another English writer. It was about the time that she met Samuel that she took note of the influence I had over many a great man and she decided that she was not to be outdone in this respect. So she set her sights on influencing Samuel. She wanted it known that she was the woman behind the man -- the puppeteer capable of pulling the strings.

Both her intentions and technique in achieving influence over others were riddled with darkness. Unlike myself as a Genie, she never wanted to truly help someone. Her goal was to ride on his coattails and take the credit for his success. As a result, Samuel lapsed into moments of depression. Sure, there were other times when he was tremendously prolific where his writing was concerned. But the ups and downs of his mood swings were troublesome. Raven grew impatient and implored him to get it together. She even planted seeds into his thoughts that the work of Shakespeare should be criticized, and that Samuel should call himself a literary critic and do the deed.

For a period, people listened to Samuel and his influence grew just as Raven had wanted. She was placated, but it didn't last because Samuel's guilt overtook his emotions once again. A physician diagnosed him as having manic-depressive psychosis and Raven was furious when he would retreat to his bed. She sought out the doctor and insisted he increase the medicine that Samuel was taking, but it was the worst thing she could have done to the poor man. He was treated with laudanum, which led to a nasty addiction to opium. One day, as she stared down at him, broken and defeated, she declared that his mind was his "Achilles Heel." It was 1840 and the first time the phrase had been used in modern culture.

Samuel asked her to explain the strange sentiment and she rolled her eyes in disgust, but recounted the story of baby Achilles and his mother, Thetis. Samuel was too despondent about their relationship to even fight back, but he wrote the phrase in his book, "Ireland."

After I recounted the story, James' thoughts whispered in my mind: *"We need to go back."*

I focused on his words, our connection and then I was able to hear him clearly. "The x-points are closing. It's like a high tide coming in. If we don't hurry, we'll be washed away."

I nodded my head sadly, feeling defeated at not having seen what was plaguing Charlotte or Samantha, when suddenly the horrible image of what was occurring struck me.

"The bluffs," I said in panic.

Through his connection with me, James saw what I did, but it was too late.

James held me close, trying to calm me.

"I can't believe we were ever friends," I choked out, hardly able to comprehend the evil that had taken over Raven.

"What do you think changed her?" James asked gently.

I shook my head. "I think her attempt to guide Samuel in the way that I have guided men over the years failed so miserably that Raven decided her powers to influence should only be used to benefit herself."

We sat holding hands, both of us realizing that for Raven to have influence over someone who is innately good, like Charlotte and Samantha, she would have to make them think that they were also doing good. And so, she continued to push Samantha onward, running into a frenzy over a fear that something terrible was coming to Charlotte.

Raven used the reality of Phineas bringing Charlotte back to the present and distorted it. For once, I couldn't fault Phineas, who was actually holding onto Charlotte and guiding her safely back. Only I didn't realize this at the time as I could only see what he had told her -- to imagine herself running in order to steady the transition of time. Naturally, Charlotte feared the unknown, although in reality no harm was coming to her.

As Raven flew in bird form, she cawed an evil laugh. Angry over Phineas and desperate to hurt the girls, she recalled the line, "kill two birds with one stone." Phineas would pay for his betrayal later, but for now the image of him chasing after Charlotte continued to flood Samantha's mind. "Very good," Raven murmured.

The vision overtook Samantha with confusion as well as desperation. She saw the two running through London streets, dressed in Victorian garb. Images of her own school neighborhood now disappeared and instead, she saw herself trailing hopelessly behind Charlotte, nearly within reach and yet, frustratingly helpless.

Raven manipulated the images so that in Samantha's mind, Charlotte stopped for a moment and was nearly close enough for Samantha to reach out and touch her shoulder, but her hand simply grabbed air. Her response was to run faster, her arms pumping furiously, and as she ran, Raven took the form of moth and nestled in her hair so as to be close to the action. The wind picked up again and leaves rustled and littered the sidewalk and street. As Samantha crunched through them, Raven's words could be heard with each of her pounding steps, "help her."

The kids had left the high school and were running the course outlined through the neighboring houses, but in Samantha's mind, she continued to see the streets of London. It caused her to veer from the course the other kids had taken and continue onto Pacific Coast Highway, where the Malibu bluffs bordered the busy street. So when she stepped off the curb, only a block from where her classmates were running in the opposite direction, she didn't see the delivery truck careening toward her. Its tires squealed with a sound that mirrored Raven's laughter, but thankfully managed to swerve into the opposite lane and avoid hitting Samantha or any other traffic.

But, the drivers of the two cars that had been tailgating the truck, annoyed at being stuck behind it for the last mile, did the opposite. As the truck swerved out of the lane, the two other cars took the opportunity to accelerate. Having long managed their impatience, Raven entered their thoughts, imploring them not to hold back any longer and reminding them of their wasted time. As the truck suddenly swerved to avoid Samantha, both cars sped up in an attempt to finally pass it. Although the truck avoided Samantha, the parade of cars following were not as adept. First one and then another hit her, sending her crashing over the bluffs and finishing Raven's job for good.

James and I had seen the horrible fate that struck Samantha, albeit too late. My only solace was in knowing that Charlotte was safe. We returned from the bluffs, followed by two police cars whose detectives were waiting to question Charlotte about Samantha's frame of mind.

She had returned to this Realm and assumed, or perhaps hoped, that I would be enjoying dinner with James and she could sneak into the apartment undetected. But the second she returned from the past, she knew that something was terribly wrong.

The moment she entered the building I could feel

her presence and I ran into the hallway to meet her.

"Suki, what's going on?"

I threw my arms around her and pulled her close, thankful that she was alive. The police officers moved around us, taking notes and speaking in hushed tones. A man in a suit approached us the moment he saw me hugging Charlotte.

"Can I get a word with Miss Bloom?"

"Just give me a minute please," I answered. "I haven't told her..."

"Suki, what's wrong?" Charlotte said pulling back from me, and then instinct and rationality took over as she scanned the room and she knew the reality before I had to break it to her. "Where's Sam? Where is she?"

"Charlotte," I said taking her hand. "She's had another accident. She didn't make it this time."

Charlotte crumpled to the ground, tears streaming down her face. The pain of it was too much for me to watch and I closed my eyes as well. I leaned down to hold her once more. "The detective wants to rule out suicide since she went over the bluffs, but they really are treating this like manslaughter. He wants to ask you a couple questions."

Charlotte was suddenly alert and to my surprise her expression changed from sadness to anger.

"Why didn't you stop this? You're tied to us and yet, you did nothing?"

"Charlotte, it's...it's not how this works. I can't use my powers for my own reasons. I can only guide my Releasors and grant their wishes. And, in this instance, I did."

"What are you talking about?" Charlotte practically spat the words at me.

"Samantha was only worried about your safety. Her visions and fear for you were so strong, that I put my focus into bringing you back safely."

Suddenly, a change crossed Charlotte's face. I saw a new emotion -- that of guilt. I hadn't wanted to tune into her mind, but given the circumstances I had no choice.

I whispered to her, "Where have you been?"

"I...I can't...," she stammered.

Once more, the officer approached, waiting to question Charlotte. That's when I saw glimpses of what was causing her so much distress. She couldn't possibly explain to this man that she had just traveled through another Realm, back in time and then returned again. Her distress wasn't just the recent news about Samantha. It was that she had no plausible explanation for where she had spent the last hour.

"You've been with Phineas."

She merely nodded.

"Listen to me," I whispered. "You've been downstairs this whole time. James will cover for you. You're helping him with prep work for the evening shift. The place was closed so nobody saw you."

Charlotte nodded and walked over to give her statement to the officer in charge.

The stages of grief affect people in different ways. Initially, Charlotte was inconsolable. She locked herself in the room of my suite that she had claimed for herself and wouldn't come out even for food. And then just as quickly as the turning of the lock, she got to work organizing Samantha's things, sorting them into piles, making notes about her funeral, listing people who needed to be called. She went into total business mode and shut down any emotion that wasn't useful to her.

As for Phineas, his name wasn't mentioned except for her to verbalize what was naturally on my mind as well...had he purposefully taken her back in time at that precise moment to separate her from Samantha? Although he stopped by the suite once, she refused to see him, and I certainly wasn't about to let him in.

I was relieved when Josh stopped by a few days later to check on her, but her reaction toward him was reserved at best. It wasn't until Josh commented on her pallor that she agreed to leave the hotel for the first time in a week.

In contrast to our moods, it couldn't have been a more beautiful day. The sun was out, but there was a slight chill in the air, which prompted us to take on a brisk pace. I purposely allowed Charlotte and Josh to get ahead of me as I hoped their time alone would heal the wounds Charlotte was feeling and perhaps build a tighter bond between them. He offered his hand and she accepted, another good sign in my book.

"I'm so sorry, Charlotte," Josh offered.

"I know. Thanks."

"It's just so random. Do they know anything about the driver?"

"Hit and run, but they said they'll find him. I have to believe that."

"They will."

The wind started to pick up a bit more, and the leaves and dust swirled in the air.

I pulled my scarf tighter around my neck. "Charlotte, this wind is going to leave my skin looking like used sandpaper. You ready to turn back yet?"

"You go ahead. I just want to walk a bit more."

"I'll stay with her," Josh said.

"Alright then. You be safe," I called out, and watched them turn the corner, putting distance between them and myself. For a few more moments, I trained my ear on their conversation, as I was still worried about her, but their talk took on a tone of Josh wanting to express himself to Charlotte and as a lady, I just couldn't continue to eavesdrop so I let them gain more distance from me as I turned to return home. It would prove to be a mistake in more ways than one.

"Charlotte, do you believe that something good can come out of something horrible?" Josh asked.

"I don't know. I suppose that would be preferable to just having the horrible thing remain by itself."

Josh stopped to look at her. "I like you. I've

always admired your strength, the fact that you never seemed to care what other people thought."

Charlotte looked down at her worn jeans and the simple grey sweater that covered it. Her feet were encased in short black boots, not of the sexy stiletto heeled variety, just basic boots more for horseback riding, and her blonde hair, which was today straight and sleek as the sharpest knife due to the wind, was tied back with a simple black ribbon.

"That's not necessarily true. I just don't know how to pull off a fashionable wardrobe as well as Ashley," she said with a wry smile.

"You don't need that. You have natural beauty."

"I think that's a euphemism for 'she'd look so much better if she'd just wear a bit more makeup'."

Josh cupped Charlotte's face in his hands. "That is ridiculous," he said leaning in for a kiss, but a sudden and cold gust of wind caused Charlotte to put distance between them. She placed her hand on his chest, stopping him in his tracks and self-consciously looked around knowing that if Phineas was nearby he would be furious. If that thought wasn't enough to break the mood, then what she saw next was sure to do the trick.

They were standing adjacent to an antique car lot that was closed for the day. The lot was protected by two Dobermans who had inexplicably gotten loose from the fenced enclosure. The two black beasts stood in front of Charlotte and Josh, teeth barred and ready to pounce.

"Just stay calm," Josh said in a tone that was

anything but. "We'll just stay still and they'll go back inside."

"Okay," Charlotte breathed, never taking her eyes off the dogs. Instinctively, her hand went to the Amulet of Pollux that she now wore around her neck. The stone felt cold under her touch, but it calmed her nonetheless, giving her focus and then as the dogs began to growl, something more.

Josh took Charlotte's hand and took baby steps backwards, but the dogs only edged closer. It was a Western shootout, with both parties wondering who would strike first although Charlotte and Josh were without weapons. The dogs stared at their quarry, growling a low warning.

Keeping her hand on the amulet, Charlotte felt oddly calm in spite of the situation. The wind stirred and she inhaled deeply. Voices filled her mind. At first, there were too many to focus on, and then, as if the words were tumbling through a funnel, one stood out and remained strong. She heard the wisdom of one of my past Releasors and embraced all of the knowledge that he imparted. She spoke in a soft voice, "It's going to be okay."

She repeated the phrase like a mantra, to herself, Josh and the dogs. First the dog on their left looked away from them as if it was becoming bored with this staring fight. When a mouse scurried just inside the car lot, the other looked away as well, and Josh audibly breathed for what felt like the first time in the last five minutes.

"We'll be okay," Charlotte said again quietly.

For a moment it seemed to be true, until a loud and sudden shriek from a blackbird sitting in the tree above them, broke the silence and caused the dogs to not only renew their interest in Charlotte and Josh, but to become suddenly agitated. The bird dove down at Charlotte, its talons reaching for her necklace.

"Charlotte!" Josh yelled.

She bent her head down and covered the back of her neck with her hands. The blackbird clawed viciously at the back of her head, but Josh batted it away. Although the bird had taken off for the trees, it was only a momentary reprieve as it dive-bombed toward Charlotte once again. She covered her amulet believing the shiny object was what attracted the vicious bird. In reality, it was Raven and she knew only too well that this amulet was more than a pretty trinket. It was what she hoped to find when she had ransacked my suite.

In spite of Raven's desires, her attack only managed to incite the dogs into action. Finally, she flew off, hoping that they would finish her dirty work.

"Are you okay?"

"I think so, but we have other problems," Charlotte said, motioning toward the dogs. She steadied her breathing and once again concentrated, hoping to hear the voices that the amulet had provided earlier.

The dogs stepped closer and as in their presumed training, each moved in opposite directions so they were no longer just in front of Charlotte and Josh, but now circling them from either side. The dogs' growling became louder, punctuated by sharp barks as they inched closer and closer, and just as one took a leap towards them, Charlotte extended her arms straight up, closed her eyes and concentrated with all her might on those dogs. The wind blew fiercely, muffling the sounds of the dogs' barks and all the while, her thoughts stayed on those beasts.

"They won't hurt us," she said with conviction.

"Charlotte, I wouldn't be so sure of that. We need to get out of here."

She opened her eyes and this time, rather than look away, she caught the eyes of one and stared him down until he sat in front of her. With a deep inhale, she looked to the other dog, which was now growling louder as if imploring its partner to get back to doing what it does best, tearing intruders apart and worrying about the remains later. She and the dog, which now appeared even blacker as its body was tinged with sweat, locked eyes.

"Charlotte, let's go," Josh said under his breath.

"You first. Just edge backwards and take off. I'll be right with you."

Charlotte waited until she heard Josh's footsteps round the corner and disappear, but instead of following suit, she continued to lock eyes with the dogs.

Nam myoho renge kyo. The chant echoed in her mind. She heard the words softly at first and then she repeated them aloud, all the while staring at the dogs' eyes until they not only stopped growling, but sat down and began whimpering.

She had the opportunity to leave at that point, but she only moved closer to the dogs as if compelled to see just how much she could get away with. She held her hands in front of her, palms outstretched toward the dogs and motioned toward the ground. Immediately both dogs lay down. Her concentration didn't waiver for a moment. Instead, she held their gaze and looked directly into their dark pupils, her own eyes never blinking, and rotated her finger in small circles. The dogs both rolled over onto their backs.

Charlotte smiled to herself, but maintained her concentration. She was no longer concerned about being on the wrong end of an angry dog, but the circumstances of her delay would have been equally disturbing to someone like Josh.

Now with the dogs on their backs, her hands still raised, she scrunched her fingers open and closed as if tickling the dogs' tummies, for she was. Each one lost control of its back leg as it did the frenetic scratching of their bellies. Gone were the attack dogs now replaced by docile pets lying at her feet. She slowly, ever so cautiously, patted each dog on its head before sending them on their way. Her eyes dilated slightly, her hands held steady in front of her and she simply waved them toward their yard where they ran off and continued their patrol like nothing had ever happened.

Charlotte took a deep breath and calmly walked in the direction that Josh took.

"Where have you been?" I demanded when she finally returned to the suite. Josh had arrived a good fifteen minutes before her and was nearly pacing a trench in the carpeting. "Your hand...what happened?" I said walking to the bathroom to retrieve a bandage and antiseptic.

"There was a crow. It was horrible," Josh said.

My eyes met Charlotte's and together we knew that this was no ordinary crow, but a massive blackbird that was in fact, Raven.

"You're okay?" I asked again.

Charlotte took a seat on the couch and reached for a cup of tea that sat on the coffee table, not caring who it belonged to. "I'm here. I'm fine."

"Charlotte, I thought you were right behind me," Josh added with equal parts concern and scolding.

Charlotte did her best to maintain the calm she had demonstrated with the dogs, but ironically it was easier for her to communicate with them rather than Josh and myself. "You can imagine that this has been a pretty hard day. Josh, do you mind if I see you at school? I think I'm going to lie down."

Josh stood up and planted a gentle kiss on her forehead. "Sure. I'm glad you're okay. See you tomorrow."

Josh had only just left, but faster than ants find watermelon at a barbecue, I implored Charlotte to spill the story.

"Why didn't you leave with Josh?"

"Because it was so cool! Suki, the amulet...I know things..."

It was the first time in the days since Samantha's death, that she had smiled. I didn't want to take that away from her, but the circumstances were worrying.

"Josh told me the dogs finally seemed to stand down. Why didn't you leave with him?" I repeated.

"I don't know. It's like I said, I suddenly heard voices, many of them, and then there was one that stood out and it told me how to evoke calm in people. So, I tried it on the dogs and guess what? Somehow, I could just tell that they would listen to me." She walked toward the kitchen and retrieved a plum, which she bit into with a flourish. With her mouth still half way full, she added, "I didn't know when I'd come face to face with angry guard dogs again. Seemed like an opportunity," she said wiping away a bit of juice that had rambled onto her chin. "All of a sudden, this weird phrase popped into my head..."

"Nam myoho..."

"That's it!" she interrupted.

"It's a Buddhist chant. Very calming, centering. One of my Releasors was a Tibetan monk."

"Well, I've never heard it before today, but with that phrase, I could focus and make them respond to me."

I breathed deeply, somewhat annoyed that she was happy about these circumstances, had risked her life unnecessarily, and was eating like a common construction worker. I handed her a cloth napkin, hoping to reinstall some sense of refinement in her before continuing. "So you communicated with them..."

She nodded, her eyes shining. "Even got them to roll over on their backs so I could tickle them!" she squealed.

"Did they communicate with you?"

Charlotte stopped mid-munch. "That can happen?"

"Sometimes. If you're just an animal intuitive, then no. But, it sounds like what happened to you was more than just a gut feeling of what would happen."

"It was," Charlotte admitted. "There was this moment when I looked into their eyes and I could see that everything would be alright. It's this necklace."

"Yes. It's called the Amulet of Pollux. I left it in the past for one of my Releasors to find. How did you get to it?"

"Phineas brought me."

"Phineas?"

Charlotte nodded.

"Does he know you have it?"

"No."

"Charlotte, don't tell him. Please."

"Suki, we don't have proof that he took me back to separate me from Samantha."

"I don't believe this," I said shaking my head. "Raven must have told him about the necklace. She's been after it for centuries. It's why she attacked me here. It unleashes all of the secrets of every Releasor that has ever been with me. And now, that information is yours. There's a reason it was you."

Charlotte stopped eating. "I know. It came to me as soon as I found it," she said lightly touching the stone. "Most people have to study, review their lectures, but not me."

You're a Pamnesiac," I told her. "It's like having a photographic memory, but it relates also to everything you've ever heard. You can recall every experience, every lesson, every detail. You are the one meant to unlock the secrets of the Amulet of Pollux because once you do so, you can be rid of it and Raven will never get to it."

I hugged her and she lightly rested her head against my shoulder. "We need to get dressed for the funeral," she said sadly.

I nodded my head.

"Suki, I've been considering the last wish..."

Chapter Fifteen

"She has the Amulet," Raven screamed. "I saw you with her, Phin."

"She found it on her own, and who cares? Don't you have enough power? When will you be satisfied?"

"When I control destiny. Knowledge is key and that amulet was meant for me. How did you get her back there?" Raven paced their living room, looking as if she may throw something.

"It's actually quite simple, Raven, but you wouldn't understand. I was happy back then, and that accounts for something. When I'm not so focused on causing humans misery, I can actually accomplish a lot. I learned to go back and every time I do, I hope with all of my soul that I will find a cure for what ailed me."

"And what would that do?" Raven hissed.

"I wouldn't have needed you to bring me back. I wouldn't be bound to you. I could have lived my life. You know Raven, would it be so bad to live the way humans do? Make this our final life? Maybe if you had ever allowed us to live normally, without so much emphasis on power, then we would be happy and stop all the drama."

"Don't even joke about that. We came here for revenge on what Suki took from me. I won't be finished until I control every last ounce of her power. So don't ever talk to me about wanting to be average, which is what your humans are."

Phineas moved toward the door without turning back.

"Don't walk away from me!" Raven exploded, her fury unleashing a fireball, which soared just inches from Phineas' face.

Phineas stopped dead in his tracks. He had seen his sister's acts of destruction millions of times, but never directed toward him. "You're wrong, Raven. You're out of control and you'll figure that out."

"Really?" she said with amusement, as if speaking to a naive child, but Phineas held his ground.

"Samantha wasn't average. She could sense evil in a person. And as for Charlotte, I guess her finding that amulet proves her abilities once and for all. She may be living a human's typical life, but she is extraordinary and you know it."

It was the first time he had so outwardly spoken against Raven. Satisfied that he had the last word, Phineas walked toward the door.

"Where do you think you're going?"

"I'm going to pay my respects and then, I'm going to figure out how to get my life back."

"You think you can waltz into that funeral and Charlotte will welcome you with open arms? She obviously thinks you had something to do with

Samantha's death."

"All I care about right now is Charlotte's happiness. It doesn't matter what she believes about me. You said it yourself...her destiny is to be with Josh and now, there's nothing standing in her way. Any feelings she had for me will be forever laid to rest thanks to your treachery."

"You're not so noble, Phin. If you really wanted her to be with Josh, you wouldn't go to the funeral."

"I'm going to ensure that she ends up with him...for her sake. And then, I'm still leaving you."

"You're such a fool, Phin. It was never about Josh. That was a lie to keep you from falling for her. So much for that plan."

Phineas' heart jumped into his throat with the very notion that he had the chance to be with Charlotte, but it was forever ruined. "Why would you lie to me? You acted like you wanted me to be with her."

"All part of the plan. The only reason Josh showed any interest in her was because you did first. And, if you believed Josh and Charlotte were meant for each other, then you would step out of the picture, which is what ultimately needed to happen," she said and shifted suddenly, soaring toward Phineas and ripping her talons into the back of his neck.

He swatted her away, and she just as quickly shifted back and laughed mercilessly at him. "Poor Phin, I just couldn't take the chance of you working too hard to influence her. You lost the girl; I'll gain the amulet."

"I still have time."

"That's doubtful. She thinks you were involved in killing her best friend. Oh, and she's planning on going into the other Realms to bring Samantha back. As if..."

Phineas didn't wait to hear any more of Raven's diatribe. He shifted into bird form and flew to find me, the one person who might be able to help, even if I was the last person who wanted to see him.

Charlotte took care getting dressed. She wore a black dress that laced up at the waist, tall black boots and an expression of utter sadness. She didn't normally wear black even though it was always in fashion, as she felt it made her fair complexion and blonde hair appear even more snowy white than usual. Today, even her eyes were heavily lined in black accentuating their clear blue as well as her mood.

"You look striking," I noted and reached to put my arms around her, but she shifted uncomfortably, and instead walked ahead of me to where James was waiting with my car. The three of us drove in silence to Samantha's funeral. The turnout was small as Samantha had no family to speak of and Charlotte hadn't been to school since the accident. A handful of teenagers, who had somehow managed to use the funeral as a reason to ditch classes, sat in the first few rows of church pews. The three of us sat in uncomfortable silence listening to the priest, who we had met with just the day before, recite the stories about Samantha's vitality and love for life that we had expressed to him. It all seemed terribly manufactured and unfair. Hearing about someone we loved so deeply from someone who never had met her just didn't do her memory justice.

When the service was over, the congregation filed out of the church and met outside to walk to the adjoining garden where an assortment of simple headstones marked the final resting place of the deceased. Samantha's grave sat under a massive California Pepper Tree whose branches stretched both toward the heavens and outward like a person extending their arms for a hug. It would have been a beautiful setting for someone who had lived a long life, but no beauty of nature could remove the truth that Samantha had been taken too early from this life and at the hands of dark magic.

I noticed that Charlotte didn't shed a tear. Instead, she wore a look of determination, which scared me to my core.

"Can I do anything to ease your burden?" I asked gently.

"You already explained that your abilities with this matter are limited," she replied coldly.

I looked to James, feeling both hurt and helpless at her comment. Between Charlotte and Samantha, I was bound to grant them three wishes and to guide them, but being bound by rules had resulted in a horrible outcome. James took me by the arm and led me away, allowing Charlotte to have a few minutes to mourn alone.

"She's hurt," he said.

"I know. It's always hard for humans to understand the laws of the Jinn -- Genies. In Arabic, Jinn literally means 'hidden from sight.' I often think that refers to our pain. If only our Releasors could see how our hearts break for them."

"You know that you had no choice regarding Samantha. To save her would have meant disobeying a major law of the Jinn. She wished for Charlotte's safety, and you were bound to grant it."

I nodded, knowing that James spoke the truth, but Charlotte was in too much pain to see it as well.

"Do you think she'll ever forgive me? I could be here awhile as she hasn't used the last wish."

"About that..." James said taking my hand.

I looked up at him and my heart felt like it was breaking once more. I suppose if one hasn't given into love for as long as I have then when it comes around, it feels all the stronger. It was unbearable to think of having to live an eternity remembering what I have with James, but not being able to be with him.

"You know there isn't a future with me," I said sadly.

"You just have to believe. I've always been with you, Suki. You just never needed me before this visit to L.A. You can find me again."

"I'm not sure what to believe...

But before I could answer fully I saw Charlotte walking back toward us.

"Are you ready to go home?" I asked carefully.

"No, not yet. Everyone else has left, and now I just want to spend some time here alone. You two go home."

"I'm not sure it's safe for you to be here by yourself."

"I'll be fine. It's a church for god's sake."

James took my hand and gave it a squeeze, indicating that I really had no argument.

"If you want me to pick you up, just call me."

Charlotte merely nodded and walked back to sit beside Samantha's grave under the shade of the California Pepper.

We walked to the other side of the cemetery, back toward our car, and saw Phineas approaching.

"Haven't you done enough?" I spat out.

"I didn't do this, Suzette. It was all Raven."

"Guilt by association, I guess."

Phineas grabbed my arm. "You have to put this behind us. Charlotte is in trouble."

James stepped in at that moment. "Let go of her," he said and brushed Phineas' hand away and gave him a shove for good measure. Phineas glared at James and sent him flying into a nearby SUV, but he merely stood up like it was nothing and then with a glance, catapulted Phineas upward and then just as easily, allowed him to plummet back to the ground in a heap.

A blackbird dive bombed onto the scene and as it landed, it shifted into Raven. She clapped her hands and smiled at the exhibition. "This is even more fun to watch than when I sent Samantha running over a cliff. Please don't stop on my account."

Phineas dusted himself off, held up his hands in truce to James. They both stared daggers at Raven.

"Ignore her," Phineas said. "Suzette, just get to Charlotte."

"Don't be such a worrywart, Phin. I'm right here in plain sight. What threat could I possibly present to dear Charlotte? Suki, maybe this is all part of another plan. I think he wants you to leave so that I can get close to James." With that, she laid her attention on James, and to my surprise, he pressed his fingertips to his temples as if in incredible pain.

I focused on James, trying to see what was happening to him, without actually feeling it. Like she had done with Samantha time and time before, Raven had planted an image in his mind, an image of souls being tortured. I stayed calm and thought of the peace of the butterflies that had calmed Samantha during her first encounter with Raven. A trail of blue-tipped butterflies, fluttering gently against the breeze entered James' mind. I brought him peace and soon, the destructive image that Raven had planted was replaced by one of beauty and serenity.

"Well done," Raven said to me when James was fully recovered. "You're getting quite good at that trick. Too bad it took you so long. My job here is done."

"You're bluffing. I've had no indication that Charlotte is threatened by you, and Phineas is right here, as well."

Phineas looked at Raven, and his connection with her revealed her plan in his mind. He took off running toward the cemetery. Raven watched him go and merely laughed. "You'll be too late," she called out before shifting and flying away.

I looked to James and in an instant, he grabbed my hand and we took off in the direction that Phineas had run.

Charlotte stood in a clearing by the graveside, her eyes closed, her hand resting lightly on the amulet at her throat. Within moments the memories of past Releasors flooded into her and she shivered with the cool of the air swirling around her as she absorbed every thought. Charlotte became lost in a trance of her intentions. A whirring sound occurred, like gears slowly gaining speed and a cloud of darkness surrounded her. As she put her arms up toward the sky, Phineas arrived and shouted her name.

"Charlotte, stop! You can't go there. You won't find her."

The cloud moved around her and he saw in horror that it wasn't mist after all, but thousands of white moths, hovering over her body, their wings beating lightly against her hair, neck, arms, and the rest. She concentrated more and never flinched, giving into the darkness of the moths.

"Nam Myoho Renge Kyo," Charlotte chanted to center herself.

"It's a trick, Charlotte. Raven wants you to be trapped in the past."

In spite of Phineas' protest, Charlotte's focus was maintained and the moths continued to hover. When they finally scattered into the skies above, Charlotte was gone.

James and I ran into the clearing, but it was too late. Phineas had slumped onto the ground beside Samantha's grave, his head in his hands. He looked up when we arrived.

"She's gone."

"Where is she?" I asked, the panic rising in my voice.

Phineas looked from me to James. "-- to the other Realms, to retrieve Samantha."

"What!? How would she even know how to do that? It's impossible even for me."

"But, she's got the Amulet of Pollux and it has released the information from all of your Releasors. Think about it, Suki," Phineas pressed.

"Charles Babbage," I said with dread.

"What could he mean to all of this?" James asked.

"He created the first programmable computer, in a sense. His analytical engine could compute anything, and now Charlotte has unlocked the secrets of Charles' mind."

"It's worse than that," Phineas added. "I left her alone when we went back in time. She had access to

Charles' computers and every program that he ever created, only she now knows the equations backwards and forwards."

"And Plan 28?"

Phineas nodded gravely.

"What's that?" James asked.

I recalled my time with Charles and told James of the most pertinent details. "Babbage developed his plans in the 1820s, but his ideas are still of interest today with tens of billions of dollars being funneled into a new project, called Plan 28, to use his computations for time travel."

Phineas turned to me. "It's my fault. I should have kept her safe from Raven."

For the first time, I saw the humanity still within Phineas and knew that he spoke from a place of love in his heart. I reached out to him. "I'm not without blame. She wanted to use her last wish..."

I told Phineas and James about the last conversation I had with Charlotte, just one hour earlier.

"Suki, I've been considering the last wish...," Charlotte said hesitantly, knowing that using it would mean sending me back to my bottle. "Samantha," she said simply.

It was true that I wanted to stay longer, but that alone could not keep me from granting a Releasor a wish. I couldn't grant her wish because it broke the rules of the Jinn. "Charlotte, you can't wish for Samantha to return to us. It has to be an unselfish plea and you would only be asking that to ease your own pain."

"I know. I wasn't going to ask for her to come back. I want to go to her."

She didn't have the chance to verbalize her request as we had to get ready for the funeral. Once at the church, the conversation was again halted when the priest took to the podium and started the service. Following the service, she nearly got her way.

Charlotte carefully slid her hand along the top of Samantha's headstone, brushing away any dust that had already dared to settle. "Well?" she prompted.

"I can't let you do what you're suggesting. It's too dangerous and I'm also supposed to protect you. I can't in good conscience grant this wish."

"But you can't stop me either. If I want it to be, then so be it. My wish; your command."

Phineas spoke up again, interrupting my story. "And that's when I arrived."

I nodded, now wishing I hadn't stood in the way of their love.

Charlotte and I had been arguing over her request when we looked up to see Phineas walking toward us. He also wore black, giving him a look that was equal parts danger and sexy. We watched in utter amazement as he boldly made his way toward us.

Although she doubted his intentions and his past actions, I could still tune into Charlotte's thoughts and I knew that she found Phineas to be utterly captivating in spite of the evidence stacked against him relating to Samantha's death. And yet, she was a woman with pride. She turned on her heel to avoid him, but Phineas easily caught up to her. I tuned my ear to listen.

"Charlotte, wait," he said taking her by the arm.

"Haven't you done enough?"

"I didn't know. Charlotte, you have to believe me that I didn't take you back so that Raven could do this," he said motioning to the headstone. "I never saw any reason to harm either of you. And you have to know...I love you."

Charlotte turned and looked at him, searching his face for any clue that his words were true.

"How can I know the truth?"

He answered her by wrapping his arms around her, and holding hers in place. She struggled against him, but he didn't release his hold. And then, when she was too tired to fight it, he bent his head toward hers and let his lips find her own. He kissed her tentatively at first, and then, when she responded, the passion in his own kiss took hold. His mouth left hers and he trailed kisses down her neck, his hands reaching around her waist, pulling her in closer to him. Finally, Charlotte recovered herself, and pressed her hands against Phineas' chest.

"Stop," she said. "There's too much sorrow between us. This..." she said indicating what had just transpired between them, "isn't meant to be."

"But it is," Charlotte. "You have to trust your heart," Phineas said.

Charlotte looked to the headstone, imploring some sort of rational answer to come to her. Phineas followed her gaze.

I arrived at that moment. Charlotte looked out at both of us and spoke the last words we would hear from her. "Learning to trust is one of life's most difficult tasks."

Ironically, they were first spoken by Isaac Watts, who Released me in the 1700s. At the time, I simply thought that Charlotte was familiar with his quotes and hymns because I had inspired him and fame became his reward. I never realized that her knowledge was first-hand, having been obtained from the amulet.

"We've both failed her," Phineas said wearily.

James saw the sorrow in both of our eyes, and spoke with the wisdom that he has achieved through so many lifetimes. "You haven't failed because you both love her. You both have trouble embracing that emotion. It's time that you give in to your vulnerabilities."

"I'm with you," Phineas said.

I nodded. "We find her and we do as she said...we trust that we'll be successful."

The Romani Realms

Released

Resurrected

Returned

About the Author

Mia Fox is a Los Angeles-based novelist who writes across varied genres including Young Adult/New Adult Paranormal Romance and Chick Lit. She received her Bachelor of Arts Degree in Communications from U.S.C. followed by a Masters Degree in Professional Writing also from U.S.C.

A lifelong reader and history lover, Mia loves infusing her own writing with details of the past. Her other interests include cooking and baking. Fortunately, she is also a yoga enthusiast, which proves useful in keeping her other passion -- eating -- in check.

Mia is happily married to her best-friend, a Brit who has inspired her with annual visits to England, an appreciation for dark chocolate, and the blessing of their three children.

Mia's books are available from Amazon, Barnes and Noble, iBooks, and Kobo.

Connect with Mia:

Website:
www.miafox.net

Facebook
www.facebook.com/MiaFoxAuthor

Twitter
@MiaFoxBooks